Honeymoons Can Be Murder

The Sixth Charlie Parker Mystery

Connie Shelton

INTRIGUE
P R E S S

Philadelphia

ISBN 1-890768-30-8

First Printing, February 2001

This book is a work of fiction. Names, characters, places and incidents are either the product of the author's imagination or are used fictitiously. Any resemblance to actual events or locales or persons, living or dead, is entirely coincidental. Although the author and publisher have made every effort to ensure the accuracy and completeness of information contained in this book, we assume no responsibility for errors, inaccuracies, omissions, or any inconsistency herein. Any slights of people, places or organizations are unintentional.

Library of Congress Cataloging-in-Publication Data
Shelton, Connie.
 Honeymoons can be murder/by Connie Shelton.
  p. cm.
 ISBN 1-890768-30-8 (alk. paper)
 1. Parker, Charlie (Fictitious character)--Fiction.
 2. Women accountants--Fiction. 3. Christian antiquities--Fiction. 4. Archaeological thefts--Fiction. 5. Honeymoons--Fiction. 6. Taos (N.M.)--Fiction. I. Title.

PS3569.H393637 H66 2001
813'.54--dc21

           00-046179

10 9 8 7 6 5 4 3 2 1

For Dan.
Ten years into the honeymoon, it just keeps getting better.

The author wishes to thank the following
people, whose help was invaluable:
Dan Shelton, helicopter pilot extraordinaire and,
as always, my technical advisor; Susan Gaffney,
DVM, Angel Fire Small Animal Hospital, for
her loving care of our pets and for her help with the
veterinarian's role here; Peggy Smith, bookseller, and
Susan Slater, writing teacher and mystery author, for
their insights and helpful comments.

ONE

"Engine failure!"

The low-rotor horn's continuous high-pitched whine screamed in my ears. My eyes automatically jerked toward the console where the rotor tachometer was passing through the bottom of the red arc.

Immediately my left hand reached for the collective, pushing down. Right pedal, cyclic back. Another glance at the instruments. Airspeed sixty. Okay. I took a deep breath and slowly let it out. Follow procedure and stay cool.

My eyes scanned the ground, looking for a landing place. Great. A hell of a spot, rolling hills and piñon trees. There was one road and it was going to be our only chance. I judged the angle and the distance, hoping like hell that my training had sunk in. I forced myself to wait until we were just at one hundred feet above the ground, then pulled the cyclic aft, flaring and slowing our rate of descent.

Gradually we ceased forward movement and I eased the cyclic forward again to level the JetRanger. We drifted the final twenty feet downward as I raised the collective to cushion the landing and gave it some left pedal. On the ground, I reduced the collective pitch again as my pent-up breath whooshed out.

"Beautiful autorotation." Drake grinned.

"Well, I *wanted* to get it lined up perfectly with the road," I said, wiping my sweaty palms on my jeans.

"Hey, at least you're *on* the road."

"No thanks to your choice of great locations to shut off my engine," I teased.

My husband winked and flashed me the gorgeous smile that had grabbed my heart the first time I met him. "Just thought I'd give you a challenge. You've done bunches of perfect autos at the airport. Gotta find out what it's like in real life."

"And I did okay?"

"You're ready for your check ride. Pull pitch and let's head home."

Ten minutes later I set the helicopter down in front of the hangar at Double Eagle Airport on Albuquerque's west side. We went through a short debriefing as Drake reviewed again what the FAA examiner would be likely to ask me tomorrow.

By six o'clock we'd safely stowed the blue and white JetRanger, CharlDrake Helicopters, Inc.'s only aircraft, into its hangar slot for the night. With our big red mutt, Rusty, in the backseat of my Jeep we were on our way to Pedro's for dinner. Practicing what to do in case of an engine failure had made me ravenous, and I was ready for the biggest plate of chicken enchiladas I could get my hands on.

"Check in at the office to see how many times Tammy called for help today," I suggested.

Drake pulled his tiny new cell phone from his pocket and punched in the speed dial code for the office I share with my brother, Ron, at RJP Investigations. Since my marriage to Drake six weeks ago, we'd been training a new girl at the office. The hope was that she'd take over some of my duties and some of Sally's, leaving me free to do more flying with Drake, and Sally free to be a mommy to the little girl she was expecting in February. So far, educating the new employee had not been smooth sailing. I'd been spoiled by Sally's quiet efficiency, and Tammy just wasn't picking it up quickly. We were down to only ten or twelve crises per day, something I wasn't sure I could live with long-term. The fact that Drake, Rusty, and I were also temporarily living in my office didn't help. It merely put me on call at all hours.

I'd taken several afternoons off recently to work on my piloting skills, hoping that Tammy would learn to cope, if she couldn't call on me any hour of the day or night.

"Two messages from Tammy," Drake relayed.

I groaned.

"Then another one saying she solved the first two."

At least I could eat my enchiladas with a clear conscience.

"Oops—another—" Drake reached for paper and pen. He jotted a name and number before ending the call.

"This one must have come in after Ron and Tammy left," he said. "A charter job up in Taos." Along with our living in the RJP offices, all calls for Drake's helicopter business were being forwarded there too.

"The guy didn't give any information really," Drake said. "I'll call him when we get home."

There was only one other car in Pedro's parking lot when we arrived and two people just walking out the door headed toward it. Once they'd backed out we let Rusty, our big reddish retriever, out of the car and he went inside with us.

"How's everyone tonight?" Concha greeted, as we made our way to our usual corner table.

From the bar, Pedro held up two fingers and I nodded. He began to salt the rims of two margarita glasses.

Rusty took his customary place in the dark corner behind our table, eying the basket of tortilla chips Concha set before us. I flipped a chip his direction before scooping one into the bowl of hot salsa for myself. He's probably the only dog in Albuquerque who has regular restaurant privileges, but I have the feeling he's unaware that Pedro breaks the health code regs only for him.

Drake and I rehashed the just completed flight, as pilots always do, sipping at our tangy margaritas until Concha appeared with steaming plates of enchiladas. After that it got quiet as we both attacked the delicious heaps of chicken, cheese, tortillas and green chile with vigor.

Another couple came in while we were eating, followed by Manny, another of Pedro's regulars. The couple gave Rusty a surprised look when we started to leave.

A wintry chill gusted through the ancient bare tree branches around the Old Town Plaza. We drove up Central Avenue about a mile and turned into the quiet neighborhood of older homes where the RJP Investigations office is. The area is still about half residential, half commercial, and has been this way for years. Several windows glowed with warm yellow light in our temporary home, the gray and white Victorian where Ron and I run his private investigation business. Luckily, downstairs showed only the nightlights, indicating that Tammy had gone home. I was eager to spend the evening reviewing questions for my checkride, then get a good night's sleep.

We parked behind the old house and Rusty raced to beat us to the back door, then promptly zoomed in to make his customary check of the perimeter before he could settle down for the night. Drake started a pot of coffee and I scanned my desk, which had been moved to our former conference room when we started living in my office, checking to be sure Tammy hadn't merely dumped her emergencies there for me to fix. While I flipped through the new mail, I heard Drake's voice returning the phone call from the customer in Taos.

"How would you like to finally have a honeymoon?" he asked fifteen minutes later when he pulled me into his arms in our upstairs bedroom. "A nice romantic getaway in the mountains, where we could have an old-fashioned Christmas, go skiing if we pleased, build cozy fires in our own private rock fireplace in our own private mountain cabin."

I scanned his handsome face and ran my index finger over the touch of gray that trimmed his dark hair at the temples.

"And?" I asked. "Why do I get the feeling there's more?"

"And I'd operate heli-skiing tours at the Taos Ski Valley."

"Isn't that dangerous, flying into those remote areas?" My eyes narrowed.

"Sweetheart, everything's dangerous to some degree. But you know me—I'm not taking any extraordinary chances in a helicopter."

He had a point. Drake is one of the most cautious pilots I've ever seen and it wouldn't be like him to take any unnecessary risk.

"And somehow, spending Christmas here in your old office doesn't quite have the same appeal, now does it?"

Another good point. And we'd never gone on a honeymoon after our hasty marriage in October.

"But what about the remodeling at home? I really need to be available for the contractor."

"True. But Taos is only a couple of hours away, and the ski area doesn't really want to start the heli-skiing program until the week before Christmas anyway. You know good and well that no contractor is going to be working full-tilt around the holidays, hon. So it wouldn't harm anything for you to be gone for a couple of weeks. Then, after the first, you can always drive back down here once a week or whenever you need to."

I thought of spending Christmas in our presently crowded living conditions, the stacks of year-end paperwork that would soon arrive, and the chaos of working with Tammy. The idea of spending the winter in Taos gained immediate appeal. But if I'd had a crystal ball to the future, I might have decided to opt for the cozy warmth of my office.

TWO

"Charlie, this is Eloy Romero," Drake said, introducing his slim, dark-haired companion. Eloy's face was deeply tanned with squint wrinkles at the corners of his eyes. He wore a one-piece red ski suit with black and white accents and a matching knit cap. "He's gonna take us up to his cabin and show us around."

"Good to meet you, Charlie," Eloy said. "I hear you're New Mexico's newest commercial helicopter pilot."

I blushed, but was secretly tempted to flash the new license in my wallet.

"You got four-wheel drive, right?" Eloy asked.

I nodded.

"Good, you'll need it to get in and out of this place."

"I can't believe how much snow you've got here," I said. "And I can already see that I'm going to have to find a store that sells boots."

He chuckled, a pleasant sound that lit up his good-looking tan face. "Yep, you city folks are never quite ready for the mountains, are you?" he said, looking at my ankle-high hikers. "And if you don't have a really warm parka, you'll want to look for one of those too."

"This is the guy who's just back from the tropics." I nod-

ded toward Drake. "He may need to be completely outfitted." Drake had moved to New Mexico from Hawaii only
a couple of months ago.

Eloy gave me the name of an outdoor clothing shop in
town that could supply us.

"Well, I guess we're ready to settle into the cabin," Drake
said. "The ship's already parked so she's safe for the night."
We were using a large metal maintenance building, owned
by the ski area, as a temporary hangar for our aircraft during the next few months. It was located on the only road
leading to the ski lifts, and Eloy had made a large sign
announcing our services, which he'd mounted on posts facing the well-traveled road.

Drake had flown up to the ski valley, while I drove my
Jeep with Rusty, our warmest clothing, and several bags of
groceries inside. His trip had taken a little over an hour,
while mine had taken nearly three.

We climbed back into the Jeep and pulled out of the
parking area, following Eloy's dented white pickup truck.

The road leading into the Taos Ski Valley is a winding
paved two-lane, passing through a forest that begins, north
of the town of Taos, in piñon and sagebrush that are soon
replaced by tall ponderosa pines at the bottom of a deep
canyon flanked by steep rocky walls. The snow in town had
been minimal—two or three inches—but as Rusty and I
ascended into the valley, the plowed snow walls beside the
road had steadily grown until they reached almost to the
height of my side windows. Now, as we followed Eloy, we
took a well-plowed dirt road even farther into the hills.

We traveled about three miles, while the road became
narrower although still plowed, past occasional driveways,

most of which were gated and uncleared. The sky was low and white, heavy with the promise of more snow and the temperature had dropped to the low thirties. I shifted into four-wheel drive to get the speed I needed to keep up with Eloy's hard-to-see white truck.

He turned eventually into a much narrower lane, one with an open metal gate and a freshly cleared path. The terrain rose steadily as he climbed over uneven places that would no doubt be fairly huge potholes after a thaw. I followed as closely in his tracks as I could.

Around the second curve in the lane we came to a clearing that served as a parking area for a log cabin. Built of smooth-peeled pine logs, the house was two stories tall, about two rooms wide, a charming little box whose squareness was broken by a covered porch the width of the cabin's front and wrapping around the west side. Wooden boxes below the second-story windows would contain flowers in summer—now they sat heaped with over a foot of snow. On the east side of the cabin an old International Scout sat parked, facing outward, with a snowplow attached to its front. We followed Eloy, parking beside his truck in front of the small house.

As soon as Drake opened his door, Rusty leaped out of the Jeep and bounded through the snow pile bordering the driveway, where he sank up to his chest. He pushed off with his hind legs and cleared the berm, landing in snow that was a couple of feet deep.

"Well"—Drake chuckled—"he's certainly having a good time already."

"Don't worry," Eloy assured us. "He can't get too far. The property is fenced, but I doubt he'll travel the whole ten acres in this much snow."

"Not as long as he knows we have the food here," I told him.

"Let me show you around," Eloy said.

He pulled a small key ring from his pocket. "Here's the key to the front door." He held one up. "And this little one is the padlock on the pumphouse. You've got your own well back there," he said, indicating a small wooden structure behind the house. And this one is for the Scout. The county plows the road, but you've gotta do your own driveway."

I looked at him skeptically.

"It's not hard," he assured me. "I'll give you guys a quick lesson. It's actually kinda fun.

"Meanwhile," he continued, "I turned the heat on early this morning. The propane tank is full, the water system has been checked out and serviced, so I think everything's ready for you."

We grabbed a couple of bags from the car and followed him to the front door. Rusty busied himself trying to unearth mysterious scents in the snow.

Inside, the cabin was indeed toasty warm. The front door opened into a shallow ski porch, with a bench along one wall and wooden pegs for hanging skis and coats along the opposite wall. A second door brought us into the main living area, with kitchen and dining to our left, the entire first floor being one greatroom. Stairs along the west wall to our right led up to a balcony, two bedrooms and a bath, Eloy explained.

I carried our grocery bags to the kitchen, a cozy nook with butcher block countertops, a modern gas range, and refrigerator.

"This freezer isn't very big," Eloy said, "but there's a small service porch through the back door. If you need to keep anything frozen, just put it out there. Extra firewood is also out there."

Drake spent a few minutes checking out the fireplace, the propane heating system, and the instructions for the well, while I carried our duffles up to the larger of the two bedrooms and put the food away in the kitchen. I was pleased to see that the kitchen was fully stocked with utensils and a set of dishes with delicate mountain wildflowers on them. When Eloy drove away a bit later, I snaked my arms around Drake's neck and kissed him, long and lingering.

"This is a wonderful place for a honeymoon," I murmured.

"Why don't I put a match to those logs in the fireplace, you slip out of a few layers of those heavy winter clothes, and let's find that bottle of wine," he suggested.

"Mmmm . . ." I headed upstairs to look for the pair of burgundy nothing-left-to-the-imagination leggings and lacy tunic sweater I'd brought with me. "The wine is out on the back service porch. I thought it might chill faster out there."

By the time I came back downstairs, a nice fire was blazing in the fireplace and Drake was lounging in one corner of the blue and green tartan sofa with two glasses of wine on the small coffee table. I snuggled into the curve of his arm and our eyes met in our own silent toast to each other.

An hour later, I peeked out from under the thick comforter we'd pulled down to cover ourselves on the lush faux-fur rug before the fire to discover that it was now pitch dark outside and our roaring fire had subsided to glowing coals.

One more lingering snuggle under the blanket, then we decided to stoke up the fire and find something to eat. At the kitchen window I glanced out to see thick silver-dollar snowflakes falling.

෯෯ ෯෯ ෯෯ ෯෯ ෯෯

By daylight the next morning, I could see that the cabin could use a good dusting. It obviously hadn't been occupied for months. Plus, I wanted to get my computer system set up soon, as it was still one of my duties to do Ron's client billing and stay in touch with his office.

Drake was already on his way back to the hangar to check on his helicopter and work out the logistics for the heli-skiing operation. We'd awakened to three inches of new snow, and he cautioned me that if there was more than about another six inches accumulation through the day, I should go out and plow the drive so he could get back. I watched the sky with some trepidation, but the clouds appeared to be moving out.

After a second cup of coffee I set out to make myself a work space. I found a folding table stashed in one of the closets and set it up in the corner and put my storage box of file folders under it, my notebook computer and small printer on top. A relatively comfortable chair came from the kitchen table, although it was nowhere near as good as my ergonomic beauty at the office. Well, I didn't intend to be spending hours sitting at my new temporary desk either. I was here to have some fun.

I tested the phone by calling the Albuquerque office to be sure everything was still all right. Sally, still working partial days to train her replacement, sounded a bit stressed but didn't go into detail. I assumed Tammy was sitting at her side. Sally put Ron on the line and I told him which clients I had billing records for. We spent a few minutes discussing office business and I told him I'd send an e-mail in the next few minutes to make sure all systems were go. Ah, modern technology.

By eleven o'clock I'd finished everything I'd brought with me and was beginning to wonder exactly how I'd fill my time in the mountains. Nothing was exactly fast-paced here. However, the cabin was still dusty so I took that up as my next cause. I located cleaning supplies in a bathroom cabinet and started giving everything the once-over. Rusty watched with ears cocked, finally getting the idea that we were staying awhile.

Dusting the bedrooms, each with simple furnishings of bed, dresser with mirror, and nightstands didn't take long and I was working my way downstairs when the telephone rang. Startled at first, I dashed for it.

"Hi, hon. How's everything going there?" Drake asked.

"Slow. But fine, really."

"I'm testing the phone we have down here at the hangar," he said. "I want to be sure I can forward the calls to the cabin phone so I don't have to stay here all day. Can't leave my sweetheart alone on our honeymoon."

I grinned at the phone. "So, how do we know it's working?"

"Just call me right back. If you get a busy signal, it worked. I'll be home in about thirty minutes."

I checked the phone then bustled a bit faster to finish before he arrived. My feather duster flicked over the coffee table and mantel. On either side of the fireplace were floor-to-ceiling bookcases filled to capacity with a variety of books and I found my attention diverting to them. The Romero family appeared to have very eclectic tastes in reading material—there were volumes of classic literature standing amid paperback romances and mysteries. I pulled a couple of favorite authors from the shelves and started a to-be-read pile.

The lowest shelf on the right-hand side was devoted to family picture albums. I pulled one at random from its place.

The faces were completely unfamiliar to me, as I knew they would be—scenes of family picnics outside the cabin here, mostly. The little log house appeared to be well-used in the summer months, when dozens of Romeros congregated here. Little girls in bright shorts and tank tops jumped rope in the driveway while the men sat on the long front porch, most of them holding cans of beer. Other shots showed the family seated at picnic tables laden with food, pretty women with fluffy hair setting bowls of corn and chile in place. Somehow, without snow on the ground, the yard looked much more spacious.

There were winter scenes too—indoor shots showing a younger Eloy and a pretty woman wearing matching ski sweaters, posed beside a decorated Christmas tree. Which reminded me that the holiday was only a week away.

I started to replace the album on the shelf and noticed that a thin photo folder had leaned into the space I was aiming for. I pulled it out and slid the thicker album into place. The folder was an old-fashioned one, dark brown cardboard with a gold swirl around the perimeter and the name of a commercial photographer in Taos imprinted on it. It opened to reveal a sepia photograph of a stately couple in mid-nineteenth-century clothing. The man was seated in an extremely straight chair, one hand propped on the head of an elaborate cane, the other on his left thigh with the elbow at a jaunty angle. The woman stood half behind him, her hands resting on his right shoulder. Neither showed the slightest hint of a smile. Eloy's grandparents?

I gently reached to the edge of the photo to pull it from its sleeve, thinking there might be names or a date on the back. When I pulled it out, a flat plastic bag slipped out with it. It drifted to my lap as I turned the photo over. There was nothing written on the back. I gently picked up the plastic bag. It was nothing more than a flimsy sleeve, about six inches square, and it contained a few scraps of brownish paper that looked like torn newspaper clippings. I carried them to my computer table and opened the sleeve to let them slip out. Picking one up, I discovered that the paper was heavier than newsprint and the black scribblings on it were not in English. They looked like a Middle Eastern language.

What on earth were they, and what were they doing so carefully hidden away in a mountain cabin in New Mexico? A chill went through the room. Despite my heavy sweatshirt, I felt the goose bumps rise on my arms.

THREE

Quickly I opened the little plastic sleeve and slipped the scraps back into it. I then slipped the plastic and the photograph back into the folder just as I'd found them and put the folder back on the shelf in its original place. I rubbed my arms to chase away the chill and glanced at the thermostat on the wall. It wasn't any colder than before, so why did I get such a strange sensation? I shook my hands out and picked up the feather duster once again, dispelling the odd feeling. It's what I deserved for snooping through other people's things.

I finished dusting the room quickly and decided to check the fridge for some idea of what to fix for lunch. Rusty was sitting by the front door, head cocked.

"Want outside?" I asked him.

He stood and wagged heartily. When I opened the door, though, he went to the edge of the porch and looked anxiously around the yard. He came back to me, staring up with his deep brown eyes topped by questioning eyebrows.

"Drake? Where's Drake?" I teased.

He wagged tentatively and glanced around the yard once more.

Hmmm. I looked at my watch and realized that it had been well over an hour since Drake had called to say he'd be home in thirty minutes. The dog had a better sense of time than I did. Now what? Had he merely gotten tied up talking with Eloy? Had customers walked in? Or could he be stuck along the road in a snowbank? I called Rusty back inside, then dialed the phone to Drake's hangar number only to get a steady busy signal, indicating that the calls were being forwarded to me at the cabin. Rats. I cursed that we hadn't made a better plan for what to do. Winter can be dangerous in the mountains. It takes a half-second for a vehicle to slip off the road, and if he'd hit a tree he could be unconscious, and it was miles back to town, and I didn't know if I had the keys to the old Scout here with me or if he'd taken them.

The phone rang and I spun so quickly I smacked into an end table and had to rescue a lamp before it crashed.

"Did you just try to call the hangar?" Drake's voice came clearly over the line.

"Yes! Where are you?"

"At the hangar. Oh, gosh, hon, what time is it?"

"Nearly one. I thought you'd be here over a half-hour ago."

"Oh, jeez, I'm sorry. I did too. I really was going to walk out the door right after I called you before. Uh, something's happened here. I'll explain it all when I get there. I'm coming now. Maybe I'll just bring Eloy with me, if that's okay. He kinda needs a place to go this afternoon." He hung up without further explanation. I stared at the dead receiver in my hand.

Wondering what was going on, I returned to the kitchen where I located some cans of homestyle chicken soup and put it on the stove to heat, set the table with places for three and opened a package of rolls I'd bought at the bakery in town. That should take care of lunch.

The two vehicles pulled into the driveway exactly thirty minutes later and Rusty jumped up, paws on the front windowsill, when he heard the sound. He raced to the door, wagging furiously. I watched as both men parked. Drake appeared to be watching the road behind them until Eloy was safely on the front porch.

They stomped snow off their boots and shrugged out of their jackets in the mud room, while I ladled soup into bowls.

"Whew! It's good to be back here," Drake said, kissing me quickly.

"What's going on with you two?" I hustled them to the table. I was suddenly starving now that I knew Drake was safe again.

We spent a few moments buttering rolls and taking test sips of the hot soup before anyone answered.

"Eloy may need your investigative services," Drake said.

"What's happened?"

Eloy took it from there. "I got word this morning that I'm about to be arrested."

"What!?"

"My cousin Steve is with the Taos Police Department. He found out that there's a warrant out for me and the county sheriff's guys are supposed to come get me."

"Whatever for?" The clean-cut, athletic Eloy didn't seem capable of anything more serious than a parking ticket.

"That's just it, Charlie. The charge is murder."

My mouth must have dropped open. "Well, surely your cousin will do everything he can to prove your innocence, won't he?" I said, dropping my soup spoon into my bowl.

"That's just the thing. This isn't his jurisdiction—it's county. And there's another family high up in the sheriff's office that wouldn't lift a finger to help out a Romero. In fact, Ray Tenorio would love to pin something this serious on me. There's been bad blood between the two families for ages—it goes *way* back."

"But doesn't there have to be some evidence? I mean, they can't just arrest a person for murder because your cousin doesn't like his brother." I knew it sounded sarcastic, even though I didn't mean it that way.

"I don't know what they've got, Charlie. I don't even know who I'm supposed to have killed. I want to hire you to check around and see if you can find out what it is and help find the truth before they come get me. Drake says you're really good at that." Eloy was ripping his bread to shreds.

I shot my husband a look and he responded with the appropriate guess-I-blew-it grin.

"Gosh, Eloy, I don't know. I don't know anyone here, don't have any way of getting to records or anything."

Rusty stood up then and nosed the front door, wagging tentatively.

"Looks like we're just about to get some answers," Drake ventured.

A white Blazer with bright blue sheriff's department markings and a bar of red, blue, and white strobes on top was coming up the driveway.

"I gotta hide," Eloy shrieked. He nearly tipped over his unfinished soup as he jumped up.

"Slow down," said Drake calmly. "That's not gonna solve anything, and you know it. Let's just find out what they have to say."

Eloy sank back into his chair and held his head with his hands. "If they take me away, just don't let my mama find out, okay?"

I wasn't sure how we would do that, but didn't have time to think about it as heavy boots stomped onto the porch and a fist hammered at the door. "Sheriff's department! Open up!"

Drake opened the door and stood with his body blocking it.

"What's up, Sheriff?"

"You probably already know that," the uniformed man responded. He was shorter than Drake, probably five-eight, and about fifty pounds heavier. His brown uniform jacket was unzipped and the shirt beneath it pulled strenuously at each of the five buttons. The name patch Velcroed to his jacket said TENORIO. His cocoa-colored face was jowly and a black mustache drew a thin line across his upper lip.

"Actually, I don't know anything about this," Drake answered. "Maybe you should explain."

"We're here for Eloy Romero," Tenorio said. "I've got a warrant for his arrest on charges of first-degree murder. This is Romero's cabin, his truck is parked outside—I think that gives me probable cause to believe he's here."

"Murder?" Drake went wide-eyed. "Gosh, what happened?" he asked innocently.

"We got a search warrant on Eloy's house. Found a weapon registered to him in a closet there. Ballistics tests connect it to a murder in Albuquerque about five years ago. Nobody's prints but his on the thing." He stroked the tiny mustache with one finger. "C'mon, Eloy," he shouted. "Let's get going." Drake stepped aside to admit him.

Eloy and I rose from our chairs. His eyes were desperate as he gave me one final look. "Charlie, see if you can straighten this out. Please. I'll find a way to pay you. I didn't do anything." He walked slowly to the front door.

The deputy accompanying Tenorio handed Eloy his jacket and waited while he slipped his boots on. Eloy tossed Drake the keys to his truck. "Just move it out of your way and lock it up," he instructed.

I took Drake's hand and squeezed tightly. We watched as the two officers cuffed Eloy and recited his rights to him before shoving him none too gently toward their vehicle. With lights strobing, they turned around and steered down the snowy driveway.

"Now what?" I asked. "Do we really want to get involved with this?"

He sighed. "Just what we needed on our honeymoon, huh? Jeez, I don't know. Maybe we can just ask a few questions. Or better yet, let's get in touch with that cousin of his with the Taos police and put him on the trail. He'll know everyone here and he should certainly be better equipped to find answers than we can."

"I agree."

We went back to our soup, which was stone cold now. Didn't matter—neither of us had an appetite anymore. I placed a call to the Taos police, asking for Steve Romero, but he wasn't in.

I turned to Drake. "How much do you know about Eloy?" I asked.

"Not much. He's employed by the ski area in the winter, and they've loaned him to me as a helper this season.

Usually he's a ski instructor but he's making more money this way."

"What about the rest of the year?"

"He told me he works for an outfitter that raises llamas down in El Prado. In the summer he leads guided pack trips and I think he guides hunters in the fall."

I carried our soup bowls to the sink, wondering if this seemingly harmless man could be capable of murder.

We spent the afternoon sitting around, mentioning Christmas—only a week away—now and then, but having no energy to do anything much about it. By three o'clock the cabin was completely in shadow and a gloom had settled inside as well as out. I suggested a walk outside before darkness fell completely, but remembered that I didn't have suitable boots. We found some snowshoes on the service porch and some Christmas decorations in a box under the stairs. Tomorrow would be soon enough to make a trip into Taos to get boots. We could ask some more questions about Eloy and the charges against him. Then we might snowshoe out into the woods and cut a Christmas tree. Eventually we might even feel like decorating it.

Drake prepared dinner that night, and we hashed and rehashed all aspects of Eloy's case, as we knew it. But that wasn't much and we soon felt stalemated. We each chose a book from the shelves and spent a quiet evening by the fire, escaping to fictional worlds.

The next morning we awoke to another six inches of fresh snow, so Drake bundled up and decided to learn how to plow the driveway. For a guy who lived in Hawaii until a few months ago, I have to say he's very adaptable.

Rusty and I watched from the front windows, both of us

impressed with the progress. He cleared parking spots for Eloy's stranded pickup truck and our Jeep, then disappeared around a bend in the driveway, throwing snow off to the side. Within a few minutes he was back.

"Milady, your Jeep awaits," he grinned. "The county road has already been plowed. They must have come along during the night. So we're off for a big day on the town, if you're ready."

Taos sits in northern New Mexico's high desert country at about seven thousand feet in elevation. The Rio Grande River runs to the west of town, cutting a treacherously deep gorge through the volcanic rock and sagebrush. Wheeler Peak, highest in New Mexico, guards the town on the east and it is in the shadow of this thirteen-thousand-foot giant that intrepid Ernie Blake cut the runs for the Taos Ski Valley. The slopes delight expert skiers and terrify beginners, but the sight of the mountain inspires awe in everyone.

The town itself began to the south and west of ancient Taos Pueblo, inhabited by Indian people for nearly a thousand years. The town's old plaza was once the site of a massive pueblo uprising, when the Mexican and Indian population rebelled against the territorial government and an enraged group murdered the governor in his own home, a block away. His wife, her sister—the wife of pioneer Kit Carson—and the children of both families escaped through a hole in the adobe wall, a hole they carved with the kitchen spoons. There's a lot of history in this little town.

Nowadays, the plaza stores carry touristy souvenirs and very pricey art, and you're more likely to see one of the handful of movie stars who live around the area than any real-life pioneers. The real people, those whose families have lived here for ten or twelve generations, like Eloy's, don't hang around the plaza much now. They're more likely to be in the snack bar at Wal-Mart, visiting and showing off their grandkids.

Drake and I first proceeded to the county jail to find out what was happening with Eloy. Tenorio was out, luckily, and the officer on duty didn't seem to have any particular objections to our visiting Eloy, as long as we didn't mind sitting outside his cell to do it. The visiting room was being cleaned at the moment. He provided us with two frigid metal chairs for our comfort. Eloy perked up immediately when he saw us.

"What have you found out?" he breathed anxiously.

"Nothing yet, I'm afraid," Drake responded.

I was glad he didn't admit that we hadn't tried terribly hard.

"Eloy, have you got yourself a lawyer yet?" I asked.

"I tried. I got one phone call last night. I called my sister's husband, Mike Ortiz. Unfortunately he was out and hasn't called me back."

"Have the police been more specific yet about the charges?"

"Well, like they said yesterday, they got my gun from my closet at home. It has only my prints on it, and they say it was used in a murder. I just don't know how that could be. The gun was always on that closet shelf. I've owned it for years, and I don't ever remember it being gone. I mean, I didn't see it every single day, but wouldn't I know if it was stolen or something?"

"I'd certainly think so," I told him. "And besides, it doesn't make much sense that someone would steal your gun and return it later."

Unless someone specifically wanted to frame Eloy, and no one else, for a murder. I didn't say it aloud.

"Why are they so sure it was you? Who was the victim, anyway?" Drake was asking.

Eloy squirmed on the thin mattress on his bunk. His hands twisted nervously. He mumbled something that neither Drake nor I could hear.

We exchanged glances in the silence. "Who?" I repeated.

Eloy looked up at me. "My brother," he said, his voice suddenly strong, his eyes ready with a challenge.

FOUR

"Your own brother was the victim, and you never thought to mention this?" I stage-whispered.

His voice dropped lower, though the cells on either side of his were empty. "It was five years ago, and it happened in Albuquerque. It tore our family apart because Ramon was Mama's favorite. Learning about his death put her in a nursing home. You can understand why I've spent five years trying to forget it, can't you?" His voiced cracked and he looked utterly miserable.

I swallowed hard. "Eloy, can you tell me about it? What happened that day, when did it happen, where were you?"

"I was on my way home from a ski instructor's trip to Santa Fe at the time they said it happened. I don't really know any details. Ramon was a priest, with a parish in Albuquerque. He rarely came to Taos anymore, and we didn't have much in common. I was always the lazy brother, the worthless one. Ramon was the saint."

He saw my eyebrows tighten. "No, really," he protested. "My mother actually used to call him that. 'Ramon is such a saint,' she'd say to anyone who'd listen. It gets really old, and you can see why he and I weren't especially friendly. But why would I kill him? I hardly ever saw him."

I didn't have any ready answers for that. However, I did know where I could go for more information on the murder. Drake asked Eloy whether he needed anything like his toothbrush or other personal items from home. We left a few minutes later.

"Let's drop in to visit Eloy's mother in the nursing home," I suggested. "Maybe she can shed some light on things for us."

The home was a modern place on the south side of town, not far from the hospital. Decorated in tones of beige, coral, and turquoise it had a southwestern flair without being overdone. Consuelo Romero had a private room, with some furnishings that had obviously come from home—an old easy chair, a hand-carved wooden bureau, and some paintings. The nightstand beside her hospital bed held a small carafe of water and a glass, alongside a picture of a young priest in white robes. There were no pictures of her other son in the room.

"Mrs. Romero has periods of lucidity and periods of complete confusion. You never know which way it will be, so don't expect too much," the nurse at the desk had told us. "It's severe senile dementia."

The same nurse introduced us to the old woman, but I had the feeling that we could have been anyone—she really had no idea who we were or why we were there, even after we repeated our story a couple of times.

Mrs. Romero sat in the easy chair across from her bed, her birdlike legs covered with a colorful crocheted afghan. Tiny hands, heavily corded with blue veins, lay passively on her lap. Her upper torso was snugly buttoned into a bulky purple cardigan with the collar of a wool shirt neatly showing at the neckline. Her coal-black hair revealed a small perfect line of white at the roots.

"Tell us about your family," I asked.

"That's my Ramon, right there," she said in a dreamy voice. "Ramon, he was such a saint." She pointed to the photograph.

"We wondered about your other son, Eloy," I began. "Eloy is a friend of Drake's and he has some problems now."

A look of confusion came over her. "Eloy? Which Eloy? I knew a boy Eloy in school when I was just a little girl."

"No, this is the Eloy who is your son. He comes to visit you here sometimes."

Her eyes were polite, but blank.

"Tell us more about Ramon," I prompted. "He lived in Albuquerque, I understand."

"Rome. Ramon went to Rome. Ramon to Rome. Roma Ramon . . ." Her voice went sing-songy.

"He served at the Vatican?" I asked.

"Israel." This time her voice was firm. "He worked in Israel."

I glanced again at Drake. Neither of us were making any sense of this.

"Roma Ramon . . . Roma Ramon . . ." Drake and I exchanged a glance.

"Mrs. Romero, thank you so much for your time. If you think of anything else you can tell us about Ramon or Eloy, just have the nurse call me." I took her fragile hand and squeezed it. She continued to gaze raptly at the photo of Ramon.

"Well, I think that was useless," I told Drake after we got back to the car. "I'll ask Eloy what she meant about Rome and Israel. Who knows if there's any reality to any of that, or if her poor mind is wandering completely."

I left a business card with the nurse on the off chance that we'd ever hear anything more from Mrs. Romero. But I had the feeling that, even in her clearer moments, we'd get nothing more than what Eloy had told us. How difficult it must be for him, I thought. Caring for his mother, paying for the nursing home, when she worshipped his brother and didn't even remember him. Awful for poor Eloy. And it might make perfect sense that he hated his brother for it. I mulled over the situation while Drake backed out of the parking lot.

"One more stop here in town," I suggested. "Then I'll get my boots and we'll head back for the cabin where we can still pretend to have a carefree honeymoon."

"Just tell me where, my love, and I'll gladly drive you there," he said gallantly.

I pulled out the Taos phone book that I'd remembered to bring from the cabin and looked up the office address of Mike Ortiz, Eloy's brother-in-law, the lawyer. According to the small map in the book, it was located on a street that ran parallel to the main highway through town. We located it without too much trouble.

Ortiz's secretary didn't seem inclined to give us a spur of the moment appointment, but Mike himself walked out of the inner office at the precise instant I was beginning to chew on her a bit for not having him return Eloy's call yet. He ushered us into his office personally.

Mike's graying hair bore tread marks through it, where he'd run his fingers as though soothing a monstrous headache. I know this because I watched him do it twice before Drake and I had taken our seats. His trim body was clad in a wrinkled white shirt and gray slacks, which, if he hadn't slept in them, he had most certainly worn for several days without the opportunity to hang them up now and again. His pale yellow tie had a big red chile stain on it and his nails hadn't seen a manicure. Mike Ortiz was probably not the town's most successful attorney.

The office itself was another giveaway to his lack of business achievement. From the appearance of the dingy armchairs and battered desk, I guessed that someone had started him out with nice furnishings fifteen or twenty years ago and he'd never had the money to replace them. The stuff that was trendy in the early 1980s was way past prime now.

"So what does ol' Eloy want now?" he grumbled. He blinked his eyes hard, twice.

"You mean you haven't called him yet?" I asked. "He placed a call from jail last night. It's now almost midafternoon."

He raked his hair again. "Look, I had a rough night, okay? Didn't even get in until noon today. I'll get down there and figure it out before the day's over. Eloy's speeding tickets aren't gonna change my day, okay?"

I controlled my impatience. "Eloy's in jail, charged with murdering his brother, Ramon. I think that deserves a bit more of a defense than a speeding ticket."

Ortiz sat up straight. "Murder, huh?"

I got the feeling he wanted to let go with something like "Whoa!" but realized that wasn't proper lawyer-talk.

"Well, in that case I guess I better get over there." He tugged at his tie to straighten it and reached for a leather jacket that hung over an artificial philodendron. "My wife's gonna have a fit when she hears this."

Meaning that he was in deep doo-doo if he didn't get her brother out of jail pronto.

"I'm with a private investigation firm in Albuquerque," I told Mike. "Eloy asked me to look into this. If you're going to be his defense attorney, we'll probably need to confer after you've talked to him." I handed him a business card, which he glanced at casually and tossed on the desk.

"We'll see. Let me see if there's any chance of getting bond set on this. Then I may let you know." He punched the intercom button. "Carla, I'll be out for an hour or so," he barked. Then he walked out the door, past her desk, and out the front door.

Drake and I shrugged at each other and followed. He drove me to a nearby store that sold footwear, while I wondered privately why a guy like Eloy, who seemed fairly bright, would trust his life to Mike Ortiz—unless the brother-in-law rate was extremely cheap.

An hour later, outfitted with warm boots that came up to my knees, we were once again on the road to the Taos Ski Valley and our private little cabin.

"Come on," I coaxed as we parked the Jeep at the cabin. "I really need to get some exercise. Let's strap on those snowshoes and hike around the property a bit before it's really dark."

"I can think of something just as physical and much more fun," Drake teased, wiggling his eyebrows at me.

"Later." I headed for the service porch and pulled out the two pair of snowshoes.

The shadows were deep already, actual sunlight having never quite appeared all day. We made one circle of the house, then ventured into the forest making our own trail between pine trees that stood like skyscrapers in nature's Manhattan. We found a stand of small blue spruce among the ponderosas and decided we'd come back tomorrow with a saw and cut one for our Christmas tree. By the time we got back to the cabin we were both starving. Drake brought out the portable indoor grill and sizzled a couple of steaks for us, while I made a salad and some garlic bread. We snuggled before a blazing fire with glasses of wine and decided that life was just about perfect.

Until the phone rang.

"Eloy! What's happened?" Drake's look of alarm gradually turned to a smile.

"What?" I nudged at his arm as he listened to Eloy.

"Tomorrow? Okay, what's the weather forecast? . . . Okay." He nodded and scribbled some notes on a sheet of my computer paper. "Okay, see you then."

He turned to me and could tell that I was about to burst.

"Mike Ortiz got Eloy out on bond. The judge ruled that he wasn't a flight risk; Ramon's death was five years ago and Eloy's never had any other trouble with the law. Besides, the judge's sister lives next door to Eloy and she'll alert him if it looks like he tries to skip."

Only in a small town.

"So," he continued, "they went out to the hangar and checked things over. Two young guys want me to fly them up to the high country tomorrow. So that's our first charter."

"All right!" I cheered.

"Eloy said he's going by the home to see his mother tonight, and he'll be out at the hangar in the morning to help me get the flight organized. Lucky for me he was there tonight."

I had to admire Eloy's devotion to his mother, knowing how difficult it must be for him to have always been the least favored son. And it was certainly unselfish of him to tend to Drake's business this afternoon, when he had such pressing personal matters. I felt myself being pulled toward finding out the answers that would free him from the murder charge.

Drake was out the next morning just after dawn, driving Eloy's truck to deliver it to him. I spent some time composing an e-mail to Ron with questions for which I hoped he could pry answers from the Albuquerque police. Our usual contact there was Kent Taylor in Homicide, but I seemed to remember that he was taking vacation about now. Mainly I wanted some details about Ramon's murder—the who-what-where-when stuff.

At eight o'clock—not holding out too much hope—I called Mike Ortiz's office to see if I could learn more about what the police had on Eloy. I wasn't terribly surprised when his secretary said he wasn't in yet, so I left a message that I hoped conveyed the idea that I really wanted to talk to him this morning. Feeling a bit at loose ends, I cleaned up the breakfast dishes and fed Rusty a scoop of doggy nuggets.

When the phone rang at eight-fifteen, I was surprised to think that Ortiz would be calling me back that soon. I was even more surprised when it turned out to be Ron.

"Hey, kid, I sure didn't expect to hear from you on your honeymoon," he joked. I could picture my brother sitting at his always cluttered desk, cup of coffee at hand, his felt Stetson hanging on the doorknob.

"What can I say, Ron? My new husband is off working

that aircraft of his, so I had to come up with a murder to solve. You got my e-mail, I guess? By the way, how are things going with Tammy?"

"I knew it; yes; and fine."

Ron has picked up Drake's habit of answering my bunched-up questions with bunched-up answers.

"We're down to only a couple of crises per day here," he said, referring again to Tammy's work. "I've got a little background info on the priest's murder."

"Wow, that was quick."

"Yeah, well, I'm just a terrific detective. Okay, here's what I've got. Seems Father Ramon was entangled in a little bit of a sex scandal at the time of his untimely death. Had an affair going with a married woman parishioner, a well-kept secret. She came forward only after he died and her husband had left her. He was shot on the steps of his church after evening mass. You may remember some of this, it made the news at the time."

"I think I do. It was late and there was no one around. A security man found his body on the steps, but he'd already been dead several hours?"

"That's the one. Anyway, at first there were no clues, but after the woman came forward about the affair suspicion fell heavily on her husband. Police were really moving in on him but it turned out that he had an iron-clad alibi for the entire evening. Was at a lodge meeting and the guys who sat on either side of him both swore that he never even got up to go to the bathroom. They even investigated the possibility that he'd hired the killer, but he passed a lie detector test without a hitch and they never found any other evidence to substantiate that theory."

"Did they ever find the weapon?"

"Not till just the other day. And the way they found it is bizarre."

I poured another cup of coffee and carried it to my computer table, where I could make some notes.

"An old priest in the same parish Ramon served died last month. The assumption is natural causes—he was eighty years old—but that may get questioned. Anyway, among the old man's possessions in his nightstand drawer they came across an old pawn ticket for a gun, dated five years ago, three days after Ramon was murdered. Luckily Kent Taylor was on the case and something clicked with him. Same parish, two priests dead, pawn ticket—it's not exactly commonplace for a priest to pawn something—with the date coincidence. He checked the registration by the gun's serial number and discovered its owner is Eloy Romero.

"Eloy claims to know nothing about his gun ever being pawned. Says he was driving from Santa Fe to Taos the night his brother was killed—alone. No one can verify what time he left Santa Fe or what time he arrived in Taos. He says he got in late that night, but the earliest any witnesses can place him back home in Taos was early afternoon of the next day. And the gun was back in his closet until a couple of days ago when Tenorio got the warrant to find it. So if somebody else pawned the gun they put it back later. That doesn't make much sense."

I let out a pent-up breath. It didn't look good for Eloy.

"What's the motive?" I asked.

"Police say there are people who witnessed a big blow-up between Eloy and Ramon about a week before the murder. Ramon had come up to Taos on some church business, but met with Eloy so the brothers could decide what to do about their mother's health situation. She was becoming senile and couldn't stay alone in her own home anymore. Ramon told Eloy that if he were a good son . . ."

Like himself, I inserted mentally.

". . . he would give up being such an outdoorsman and stay home to take care of his mother. Eloy apparently screamed a bunch of obscenities and shoved his brother around. Reports vary on whether he actually punched the priest, but a number of people witnessed the altercation in the parking lot of some popular restaurant up there."

"Sounds like Eloy'd just had his fill of being told he wasn't good enough," I commented. "The mother is still saying it, in her more lucid moments. That Ramon was a saint. Eloy just couldn't compete."

"Another factor comes in here," Ron continued. "The family isn't wealthy, by any means, but the mother does own some property there in Taos. There's one bit of commercially zoned land that got tied up in some kind of building moratorium but was released a few years back and some big corporation wants it—bad. They've offered, and she's turned down, over a half-million dollars for it. Then there's the family home. Not much of a house, but the property is fifty acres and it borders some movie star's ranch. A fairly generous offer has been made on that property too. Even the cabin property is probably worth ten times what the family paid for it way back before the ski area was developed. Only problem is, the mother's mental state isn't good enough that she can handle such matters anymore. Ramon wouldn't agree to sell either property. Now that Ramon is dead Eloy and his sister would be beneficiaries of all that money if they wanted to sell them."

"And the police believe this all adds up to a pretty substantial motive," I filled in.

"You got it."

I told him to let me know of any new developments, then I slowly hung up the receiver. Things were suddenly looking complicated. My mind was trying to work its way around all the implications when the phone rang again. I jumped, sloshing coffee onto my sweater.

"Mike Ortiz here," said the voice.

"Oh, yes, Mike. What's up?"

"You called me."

I had. I feverishly tried to remember what I was going to ask him. "We hear that Eloy's out on bail. That's good news."

"It wasn't too difficult. He can't go too far in this town without people keeping an eye on him."

"I guess that's true." I let forth a small chuckle that fell flat when I realized he wasn't laughing along with me. "Mike, I've gotten a bit of background about Ramon's death. I guess he and Eloy had some kind of a fight a week or so before he died?"

"That's right."

"Well, I was just wondering . . . I mean, I guess I'm trying to get a feel for their relationship in general. You don't believe Eloy killed him, do you?"

He let out a breath. "No, I don't think he did it. But the evidence looks pretty bad and there aren't too many other people who had any motive for it."

"What about the husband of that woman in Albuquerque?"

"You know about that?" His voice was sharp.

"It's part of the police record, Mike. Not that difficult to find out."

"From what I understand—and you probably already know this—his story is that he was deeply hurt about the affair and insisted they attend a different church afterward. But he'd never harm a man of God. He left his wife when he first found out about it, but later they got back together and patched things up. And he had a solid alibi for that night. The police must have believed him because they released him after questioning."

He was right, I knew that, but was just scrambling for theories.

"You've been in this family quite a few years, Mike. Give me a little background to go on."

"You've probably already heard it. Eloy was the youngest, the fun-loving one, loved the outdoors, worked just enough to meet his bills but wasn't really going anywhere. Maria, my wife, was the middle child. It was always assumed she'd marry a man who'd take care of her, and she did. Spanish families around here don't generally think of their daughters as needing careers of their own. Ramon was the special one. Their mother was of the old school who believed that at least one son from the family should be a priest. She raised those kids alone, you know. Their father was killed in a construction accident when Ramon was about twelve. I think Eloy was only four or five.

"Consuelo did a good job with all the kids, but Ramon got the special attention. By the time Eloy was a teenager I think she was just tired. Maybe her mind was starting to go a little bit by then too—I don't know. While Ramon was off to Rome and off to Israel and all those other places, Eloy was running a little wild. Nothing too illegal. He just spent a lot of time unsupervised. It's probably a miracle that he's turned out as normal as he has."

"His mother mentioned that Ramon had worked in Rome. Then she said it was Israel. Was it both places? I thought she was just confused."

"Oh yes, he went to the Vatican for a while. That created quite a stir here in little old Taos, I'll tell you. We were one proud town when one of our favorite sons went to Rome."

"Then Israel? Why there?"

"It was some special thing the Catholic church was doing there. Remember the discovery of the Dead Sea Scrolls? Well, it was in the 1940s so I'm sure you don't remember it personally, but you've read about them?"

"Yeah, saw a couple of television specials about the find," I said.

"Then you know that it's only been in recent years that much of the text has become public? For decades, the churches kept it to themselves. The Catholic church opened a facility in Israel, sent a whole delegation of priests down there to oversee the recovery and translation of every scrap of parchment." He chuckled. "As a not very devout Catholic myself, I've wondered if their interest wasn't an all-out attempt to be sure nothing would come to light in those scrolls that would contradict centuries of church teachings."

"And Ramon was one of those priests?"

"For a while. I guess he spent two or three years at the facility. Then his mother's health took a downturn again and he requested reassignment to New Mexico."

Scroll pieces. My mind flicked back to the tiny scraps of

brownish paper I'd found yesterday in the photo folder.

"Mike . . ." I faltered. "Oh, never mind." I thanked him for the information and told him to stay in touch, that I knew Eloy still wanted me to work on clearing him.

The minute I hung up the phone I pulled the photo from the bookshelf again. The flat plastic bag slid easily out and I looked at the scraps of paper through their protective cover. The writing certainly did look like a Middle Eastern language. I remembered thinking that when I first saw them. But pieces of the Dead Sea Scrolls? Could I possibly be holding such a valuable piece of history? I got a fluttery feeling in my stomach.

FIVE

My brain was still trying to wrap itself around all this new information when I noticed Rusty at the door, pawing at the rug and whining softly. Only then did my own ears pick up the sound of an approaching vehicle. It's amazing how clearly sounds come through in the dead quiet of a snowy mountainside.

Eloy's truck rounded the curve in the driveway a minute later and Rusty bounded out to greet Drake the instant I opened the door. Eloy waved as he turned around and headed back toward town.

"You'll never guess where we're invited tonight," Drake said, stomping the snow off his boots in the entry.

"You're probably right about that," I teased, "unless you want to give me a clue or two."

"Hint: Jason Kirk invited us."

"What? No way! The guy we saw in . . . okay, what was the name of that movie?"

"The remake of *Love Story*," he gushed.

Oh, yeah. "Okay, so it was a sappy movie that we probably wouldn't have gone to if it weren't for the free passes, but you have to admit that Jason Kirk is a heartthrob. Okay, you don't have to admit it, but *I'll* admit it even though he is young enough to be my . . . my much younger brother."

"See, I knew you'd want to go."

I hung his heavy parka on one of the wooden pegs as he unlaced his boots. "So what's the occasion?"

"He was one of my passengers this morning. Hollywood types never think twice about spending the money for a helicopter ride." He set the boots under the bench and we went inside. "So I flew them up to the high country, where they made a couple of spectacular runs, then I took them back to Kirk's ranch between here and town. I did mention that my wife was one of his biggest fans."

"Oh, Drake, you didn't." He knows I'm not the type to go googly over a movie star, even though I might enjoy sneaking a peek at his smooth young body.

"No, actually I just told him truthfully that we'd just seen his latest movie. I didn't mention our opinion of it. So he said he's hosting a reception tonight for a new artist at one of the galleries in town and he invited us." He pulled a thick ivory card from his shirt pocket, an engraved invitation personally signed by Kirk. "So if you want to go, we're in."

I said, "Probably crowded. Probably way overpriced art. Probably won't be able to get a parking spot blocks away. So . . . let's do it! Maybe all his rich friends will be there and he'll tell them how much fun it was to fly with you. It could be good for business."

"And with free hors d'oeuvres we won't have to make dinner," he added helpfully. "I could, however, use some lunch."

Over peanut butter sandwiches, I filled him in on what I'd learned about Eloy's situation, making light over the fact that we might actually have pieces of the Dead Sea Scrolls here in the cabin. First, I wanted to find out what Eloy knew about them and suggest we get them to the proper authorities.

"How was Eloy today?" I asked.

"Subdued," he said. "This took him completely by surprise. He said his mother really went downhill when Ramon died. He's worried that finding out about his arrest could kill her. You know, from what you've told me, the way she treated him all along, I'm surprised he would care—sorry—you know I didn't mean that."

"I know, hon. Families create some strange dynamics, don't they?" I stared into my glass of milk for a long time.

"Hey, we've got the rest of the day to enjoy. Let's do something fun," he suggested. "Eloy told me we should cut a Christmas tree from the property here. I described that little group we saw yesterday and he knew which ones I meant. Said we should definitely take one of them because they're growing too close together."

"Okay." I brightened up. "You find a saw and I'll stock some provisions."

I filled a Thermos bottle with hot chocolate and stuck it into a small backpack I'd noticed hanging on the ski porch. We strapped on our boots and snowshoes and let Rusty know that we were embarking on an adventure he could share.

The sky was deep blue, with a clarity unmarred by the brown air Albuquerque so often has in the winter months. Bright sunlight sparkled off the snow, creating fields of glitter, as if an incredibly wealthy woman had flung a box of diamonds over the ground. Clumps of whipped cream perfection dolloped the pine branches above us, with an occasional mound letting go to fall to the ground. Rusty bounded through snow up to his chest, while we walked easily on top of it, sinking only a few inches with our mammoth paws.

In about fifteen minutes we came to our little stand of trees and stood back trying to decide which would be just perfect. We finally agreed on a little blue spruce that looked tiny in the forest but was taller than Drake in reality. He cut through the tough little trunk with a few swift pulls on the saw, then we broke open the hot chocolate.

"I love this out here, don't you?" I said.

"Umm, definitely. Let's toast to taking a honeymoon like this every year," he said, raising his mug of chocolate.

We allowed Rusty to lick the dregs from our cups, swearing that he really wasn't consuming much chocolate from the tiny bit left there. It was really just the flavor he was after anyway. We spun the tree trunk toward the cabin and, each of us taking a lower limb with the tree between us, began the trek back. Rusty raced back and was sitting on the front porch, ears cocked toward us, when we arrived.

"Boy, my thighs are gonna feel this tomorrow," I said. "I never realized how much work snowshoeing could be."

We stomped the snow off our boots, hung the snowshoes to dry and batted the clingy snow from our legs. I offered to scrounge around for the Christmas tree stand while Drake pulled the tree onto the porch. I located the box marked CHRISTMAS ORNAMENTS under the stairs, and pulled it into the living room. Delicate decorations like glass figurines and feathery tinsel were on top. I felt a pang of regret as I recognized a few things similar to my own childhood decorations, ones I'd put on my tree every year of my life. All were gone now, lost in the fire that had consumed a portion of our home a couple of months ago.

I set items aside as I delved deeper into the carton. Near

the bottom I spotted the tree stand under a newspaper-wrapped packet, heavy for its size. I couldn't resist a peek. Inside, wrapped in deep blue velvet were two small crosses, each about six inches tall. By their weight, I guessed they had to be solid silver. Ornate with decoration, one had a delicate filigree of silver wire around the edges with tiny, intricate designs carved into the cross itself. The second cross had its shape embellished by fleur-de-lis points at each of its four tips and an incredibly detailed motif of leaves and fruit crafted from separate pieces of silver and applied so seamlessly that the welds were invisible.

"Hon, have you found the stand yet?" Drake called.

"Oh, yeah, it's right here," I replied, setting the crosses in their velvet wrap on the end table by the sofa.

"And maybe a blanket or some towels that we can set under this thing to catch the melting snow."

I handed him the stand and dashed off to find the other required items. When I returned from the bathroom with three towels, the tree was coming stand-first through the door.

"Let's set this in the corner," he suggested, "with the towels under the branches. I have a feeling when it warms up this last bit of snow will melt off and I'd hate to stain the hardwood floors."

"Look what I found in the decoration box," I told him, showing him the two crosses. "Elaborate, aren't they?"

"These must be family heirlooms. They sure aren't any modern-day ornaments bought at Wal-Mart."

"A mountain cabin seems like a strange place to leave them, don't you think? They have to be valuable. Maybe we should ask Eloy if he'd rather take them home or put them in a safe-deposit box."

"Good idea. Stash them back where they were and I'll remember to ask him tomorrow," he offered.

We decided that we'd better take showers and change clothes to be ready for the gallery reception at six. Our two showers ended up being one, long and shared under the hot spray, and the wardrobe change took a while, as articles of clothing kept getting pulled back off again before they finally stayed on.

The reception was crowded and our fears about having to park blocks away proved true when we arrived a half-hour late.

As it turned out, we were fashionably late in the Hollywood style because Jason Kirk and his entourage of four arrived just as we did, and Drake performed quick introductions on the sidewalk outside the Dumont Gallery. Jason was, predictably, devastatingly good looking and quick in his acknowledgement of our meeting. The four keepers followed Kirk into the gallery, so they could begin setting glasses into his hand, seeing that he spoke to no one for longer than one point three minutes, and generally bowing and scraping to him while putting on unbelievable airs to everyone else. I knew I would have to take an interest in the artwork or risk being sick.

Inside, we shed our coats to the outstretched arms of a young lady brought in for that purpose. She vanished to a back room with them and a tuxedoed waiter immediately appeared at our sides with a tray of bubbling champagne glasses. We each took one and were raising them to each other when a woman appeared at Drake's side.

"I saw you walk in with Jason," she cooed. "I'm Daphne Dumont. Welcome to my gallery."

Daphne's look was Taos art chic with a fine polish of some eastern school spread over the surface. Her broomstick skirt was silk, in a rich teal color, and the dyed-to-match top was velvet, with rows of tiny dyed-to-match teal beads. Her suede boots were silver, as was the silk band caressing her neat chignon at the back of her sleek silver-blond head. She'd carried the silver and teal theme to the tips of her fingers (silver) and to the six rings of Indian silver with perfectly matched turquoise stones that adorned those fingers. I instantly felt like a clod in my cotton skirt and beaded holiday sweater.

Drake looked somewhat taken aback that she'd wound her silver-laden hand through his arm but wasn't sure how he could gracefully untwine her.

"Jason tells me he went for a perfectly *marvelous* helicopter ride with you today, Draper."

"It's Drake," he said. "Yes, he did, and I'm glad to hear he liked it."

"I'm Charlie, Drake's wife," I introduced, extending my hand and forcing her to withdraw her arm from my husband's. "I'm so interested in the paintings. Do tell me about the artist."

Businesswoman that she was, Daphne couldn't ignore my apparent enthrallment, even though she clearly would have rather led Drake around the room by his elbow. I glanced back toward him and he shot me a thank-you look before heading to the refreshment table. For my rescue attempt I was rewarded with ten minutes of Daphne's gushing about one particular painting before she spotted someone she knew who apparently had a bigger Visa card limit.

"If I hear the word *marvelous* one more time, I'm gonna

puke," I whispered to Drake when we met again.

"Thanks for bailing me out," he said. "Here, I've fixed you a plate."

He handed me a saucer-sized bit of china with an array of things I couldn't identify. "The round ones with the little curly orange thing on top are pretty good," he confided.

"I bet you tried some of everything," I teased.

"I did. And I didn't put anything on your plate that hasn't passed my own personal taste test."

"You are just *mahvelously* kind, my dear."

"Too much Daphne, I see." The female voice startled me and I was instantly mortified that someone had overheard me joking about the hostess. "Don't worry. I'm no fan, and your secret is safe with me," she said.

I turned to face the speaker.

"I'm Margaret Collins. Call me Maggie. And please don't be under the impression that I actually fit in with this crowd."

"Hi, Maggie." I introduced myself and Drake and explained briefly why we were visiting Taos and how we happened to be at the showing.

"So if you don't fit in with this crowd, how do you happen to be here?" I asked. I got the sense that, with Maggie, the question wouldn't be considered rude.

"Same way you did. Knowing somebody. Actually the caterer is a very good friend and she asked if I'd like to be in on the free food and drink. I'm really a farm girl myself, own a small spread near El Prado, and you're more likely to see me in Levi's and a flannel shirt any day of the week. But I clean up pretty good and can do this kind of thing now and then. Plus, I thought Beth might get short-handed tonight.

One of her waiters isn't too reliable and they knew they'd get a big crowd."

Her grin was infectious and I noticed for the first time what a pretty, natural face she had. Unspoiled by makeup of any kind, her skin had the texture of a summer peach and her cheeks had just a hint of wind-kissed pink to them. Her hair was her most striking feature, completely gray with an interesting white highlight at the hairline, it fell thick and luxurious past her waist. I liked her immediately. I glanced toward Drake, but he'd wandered to the far side of the room to look at the paintings.

Maggie tilted toward my ear, her voice low. "There's Sam Begay, our artist, now." She indicated a Native American man in his mid-twenties with flowing shoulder-length black hair, a lean body, and a face whose planes might have been chiseled from the reddish sandstone of the desert. "I'm sure Jason Kirk will do an introduction to the whole room soon—after all, that's what he's here for. That, and the fact that Daphne's daughter is sleeping with him.

"The older gentleman who just came in the front door"—she flicked her chin that direction—"that's Anton Pachevski, the art critic. Watch for the stir, because it's big news that he's here."

Sure enough, once Daphne spotted Pachevski she made a not very subtle beeline for him. He greeted her out-stretched hand with a quick goateed kiss, while reaching for a glass of champagne with his free hand. His white receding hair was combed straight back and plastered closely to his head. The goatee was probably trimmed every other day. His clothing defied the typical art world slouch—he was stylishly European looking, like someone with a minor title.

"No one seems to know when Anton came on the scene exactly. One day he was simply *the* art critic to please. You'll certainly see some major sucking-up from both Daphne and the artist. A mention of the Dumont Gallery in Pachevski's column will mean big sales," Maggie told me. "I was an art major before I bought the ranch." She winked.

I watched the critic from the corner of my eye as Maggie steered my attention elsewhere.

"The older couple over there are from Santa Fe. The green aura you see around them is envy. They own a gallery there and have been trying for a year to get Pachevski to one of their showings. They don't give a shit about this artist tonight, but they'll eventually join the groveling at Anton's feet."

I chuckled along with her. The party really was more fun when you knew the identities of the players.

"Who's the elegant woman in black?" I asked.

"Rita Trujillo. She owns this building and odds are she's here to see if there's a good crowd and if sales are brisk. She lives on the ranch next to mine and is another lady who's more likely to be seen about town at Wal-Mart wearing jeans. But she told me a while back that Daphne's two months behind in her rent. The last Dumont showing was a bust."

So her presence might account for Daphne's almost frantic catering to the "important" guests. Interesting.

Drake sidled by, working his way around the walls of bright paint splashes. "Seen about all the art I can handle, hon."

"Do you need to be rescued, dear?"

"I think I'm ready, unless you see something here you just can't live without."

"Not at four thousand and up," I assured him. "Maggie says Jason Kirk is going to do an introduction of the artist pretty soon. I think right after that will be our chance to escape."

Maggie excused herself to make sure her caterer friend was doing all right, and Drake and I edged toward the coat rack.

Ding-ding-ding. A silver spoon tapped melodically against a wineglass. "Attention, everyone," Daphne called out. The crowd came to a gradual hush. "I'd like to thank you all for coming tonight. We're just *thrilled* with the turnout to honor our *talented* young artist. As you know, Jason Kirk, one of the *brightest* new stars in Hollywood, is hosting tonight's party and I'd like to have him say a few words and introduce you to Sam Begay."

Polite applause greeted Jason as he stepped forward. He swept one hand through the longish hair above his forehead, only to have it fall back into exactly the same casual cascade that brushed his eyelids. He grinned the slightly crooked smile that had launched him into America's female hearts and his eyes sparkled as he began to speak.

I felt myself becoming antsy, impatient with the lengthy protocol that dictated our listening to one person introduce another, who would then introduce a third. Drake caught my eye and eased our jackets off the coat rack. Jason's talk ended with his arm across Sam Begay's shoulders as the two posed with frozen smiles for cameras. I slipped my arms into the jacket Drake held up for me and we edged outside quietly.

"You looked like you and Maggie hit it off," he said, once we were safely outside, bustling toward our car in the brisk night air.

"She's funny. A sweet, ordinary person who's obviously into all the small town gossip. Maybe I'll call her again while we're here."

Drake unlocked my door and I slid onto the frigid seat. "Look, hon, it's starting to snow."

"Then our timing was perfect for heading back out to the cabin," he said. "But let's do one quick thing first."

The Dumont Gallery was on Kit Carson Road, but it was so crowded we'd been forced to park in a municipal lot about three blocks away. Our route back would take us down that winding historic road, past its namesake's home. Drake made the additional detour to circle the plaza once to savor the magic of northern New Mexico at Christmas. The adobe walls and buildings were topped with luminarias, more correctly called *farolitos*, meaning little lights. Although originally these were small paper bags with a couple of inches of sand in the bottom of each, and a single votive candle placed in the sand, modern ones are now plastic brown bags with electric lights. The flickering magic of the real flame may be gone, but these hold up much better in snow.

Slowly driving around the plaza square, seeing every building topped with the glowing golden lights, the sidewalks also rimmed with them, and the snow falling softly in big wet flakes, made the Christmas spirit of northern New Mexico suddenly very real.

There was about an inch of new snow by the time we reached the northern town limits, close to four new inches as we ascended the road leading to the cabin.

"If you're ever driving this road in a storm, be extra careful," Drake said, switching to four-wheel drive. "It has some sudden turns and it's a steep drop if you go off."

SIX

"Maggie! Charlie Parker here. We met last night at the Dumont."

"Of course, how are you today? I noticed you were lucky enough to duck out early."

"Well, the weather really started to close in. We had quite a long drive up here to the ski valley."

"I wish I'd thought of that one," she said. "I stayed till the deadly boring end."

"Look, I've got a question for you," I said. I'd called Eloy earlier to suggest he come by the cabin and get the silver crosses and take them to a safer place. He sounded surprised and said his family never had any silver crosses and he couldn't imagine where they'd come from. So now I was off on another tangent, trying to get some background information to find out who they belonged to. "Maggie, you seem to know lots of people, especially in the art world."

"Well, some."

"Do you know anyone who might have some expertise in religious artifacts? Crosses, in particular."

"Hmmm . . . let me think. You could try Sandra Chavez at the museum. They have some religious items there. Wait, I think I have her number here somewhere—" She read it off to me and I thanked her, suggesting that we meet in town for lunch soon.

A call to Sandra Chavez netted me an appointment at eleven A.M. After dropping Drake at the hangar, I headed into town and arrived at her office ten minutes early with my velvet-wrapped bundle.

"Charlie?" The woman who greeted me was petite with short, dark hair and an elfin face in subtle makeup. She wore the Taos uniform of broomstick skirt and pullover velveteen top, with two strands of silver *heishi* around her neck. She invited me into an office that was neat but crowded with books, files, and papers.

"As I explained on the phone, I'm looking for some background information on these." I laid the packet on her desk and spread open the velvet wrapping.

"Oh!" She lifted the cross with the delicate leaf work. "These are exquisite," she breathed.

She examined the cross she held, set it carefully down and picked up the other one, turning it over and carefully perusing it from all angles.

"Do you recognize them?" I asked.

"Not specifically. They're obviously very old and of the finest craftsmanship. I'd say Spanish or Italian, sixteenth century, most likely. How do you happen to have them?"

"You don't know whether they may have come from a museum or a private collection?" I dodged her question.

"No, I'd remember if I'd seen them before."

I wrapped the velvet covering around them again. "Maybe someone connected with the Catholic church would know," I ventured.

"You could meet with one of the priests at St.

Augustine," she suggested. "Father Sanchez is the younger one but Father Domingo has been here for about sixty years. He's very knowledgeable in church history, particularly if the crosses are somehow connected locally."

This last was a hint, which I ignored as I picked up the crosses and thanked her. I remembered the old church—we had passed it on the way to Mike Ortiz's office. I drove there and walked into the peaceful church. The nave was empty except for a lone figure near the altar.

"Father Domingo?" I queried of the black-clad man who was straightening candles.

"No, my dear." He chuckled. "He's in his office." On closer look, this man was in his early fifties, not even close to the age Sandra Chavez had estimated for the elder priest.

"Could you show me the way? I'd like to speak with him."

"Certainly."

I followed him through a small side door, down a hallway, and into a plain square office.

"Father, there is a lady to see you."

The elderly man was robed in a black cassock, probably more comfortable than slacks in the chilly room. His thin, white hair covered little of his shiny pink scalp, and his face settled into creases that gave him the kindly character of a basset. His smile revealed good strong teeth and a peaceful soul. He extended his hand to me, his eyes questioning.

"I'm Charlie Parker," I said, taking the proffered hand. "I wonder if I might ask for your expertise on something."

"It has been a long time since someone your age has called me an expert," he grinned. His voice was quiet and rounded with the soft tones of Spanish. "Come, sit down."

The other priest left, gently closing the door behind him.

I laid the crosses on the desk, again peeling back the velvet covering.

"Madre de Dios!" the old man exclaimed. He clutched at his chest and my own heart lurched. Father Domingo's breath came in short gasps. His fingers had grabbed a fistful of his robe.

"Are you all right? Shall I get help?" I glanced back at the door where the other priest had disappeared.

"No!" He put a hand out toward me. "I will be fine. I . . . just . . . I just want to . . ."

He reached toward the crosses and pulled the edge of the velvet cover so the packet slid across the desktop to him. Gently, as one might handle a fragile flower, he lifted the cross with the delicate silver wire.

"The Cross of Lamonde," he said reverently. "I never thought to see it again."

He held the cross to his heart, gently rubbing it against the fabric of his robe. His eyes were closed, his lips pressed together.

"Where ever did you get this?" he asked after a couple of minutes.

"This is a famous cross?" I countered. "I take it that it is very well known."

"They both are." He set the Cross of Lamonde down and picked up the other. Holding it in both hands as if it were a tiny baby, he gazed lovingly at it. "This is the Cross of Santiago."

My expression must have shown that my knowledge of Catholic tradition is nil.

"You have never heard of them, I guess." His face showed great compassion for my state of complete ignorance.

"These crosses are treasures of the church. It is so good to have them back again."

His stare became sharp, his anthracite eyes piercing mine. "I ask you again, Ms. Parker, where did you get these crosses?"

It was time for confession.

Without naming names, I told him how I'd found them among a box of decorations, carefully hidden away in the mountain cabin. I said that the owner of the cabin knew nothing about the crosses being there. Which was almost true—at least I *believed* that Eloy knew nothing about them.

"Father Domingo, I'm a partner in a private investigation firm. Could you give me some background information on them? It would really help with a case I'm working on. For instance, where did the crosses come from?—recently, I mean."

The old man settled back in his chair, his color finally looking a bit better. He kept the crosses in front of him on the desk, still watching them protectively.

"As far as I am aware," he began, "the Cross of Lamonde was kept at St. Patrick's Cathedral in New York. I have never visited there myself, but when the story came out about the loss of it, pictures were released so we would all be watching for it. It was stolen from the sacristy and the cardinal actually received a ransom note. It was the most valuable item in the parish's collection and the thief knew exactly what he was taking. The cardinal answered the ransom demand publicly on the radio, saying that the thief would do well to return God's property without delay and without demanding a payment of money.

"It was apparently the wrong thing to do because the cross vanished and no further word came from the thief. Many believed that he had followed through on his threat and melted it down. Others believed that some unscrupulous person had purchased it for a private collection and that was the reason it was never seen again.

"When the Cross of Santiago disappeared from the Vatican collection, it was decided not to make the theft public, for fear of the same thing happening."

Vatican. My coincidence meter shot up. "How long ago did this happen?" I asked.

"Let me think." He squinted his eyes and looked upward. "The first theft was probably seven or eight years ago. Father Ralph had just come to our parish here for the first time. He's usually with us around the holidays each year, but Father Sanchez is our regular priest."

"And the second cross?"

"A year or two after the first, I believe." He rubbed his temple. "Yes, I think that is about right."

"Were the police involved? Did they have any suspects?"

"Oh, yes. And the FBI, I seem to remember that they had suspects." He smiled as he swiveled in his chair and opened a file drawer in the desk. "Forgive an old man with an interest in crime-solving," he said. Pulling a thin folder from the back of the drawer, he withdrew a small stack of what appeared to be newspaper and magazine clippings. He scanned each one slowly.

"This one mentions a man named Leon Palais, who was someone important in the art world. The police suspected that he might have been working with someone on the inside."

I settled back in my chair and read the whole article.

Palais had indeed been the number-one suspect. He was referred to in the article at different times as an art dealer, a collector, and an expert on religious artifacts. He'd been in both New York and Rome, coincidentally at the same times the two thefts had taken place. Although he didn't have direct access to the places where the crosses were taken, and could not be placed at either scene, authorities believed that it would have been easy enough for someone on the inside to slip the small silver crosses to him. No suspects were named as the possible insiders.

Palais was a slippery character. The only photo known to exist of him was on his passport. Reprinted with the article, the photo showed a burly man in his forties with fluffy hair and a thick beard. The last place Palais had used his passport was on the French/Dutch island of St. Maarten in the Caribbean. He had entered on the French side and blended so well with the dozens of different nationalities who inhabit the place, that he'd not been seen again. The last of the articles Father Domingo handed me was dated five years ago, when the trail had dried up.

Five years ago, Ramon Romero, the priest from Taos was killed, returning from an assignment at the Vatican. Too much coincidence for my taste, although I couldn't imagine Ramon the saint actually breaking and entering, or sending ransom notes. How would this all fit together?

I asked Father Domingo if he would assure that the crosses were returned to their proper homes. I would leave them with him on the condition that the returns were done quietly with no publicity. For Eloy's sake, we couldn't afford to alert any others who might have been involved.

SEVEN

I left the church, feeling relieved that I'd found someone to take care of the crosses for me, but more confused than ever about the implications of the thefts and the number of people involved. I couldn't help but feel that Eloy's brother had somehow been tied in, but how?

I called the hangar to see if Drake could break away for lunch, but he was out on a flight. I called Maggie Collins to ask her the same question and got an answering machine. So I opted to do some last-minute Christmas shopping. I'd already taken care of everyone in Albuquerque, leaving gifts at the office for Ron and his boys, Sally and her husband Ross, and a little trinket for our new girl, Tammy. I had mailed gifts to my brother Paul and his family in Phoenix, and left a little something for my grandmotherly neighbor Elsa. So everyone was taken care of except the most important—Drake.

The problem was, I was really stuck for ideas for my sweetie. By the time men hit forty, they've usually acquired everything they really want for themselves. And if some new gadget came out, he'd buy it without waiting for an occasion. I parked behind the plaza and decided to browse the shops. Maybe something that would be a lasting reminder of our honeymoon winter in Taos would be fun. I climbed the stairs to Ogilvie's restaurant where I ordered a salad and tried to hatch a brainstorm in the gift department. Unfortunately all the confusing, conflicting complexities of the silver crosses and Ramon's murder intruded unmercifully into my thoughts.

Wind whipped the bare branches of the plaza trees as I emerged from the restaurant forty minutes later, the brisk remains of the storm that had passed through last night. I discovered by staying on the covered sidewalks that ringed the plaza, I avoided the bitterest of the chill. I ducked into a couple of shops but found the touristy little things trite, and the pricey galleries held nothing that would interest him. Midway down one side of the square, however, I hit upon the perfect idea.

At our hasty wedding ceremony the previous October, we'd not exchanged rings. The whole thing was put together on less than two days notice after the investigation I was working on turned ugly. Our joy and relief at being reunited had left little time for a real ceremony, let alone shopping for the extras. All we knew then, and still reinforce daily, was that we wanted to be together forever. In a jeweler's window, there was a display of unusual wedding bands, some with distinctly southwestern looks, others with intricate gold work, and others with precious and semiprecious stones. A tiny card in the corner of the display announced that custom-designed rings were their specialty. I went inside.

"I hear he's getting a *rave* from Anton Pachevski," a blond woman at the counter was saying to the clerk. "Last night's showing was a *smash*."

I made a pretty good show of browsing the jewel cases,

although my ears had definitely perked at the mention of the show we'd just attended.

"You were there, weren't you, dear?" It took me a second to realize the woman was addressing me.

I raised an eyebrow in question, just to make the point that I hadn't been eavesdropping.

"At the Dumont Gallery, last night." She waved a many-ringed hand in the general direction of the gallery's location down the block. "I seem to remember seeing you there."

"Oh. Yes, my husband and I attended."

"*Lovely*, wasn't it? Just *fab*ulous."

I really hoped she wasn't about to launch into *mahvelous*. Daphne Dumont had already worn that into the ground. "It was very nice," I responded.

"I took *Canyon at Sunset*. I really do think it was the best piece in the show. And a steal at only ten, didn't you think?"

"A little out of our range, I'm afraid." I didn't specifical-ly remember *Canyon at Sunset*, but everything I'd seen that bore landscape-sounding titles looked more like genitalia. I'd gotten the feeling that the artist definitely had a one-track mind.

She turned again to the clerk, having gotten all the mileage she needed from me.

I browsed the rings in the display case and found several sets I liked, but decided that this was a decision Drake and I should make together. I opted for taking the card of the jewelry maker and decided to present Drake with a gift of the rings, with the provision that he and I would return after Christmas to choose them. I left the store a few minutes later, leaving the female gusher still in full form with the hapless store clerk smiling woodenly.

I arrived at the cabin and called the RJP offices to see if there were any messages. One, from the contractor who was doing the remodeling on our house. Since the fire in October I'd been more or less the full-time supervisor of a construction job. One end of the house had been gutted, so the construction included a new master suite for us, a new guest room and bath, and a customized office for Drake. Since the original house was built in the 1950s, we had to keep the exterior look consistent with the original but wanted to update the interior and give ourselves a few of the modern luxuries. I'd learned the finer points of bathroom fixtures and more than I ever wanted to know about drywall texture. Drake was so involved in getting his new business going that I really couldn't expect him to do mundane chores like picking wallpaper patterns.

I dialed the contractor's number and the phone rang twice before a perky-sounding voice picked up.

"Hi, Ms. Parker," Cori Smith greeted. "Walt's got a question about your windows. What was the model number you chose for that area around your Jacuzzi tub?"

Cori was the daughter-in-law of the contractor and she ran his office quite efficiently. Evidently this was one item she hadn't written down.

"Gosh, Cori, I don't remember. And I forgot to bring my Construction Project folder with me on my honeymoon."

"Oh, I'm so sorry, ma'am. I didn't realize you were away. I thought you'd be here in your Albuquerque office."

"Is it urgent?" I asked.

"Well, I know he wanted to get the exterior closed in before weather hits. It'd be a shame to have snow come through on your new flooring."

"Um, I see what you mean." But I wasn't too inclined to dash to Albuquerque to find my folder two days before Christmas. "He could try calling the window place. They probably wrote down the information. If not, I'll plan on making a trip to town right after Christmas and I'll catch up with him then. Would that be okay? Meanwhile, just have the men keep that heavy plastic stretched over the window openings."

"Okay, Ms. Parker, I'll tell him." She didn't sound too thrilled about it, but hey, those are the breaks.

I was just debating the merits of finishing the Christmas tree decorating when I heard Eloy's white pickup truck lumbering up the driveway. The poor lonely tree had sat in the corner, surrounded by towels, with the box of decorations beside it where I'd left them after finding the silver crosses. With only two days to go, it was beginning to nag at me that we hadn't hung a single light or ornament yet. Now Drake was home and I decided we could do it together this evening.

"Ask Eloy to come in with you," I shouted from the porch as Drake climbed out of the truck.

Eloy cut the engine and they both clomped up the steps. Rusty pranced around Drake, wagging and rubbing against his human's legs, excited that he now had three people to beg treats from.

"I thought you two might be interested in knowing what I've learned about your situation," I said to Eloy. "You guys want some coffee? Beer? Wine?"

I busied myself getting drinks organized while they shed their snowy boots.

"How was your day, sweetheart?" I asked Drake, kissing

him, when he came into the kitchen.

"Nice—yours?" He'd slid his arms around my waist and probably would have gone farther if Eloy hadn't come into the room.

I handed out beers to the two men, picked up a glass of wine for myself. We carried them to the living room, where Drake set logs in the fireplace and struck a match to them. I settled back into the tartan sofa cushions and put my feet up on the coffee table.

I filled the two men in on my findings from Father Domingo.

"So how did the stolen crosses get into my cabin?" Eloy snapped.

I shrugged, not sharing my speculation that Ramon the saint might have been involved with artifact thieves.

"I'm just concerned," I told Eloy, "about how your gun gets connected with all this."

He sighed. "I know, Charlie. I don't understand it. That gun was always stored in my closet. I can't figure out how it could have been used in a killing, and returned to the closet without my knowing it was missing."

"So you didn't use it often yourself?"

"No, hardly ever. I took it out to the shooting range three or four times a year, maybe."

"And aside from those times, you didn't actually see it or handle it every day?"

"No. I put it on the closet shelf near the front door. Always covered it up with a folded jacket, so nobody would see it there. You know, didn't want anybody who might look in the closet to just spot it."

"So it's possible that it could have been 'borrowed' by

someone and put back later without your knowing it?" Drake asked.

"I guess. But I can't imagine who that would be. I mean, wouldn't I have seen them carry it out?"

"Only if you were there at the time. Did anyone else have a key to your house?"

"No—well, I have this girl come over and clean about once a month. I leave a key out for her. But only on the day she's coming. It's not out all the time."

We sipped our drinks silently, each of us wondering how this whole thing came together.

"On a happier note," Drake said, "a woman called today to book a flight for a couple of her nephews. Introduced herself as Hope Montgomery. You don't suppose . . .?"

"Hope Montgomery, the elusive heiress to that microchip fortune?"

"Maybe."

"I remember reading about that," Eloy said. "The one who showed up and claimed all the stock in Monty Enterprises after Monty was killed in the plane crash."

"Yeah," I said. "A couple of years ago. It made the papers because no one knew he had any heirs, but she apparently had all the proof she needed to show she was his daughter. I wonder if it could be . . . Well, I guess she's got the money to buy helicopter flights for anybody she wants to, huh."

"Yep. And I'm gonna make sure they have a good time so they'll want to do it again." Drake laughed.

"Eloy, you wanna stay for dinner?" I asked.

He glanced at his watch. "Oh, I almost forgot. I've got a date tonight. A Christmas party for my girlfriend's company. She'll shoot me if I don't take her. Sorry."

He set his glass down and headed for the door. "Oh, Charlie." He turned. "Thanks for all you're doing to help me out."

Drake rose and showed Eloy out, watching as he navigated the snowy driveway.

"I'm kinda glad he didn't stay after all," I admitted. "It's nice to have you to myself."

We spent the evening trimming our tree and snuggling on the couch by the light of the Christmas tree and fireplace. Murders aside, I was determined not to let the world's problems ruin our honeymoon.

EIGHT

"Hon, that was Eloy," said Drake, hanging up the telephone and rolling to face my side of the bed. "Guess he had a bit too much fun last night at that party. He can't make it to the hangar to help me today."

"And you're wondering if I might be able to come with you and load your passengers . . . and maybe help out . . .?"

"Well, if I were really, really good to you later, would you think about it?"

"Show me what really, really good means," I teased.

Trailing his lips across the soft inner skin on my arm and heading toward even more enticing locales, he smiled up at me. "That's a little sample." He grinned.

"And what time are these passengers going to show up?" I asked.

"Ugh. In about an hour. We better get going."

We shared a quick shower in the cabin's tight fiberglass stall, teasing each other with little accidental brushes against sensitive places and promising each other that our first Christmas Eve together would be memorable.

"You know, I was thinking . . ." Drake said, thirty minutes later as we were driving down the mountain toward the hangar in the ski valley, Rusty fogging the back windows with hot doggy breath, ". . . that it would be much handier if we had two vehicles here. You or Eloy wouldn't always have to drive me to work each day."

"I don't mind your using the Jeep anytime you want," I told him. "I'm doing most of my work from the cabin anyway. Or I was until I started running all over town trying to gather evidence to help Eloy."

"Exactly. So maybe now it would help if I had my truck here. I was thinking that, next time you want to go to Albuquerque, I'll ride along and bring my truck back."

"Okay, sometime between Christmas and New Year's Day I told the contractor I'd come down and settle a question he had over some windows. Can you get away then?"

"We'll see what the flight schedule looks like, but I can probably squeak out a day off."

Our passengers were waiting in a dark red Suburban when we arrived. Drake unlocked the door to the office, then headed into the hangar section of the building to do his preflight check before rolling the aircraft out to the concrete pad behind it.

Two young men were taking the flight, carrying snowboards that they planned to ride back down. The woman with them was none other than the blond lady I'd encountered at the jewelry store yesterday, the one who'd gushed over the paintings at the art show. So she was Hope Montgomery, heiress to a fortune. She recognized me immediately.

"Did you find something nice at the jeweler's?" she asked.

I shook my head and made a little *Shh* motion with my mouth. I didn't want Drake to have a clue about the gift.

"Are you enjoying your painting?" I changed the subject abruptly, while I directed the two young men to step onto the scale with their snowboards so I could calculate the weight and balance for the flight.

Ms. Montgomery went on about the gallery showing and how she just knew the young artist would go far, while I processed her credit card.

"Okay, I think we're set," I said briskly. "Do you gentlemen have a check-in plan after you make your run?"

They held up a tiny cell phone.

"Okay, we require that you call this number." I handed them a business card with Drake's cell number written on it. "At the end of your run. We'll expect to hear from you within an hour after we drop you off. If we don't hear from you within two hours, we're required to notify search and rescue, and there's a six hundred dollar per hour charge for the helicopter to go out looking for you." I directed this last bit to their aunt, since it was her credit card I'd be putting the charge on. "These releases you've signed authorize us to do this, so it's very important that you check in."

"That's cool." One of the young dudes answered while the other gazed around the room, not paying any attention at all.

"Do you also have a plan about meeting up with them somewhere?" I asked Ms. Montgomery.

"Oh, yes. But I'm not staying up on that mountain all day," she said. "I have some shopping to do in town and they'll stay up there with their snowboards until four o'clock. Hear that, boys? I'll be back to pick you up at the base of the ski lift at four."

They waved her off as she turned.

"Oh, Charlie," she said, turning back to me. "I'm have-
ing a little 'do' at my place on the twenty-sixth. You know
how the day after Christmas always feels like such a let-
down. Like all the fun's over? So I always like to stretch it
out with a party. You and Drake plan to come, will you?
Seven-ish?" She pulled a card from her purse. It was a printed invitation with a map to the house printed on the back.

"I'll check with him and let you know," I said.

Drake had the aircraft out of the hangar by now and I
helped the two passengers into their seats, buckled belts,
placed headsets on. We slipped the two snowboards onto
the floor of the backseat.

"I'll be back in about fifteen minutes," Drake said.
"Then I'll take you out to breakfast if you'd like."

I nodded and stepped back as he fired up the turbine
engine. Even though I was also a pilot now, I still watched
with some trepidation every time he took off, especially
when flying into the mountains.

The helicopter lifted off, creating a flurry of loose snow
that whipped around me. I waved to them and went inside
to wait where it was warm. Rusty and I rooted around and
came up with a fairly clean mug, a tea bag, and a box of dog
treats. I nuked some water in the microwave for tea for
myself while he got a couple of the treats. A few minutes
later we heard approaching rotor noise.

"Helicopter," I said.

Rusty perked up his ears and raced to the front window.
He was already learning that this was a sound we anticipat-
ed with joy.

It took another thirty minutes for Drake to shut down
and to wheel the aircraft into the building. We were nearly

at the Thunderbird Lodge, where we planned to have breakfast, when Drake's cell phone rang.

"Okay, thanks. Have a good one," he said.

"I'm kinda surprised they remembered to call," I commented. "They both seemed distracted when I gave the
briefing."

"I sorta turned them into mission commandos while we
were on the flight." He chuckled. "They seemed like the
kind of kids who'd respond to that. Told them I was dropping them off at a top-secret location; their mission was to
ride down to the base lodge and check in with their unit
leader. That's me."

"Good thinking. I had the feeling that reporting to Aunt
Hope was not among their priorities for the day."

Over breakfast I told him about the invitation to Hope's
party the day after Christmas. "Normally I'd be bored stiff
at something like that," I said. "But she seems connected in
the art world. I'm thinking there's a remote chance that I
might pick up some tidbit about Eloy's case, although I
don't know what I'm looking for exactly."

"Sure, anything's fine with me."

"As long as we get tonight and tomorrow together alone.
I want our holiday to be special."

And it was. Starting with a romantic candlelit dinner,
followed by another romp on that fur rug and a night of
ultra-sound sleep as the clouds let go with another round of
huge flakes. We made eggs Benedict for Christmas brunch
and opened our few gifts by the roaring fireplace. Drake got
me a lovely, delicate pendant, a gold helicopter on a chain,
and he loved the idea of our choosing rings together. We
read books, cooked a turkey dinner, and ventured out once

to trek up the hill on our snowshoes while tiny snowflakes swirled around us, clinging to our jackets and beading our hair with crystals. Which, of course, had to be followed by another warm shower together, and afterward we bundled into sweats and feasted on the turkey. A perfect day.

The problem with perfection is that it could only go downhill from there.

NINE

"Darlings! I'm so glad you came," Hope Montgomery gushed as we walked through the foyer of her spacious hacienda, after a uniformed maid had taken our coats. Set in the foothills above Taos, the huge adobe could be seen from miles away. I'd noticed the house on previous trips into town, but didn't realize who it belonged to until we'd begun to follow the little map she'd given me.

From the quarter-mile-long driveway, we'd been directed by valets to leave our car with them and follow a luminaria-lined walkway through a heavy wooden carved door into an inner patio, where snow-laden pines glowed with strands of blue Christmas lights. Following the path led us to the front door to the house. More luminarias topped the adobe wall around the patio as well as the varied levels of the many-tiered house. Although the bagged lights atop the house were electric, the ones along the pathway were the real thing. I wondered where the sand had come from to assemble them, since the ground was entirely covered in a blanket of unbroken white.

The foyer we stepped into was small, but it opened into a huge circular atrium that rose two and a half stories to a vaulted ceiling. The walls of the atrium contained a half-dozen arched doorways that led off to other parts of the house. Each arch was rimmed with an elaborate garland of fir, cones, fruit, and gold bows; from the center of each arch a ball of mistletoe hung from a delicate gold ribbon. A thirty-foot pine tree, adorned solidly with gold and burgundy toys, bows and cherubs, rose in the center of the room. I made a conscious effort not to gape.

Hope Montgomery had taken Drake's arm and was leading him past the enormous Christmas tree. I trotted along, afraid of becoming lost in the place unless I knew where they were headed.

"The boys had such a *won*derful time this morning on their flight," she was saying. "They told me you're a *fab*ulous pilot."

I smiled through clamped teeth.

"Now, you make yourselves at home," Hope continued. Like this cozy little place wouldn't hold three of our house. "The bar's set up over there and Mario will make you anything you want. Munchies are on that table." She indicated a spread that took up an entire side of the room. "And we've done a kalua pig, which is being carved and served on the sun porch." She waved her many rings toward the back of the house. "Oh! There's Jack—I'll be right back."

She rushed off and I saw that it was Jack Nicholson she was greeting. I spotted at least three other famous stars of stage and screen, including Jason Kirk, who waved at Drake but stared right through me.

"Let's get something to drink," I suggested. "I hate this feeling that my hands have nothing to do."

We edged our way to the bar and I was surprised to see that I recognized a few of the locals in the crowd. Daphne Dumont was deep in conversation with Sam Begay, the

Indian artist, near one of the arches, and I spotted Maggie Collins's long gray hair across the room. Drake handed me a glass of wine and we silently toasted each other with our eyes.

"Let's wander around," he suggested.

Music wafted its way toward us from the direction of the largest arch, one that led to a crowded room. In most homes, this might have been called the living room but I had a hard time imagining living in it. The room was a good sixty feet long with fourteen-foot ceilings that were supported by massive squared-off vigas and finished out with diagonally placed latillas of peeled pine limbs. Different corners of the room attempted to be cozy—a grand piano in one, a traditional adobe corner fireplace in another. The wall behind the grand piano featured a montage of movie posters and other movie memorabilia from the sixties. Groupings of sofas and chairs sat on Indian rugs in the standard colors of black, gray, and red, and most of the furniture was occupied by guests who balanced plates of food on their laps.

"Welcome to my little mountain place," Hope said, again linking her arm through Drake's.

"Do you live here full time?" I asked, edging toward his other side.

"Oh, no. I'm usually just here in the summer. Actually, this is the first Christmas I've done here in the house. I thought it would make a nice change from Rio."

"So you have several homes?"

"Just a couple. Usually I'm in La Jolla. But the apartment in New York is nice when I want a dash of East Coast, you know. And the villa in Nice gets me to Europe now and then. I come here mainly for the solitude and because the New Mexico artists are so talented—their work is so different from the mundane stuff I find elsewhere."

"Are you an artist yourself?" I asked.

"Oh, heavens no." She laughed, raising a bejeweled hand to her chest. "I just appreciate good art, but I couldn't do a thing with a brush. Besides"—she leaned in closer—"even the very successful ones don't make any *real* money. Talented as they are, they just don't have the business sense to be financially well-off."

I wanted to ask whether she'd made *her* money, but Drake shot me a look that said it would be extremely rude of me to do so.

"I better check on the caterer," she said. "Do enjoy yourselves." She breezed away in a flurry of burgundy crepe.

"Maybe we should get some food," Drake suggested. "Otherwise, I'm likely to die of hunger."

"Or boredom," I poked. These parties were not his idea of a good time.

We worked our way through the crowd to the dining room, which had been set up with a huge buffet of traditional southwestern fare such as posole, green chile stew, chile con queso, guacamole, taquitos, fajitas, and all the trimmings, along with the roast pork and a varied spread of salads, fruit, and assorted hors d'oeuvres. I honed in on the green chile stew and a flour tortilla while Drake, missing his Hawaii days, couldn't resist the kalua pig and tropical fruit.

"Oh, pardon me," a softly Southern voice said at my shoulder. The woman had leaned over to spear a slice of pineapple and her purse strap had slipped off her shoulder and bumped me.

"No problem," I answered automatically. I glanced at her for the first time. Her clothing was casual. She didn't appear to have dressed for a party, wearing a warm-up suit of silky pink. She was attractive, with chin-length blond hair and sapphire eyes, but her hair and makeup hadn't been retouched, probably since first thing this morning.

"Do you live here in Taos?" I asked.

"Me? Oh my, no. We—my brother and I—just got in from California. I'm Susie Montgomery."

"Oh, are you related to Hope?"

"We're her cousins. We come from Texas—Dallas—but we've been in California for 'bout a week, tryin' to get together with Hope."

"Well, it's nice to meet you, Susie. I'm Charlie Parker and this is my husband, Drake Langston. We're from Albuquerque, but are working up here for the winter. I'm a partner in a private investigation firm in Albuquerque, actually." I don't know what made me drop in that last part, but Susie's eyes somehow shifted when she heard it.

Drake and I carried our filled plates back to the living room and found empty seats in one grouping of couches. I saw Susie pass by the archway, walking with a man dressed in jeans and a plaid shirt. She must have meant it when she said they "just" got in. They both looked a bit road-weary and unprepared for the glittering party in which they'd found themselves.

"Charlie!" It was Maggie Collins. "It's so good to see you again."

I introduced Drake.

"Some spread, huh," Maggie said. She dropped her voice to a tad over a whisper. "Hard to believe Hope Montgomery just stepped into all this, isn't it?"

I raised an eyebrow. I was quickly learning that Maggie was an unabashed gossip, and I let her go on.

"Oh, yes. She inherited everything. She's the daughter of the guy who invented the first computer microchip. Actually he didn't invent the chip itself, but invented something that's crucial to manufacturing them. I don't know what exactly, but he made a shitpot of money. Maybe several shitpots."

"Really?"

"I saw this in *People* years ago. He had homes all over the world. Was married once, but the wife had left him years earlier—because he was always locked away in his lab, never paid any attention to the family. Well, of course, after he hit it big she wanted a part of it all, but by then it was too late because she'd walked out long before that. But there was a daughter, Hope, and I guess he felt obligated to her. He died, oh about two years ago, and she got everything."

She paused for a breath and took a sip from her wineglass.

"And"—she dropped her voice even lower—"there was a brother. I mean, old Monty had a brother. And his side of the family made a big stink about it because he'd helped Monty develop the process with the chips and the brother thought he should get the inheritance. But Monty had patented everything in his own name and the brother's claim fell flat. You haven't already heard all this? It made the news big-time for a while."

I had to admit that I hadn't. Social intrigues have never been tops on my list of newsworthy items.

"Well, Hope sure stepped into a gold mine. From what I heard, she and her mother had lived a very average existence after the mother left Monty. She was a bank teller with very little contact with her father until she joined the ranks of the rich and richer."

"I may have just met some of the brother's family," I said. "Two people who said they were Hope's cousins."

Drake had cleaned his plate and went to dispose of it, taking my empty one too. He offered to get second drinks for Maggie and me, but I think he was secretly wanting to move around instead of being trapped in the gossip-fest. I, however, had one more thing I wanted to get out of Maggie.

"Changing the subject, can I ask whether you know Anton Pachevski?" I asked her.

"Not well, but we've been introduced. I'm not sure if anyone knows him well. He seemed to appear here in Taos rather suddenly."

"Could you introduce me?"

"Getting into the art crowd's groupies, Charlie?"

"No way. I just wonder if his art expertise extends to religious items. I have a question I'd like to ask him."

We edged our way toward the bar, where Drake was beginning to look like he could use help with the three drinks. Maggie and I took ours and worked our way through the rooms until we spotted Pachevski with a group of beautifully clad women circled around him. This wasn't a good time to question him about his knowledge of religious art items.

"Don't worry about it, Maggie," I said. "I'll catch his attention when he's less involved."

"Whatever you say," she said. "I think I'll go check out some of that food."

I gradually worked my way to the edge of Anton's little group, eavesdropping shamelessly, but making no apologies for it. When the conversation turned toward historical art in New Mexico, I popped in with my question.

"Mr. Pachevski, are there many showings of religious

artifacts, like maybe silver crosses, around here?" I asked.

Pachevski's dark eyes held mine. "Actually I've not seen any," he answered. "Of course, my field of expertise is in *fine* art, not folk art. I rarely trouble myself with craft shows." He'd let the group know that he was a cut above all that and made me feel like the dumb kid in class.

Sam Begay approached the group just then and all attention, including Pachevski's, turned toward him.

"Here's the artist of the day," Pachevski said grandly, putting an arm around the young artist's shoulders and beaming. The women began pummeling the Indian artist with questions and I slipped away from the group.

Drake was still in the cavernous living room—I spotted him at a distance. I started in that direction when I noticed Susie Montgomery and her brother standing alone near the glittering Christmas tree in the atrium.

"Did you enjoy the dinner?" I asked.

"Oh, yes," Susie answered. It came out as yea-us, her Texas twang drawing out each word. "Ready to get to our hotel though. I'm bone-tired."

"We drove all the way from Flagstaff," Fred added. "Then couldn't even get her to talk to us." His voice was bitter.

"She didn't invite you to stay here? The house is huge." Even as I said it, I realized the comment was rude. "I'm sorry—I didn't mean to be nosy."

"No, it's all right," Susie said wearily. "This whole thing has been such a mess. I'm not terribly surprised."

"Did my sister tell me that y'all are private investigators?" Fred asked.

"A partner with my brother. He's the investigator. Is there something he might do to help you?"

"Let's not talk about it here," Fred said. "Can I call you? We'll be at the Holiday Inn here in town."

I scribbled down the phone number at the cabin and told him we'd be going to Albuquerque in a day or two. They were retrieving their coats when I returned to the living room to look for Drake. We made our excuses and left shortly afterward.

ᵖᵃ ᵖᵃ ᵖᵃ ᵖᵃ ᵖᵃ

We were in the middle of discussing plans to go to Albuquerque the next morning when the phone rang.

"Ms. Parker?" It was Fred Montgomery. "I want to apologize for being so short with y'all last night at the party," he said.

"No problem." I didn't admit to him that my curiosity about Hope Montgomery was killing me. "What can I do for you?"

"Would you be able to meet with Susie and me, here at the hotel?" he asked. "I'd like to talk to y'all about taking us on as clients."

I turned to Drake and mouthed a few words. He nodded.

"Sure, Fred. We're on our way to Albuquerque, so we'll stop there on the way. In about an hour?"

We gathered a few essentials for an overnight stay in the city. Rusty watched nervously as we stacked things near the front door, following closely on my heels, making sure I knew he was going too. Lowering the thermostats and leaving a couple of lights on, we all piled into the Jeep and made the trip into Taos in just under our allotted hour. Fred and Susie Montgomery were waiting in the hotel's coffee shop.

"Would y'all like some coffee?" Fred offered.

While we all ordered coffee, I noticed that Susie looked

much more rested this morning. Her blond hair was fluffy and freshly styled and her makeup told me that she'd been to at least one Merle Norman makeover class in her lifetime. Although her clothing was inexpensive, she dressed with that flair that meant she watched fashion trends and was emulating Texas chic on a budget. Fred wore western-cut Perma-Press slacks, a plaid western shirt, and bolo tie with a hunk of agate at the throat. We discussed the weather until the coffee arrived.

"Well, Miz Parker," Fred began, "I guess Susie's told you that we're the rightful heirs to ol' Monty's money."

"Actually, she hadn't," I told him, stirring cream and sugar into my cup.

"Well, we are. I know you might have read some stuff about this. We fought it in court and got ruled against, but it's the truth. I cain't exactly tell you how I know this, but that woman Hope ain't who she says she is."

"She isn't Monty's daughter?" I asked.

"She ain't even Hope Montgomery," he said emphatically.

"Maybe we better back up a little," I said. "I'm not sure I'm getting this."

"You tell it, Susie," Fred offered.

Susie shifted in her chair, her eyes switching between Drake and me. "Monty Montgomery did have a daughter, that part's true. His wife left him years ago and took the daughter with her. That part's true. As far as we know, he didn't have any contact with the daughter for at least ten or fifteen years."

"Now that ol' Monty's dead, this woman shows up claiming she's his daughter, Hope."

"Surely the executor of his estate required proof of her identity before turning over this fortune," I suggested.

"Well, sure he did," Fred said. "But this ain't her."

"And . . ." I prompted him, getting more confused by the minute.

"And, well, I think this lady come in somehow and replaced the real Hope and took her identity."

"Did you bring this up in your court case?" I asked. I couldn't imagine that, with the kind of money involved, there wouldn't have been a serious investigation into it.

"That's just the thing. No, we didn't," Susie piped up. "Course nobody knew what Hope would look like. She was a teenager last time anybody in the family saw her and now she's fifty-somethin'. Fred, he was just a little kid, met her only a coupla times. I wasn't even born yet. Then her mamma takes her off to someplace like Philadelphia to raise her. Now she comes back with all these manners and fancy ways and she's got the court convinced of whatever she tells 'em."

"What about the mother?" I asked.

"Dead. Been gone for years."

"And how can Charlie help you with this?" Drake asked.

"Well, we was hoping . . . You see, we never had our own investigator on this. Just relied on the court. We kinda hoped you could find us some proof."

"We can pay you," Susie added.

I felt sorry for them and their predicament, but I also felt like I was getting sucked into something I had no idea how to handle. I wanted to tell them so, but the hangdog looks on their faces started to get to me.

"Let me see what I can do," I told them.

"Are you *nuts*?" Drake asked me as we got into the car a few minutes later. He had a half-smile on his face. "That whole theory sounded like pure wishful thinking on their part."

"*How* do I get myself into these things?" I wailed. "Why can't I just learn the word no?"

"I was kind of wondering that myself," he laughed. "Now what?"

"I'll talk to Ron when we get to Albuquerque. Maybe he'll have some ideas."

I stared out the windows while Drake did the driving. The snow was mostly melted in Taos, with only sparse patches remaining. By the time we entered the canyon south of town, there was no trace of it, although the rushing water of the Rio Grande on our right-hand side looked frigidly clear and the river rocks were rimmed in ice. The tiny towns slipped past and we decided to stop for lunch in Santa Fe.

We rolled into Albuquerque about two o'clock and stopped first at Ron's and my office in the old Victorian just off Central Avenue. Rusty raced around the yard, then through the back door and up the stairs, happy to be on his old turf.

"Hi, Charlie. Hi, Drake," greeted Tammy, her pudgy face beaming. "Here are a few messages." She handed me a handful of pink slips. Welcome back.

I went up to Ron's office, leaving Drake to search for extra clothes in our current bedroom, which used to be my office. My desk had been moved to the downstairs conference room after we'd discovered that we simply couldn't live and work in a fifteen-by-twenty-foot room. As it was, the room was crowded with a queen-size bed, dresser, and a makeshift rod we'd set up for the few hanging clothes we'd accumulated since all our old ones were lost. Our personal toiletry items had to be stacked on the dresser top, since the bathroom's old fixtures didn't include spacious vanity tops and since customers occasionally used that room. I was more than ready for our home to be occupiable, but it looked like it would be at least a couple more months.

Ron sat planted in his customary position at his desk, phone growing from one ear. He wore his usual Levi's and plaid shirt. His felt Stetson hung on the rack near the door. I waved to indicate that I wanted his attention. He nodded and began to wind up the phone call.

"What's up?" he asked. "Having so much fun on your honeymoon that you had to come home early?"

I shot him a poisonous look. He knew I wasn't thrilled about having to keep in touch with a contractor during the holidays anyway.

"For your information, smarty, I think I've gotten you a new case," I said. I filled him in on the Montgomerys' situation.

"So, if I discredit this heiress as a fake will the real heirs give me a percentage of the estate?"

I laughed out loud. What a dreamer. "How do you plan to do it?" I asked. "Our resources are pretty limited as far as finding out about someone who grew up in Philadelphia, lived in California, and has relatives in Texas."

"Could you get something with Hope Montgomery's fingerprints on it?" he asked.

"Hmmm. Hadn't thought about that. Let me work on it." Too bad I hadn't swiped something from her house.

"It's a long shot, but if it turned out that the imposter had a record we might expose her pretty easily," Ron said. "On the other hand, if she has no criminal past it's going to be trickier. And proving this lady an imposter won't necessarily insure that Fred and Susie get the loot. The real Hope could be alive somewhere."

Or not. I had a feeling that if someone went to the trouble to impersonate her, fight it in court, move into her homes and start living her life, they wouldn't leave a minor detail to chance, like the possibility of the real heiress walking into the picture. The other possibility was that Fred and Susie were dreamers and were letting their hopes for untold riches get the best of them.

"Any other ideas on the Eloy Romero case I e-mailed you about?" I asked.

"Well, I thought a contact at the local FBI office might help, and I do have that," he said. He pulled his amazing Rolodex out and flipped through the cards. I can never figure out how to look up anything in Ron's card system because he never files anything under the person's name and rarely under the business name. He found his FBI contact, James Burns, under P for police.

I wrote down the number and went downstairs to my desk to make some calls. First I called Fred Montgomery at the Holiday Inn in Taos.

"Yes, ma'am," he greeted, after I'd identified myself.

"I need you and Susie to do a favor for me," I told him. "You were planning to contact Hope today, weren't you?"

"Yes, ma'am. We called her this morning and we're going up to her place for supper tonight. I'm not tellin' her we got a private investigator though. Just wanna see if we can at least get her talking to us and to recognize that we're her cousins."

"Okay. That's perfect," I said. "I need you to get something with her fingerprints on it. A smooth surface like a drinking glass or soda can would be perfect. Figure out a way to pick it up so you don't leave your own prints, if you can. And don't let her know you're taking it."

"Yes, ma'am. I can do that." His wide grin nearly came

over the phone line.

"Wrap it up carefully and mail it to this address." I gave him the office address here in Albuquerque. After we'd hung up I told Ron to expect a package in the next day or two.

"Okay." I said it to Rusty and he wagged supportively. "We've done what we can on that case. Now, let's call this FBI man. Then we'll find out what our house looks like." More wagging.

"Burns here." The voice was a deep bass that I envisioned coming from a very tall bearded man. I'm not sure why.

I introduced myself as Ron's associate and explained that we were investigating an old murder case.

"I have reason to believe that this case might be connected in some way with a case you worked on several years ago," I told him. "Two silver crosses, stolen from the Catholic church, have recently been recovered."

"I remember the case," he said.

"The crosses are in the possession of Father Domingo at the St. Augustine church in Taos. He's planning to return them to Catholic authorities, may have already done so. The reason I'm telling you all this is that I believe these two crosses may somehow be connected to the murder of Father Ramon Romero, who was killed here in Albuquerque five years ago."

"Hold on a moment," Burns told me. He set the receiver down a bit roughly on the desk and I could hear papers rustling in the background. "Okay," he continued, "I've got the file here."

More rustling. "I don't see any Ramon Romero mentioned in our case," he said. "I'm beginning to remember some of the details now. We had a guy named Leon Palais pretty well cornered on this. Dates, times, contacts—all those things fit. Only problem was that he vanished. I personally went to St. Maarten in the Caribbean to track him down, but he'd just disappeared. He was known to be good with languages and different looks. A chameleon, basically. Once he hit that island, small as it is, he blended in with the population. It couldn't have been too hard—he could appear Spanish, French, Italian, Indonesian—he had that international look about him. I guess he knew it and used it to blend. The guy's sharp, and gutsy."

"Any idea where he is now?" I asked.

"Could still be there on that island, as far as I know. His passport hasn't been used to get him back into this country. At least some of the missing items have been found," he concluded.

"Was it a big theft ring?"

"Huge. We estimated well over a million dollars worth of artifacts had been taken. But no one knows how to value some of this stuff. They aren't the kind of items that show up at art auctions, you know. On the black market, these things might have brought in several million."

Wow. "And all of it's still missing?" I asked.

"As far as I know," he acknowledged. "Except for these two crosses you mention."

I thanked him for the information and hung up. I hadn't learned anything that would spare Eloy, although it was good to know that he'd never been an FBI suspect. My own gut feeling was that Ramon's murder was somehow connected with the theft ring. Millions of dollars can be a powerful motive.

TEN

Two pickup trucks with LOGAN CONSTRUCTION painted on their sides sat in our driveway. The whine of a saw came through the clear, cold air as we emerged from the Jeep and stood in our mangled front yard. Vehicles had driven across the lawn and the winter-bare shrubs and trees looked pitiful against its brownness. The front door still consisted of a sheet of plywood held in place by a hasp that was padlocked at night. It tore at my heart to see my childhood home, which I'd cared for so diligently since I'd inherited it, in this condition.

The October fire had destroyed the entire north end of the house, which encompassed our master bedroom and bath, the guest room and bath, and the spare bedroom that we'd converted into Drake's office. Other areas of the house, the living and dining rooms primarily, had suffered smoke and water damage. We'd spent a good part of November removing what furniture could be salvaged, taking it out for cleaning and storage until the house was ready for it. The new construction would include a much larger master suite, an exercise room, and a custom office for Drake. As a concession to the few times we had overnight guests, there would still be a guest room and bath—these near the front of the house with their own outside entrance. I was also using the remodeling as an excuse for new furniture in the living room.

Rusty immediately raced to his old backyard, sniffing excitedly to make sure hoards of other dogs hadn't invaded while he'd been away.

"Hey, Ms. Parker, Mr. Drake," called Hank Logan as we entered the living room. "Glad you came by."

"I brought those window brochures you needed," I told him, pulling out my folder, the only thing that was keeping me organized through this whole project.

Hank and I carried the folder to the kitchen counter while Drake wandered back to the newly framed area. I joined him a couple of minutes later, after writing down model numbers for the windows Hank still needed to order.

"It's looking good, hon," Drake said.

No trace of blackened wood flooring or walls remained. Three weeks ago, this section had been open to the outdoors, but with winter moving in, Logan had done a great job of finishing the framing, the flooring, and getting the new section under roof. The windows and new exterior doors were in place, with the exception of the Jacuzzi area of the master bath, where we planned to have double glass with automatic shades between the two layers. We would be able to look out from our tub into a small private garden with a high wall or, if we felt insecure about peepers, could push a button to lower the shades. The open spaces, which were currently covered in heavy plastic, would soon be done and I was beginning to visualize the finished product.

"I'll be so glad when this is done," I told him. "Won't it be nice to get into our own home, finally?"

He gave me an answering hug. "I'll settle anywhere with you," he whispered.

"Here are the catalogs—" Hank Logan stopped. "Sorry to interrupt." He blushed.

I laughed. "No problem."

He handed me several catalogs of bathroom fixtures. "We'll want to get these ordered right away," he said, "to keep the whole project on time."

"We'll get some decisions made right now," I promised.

Drake and I carried the catalogs to the kitchen, where we could spread them out and the light was better. I scanned quickly past several pages of ultramodern things I didn't care for and concentrated on some that would be in keeping with the traditional look of the house without being outdated.

"Knock, knock . . ." Elsa Higgins's fragile voice came through the kitchen door. "I saw your car out front." My neighbor's velveteen-smooth cheeks were pink from the winter air, her puff of downy white hair faintly ruffled. She'd bundled into a tan overcoat atop her purple knit pants and lavender flowered blouse.

I ushered her in and gave her a big hug.

"I thought you two were on your honeymoon," she chided.

"We are," Drake answered. "We're always honeymooning." He squeezed my hand.

"We had to come back and make a few decisions to keep the remodeling on schedule," I said. "It's coming along pretty well, don't you think?"

"It sure is. I've been peeking. Usually come over in the afternoons after the workmen all leave. It's a pretty big addition you're making there in the backyard."

"Yeah, the master bedroom and bath are quite a bit larger, and that spot where they cut away the grass will be a big patio. Nicer for cookouts than the little porch we had before," Drake added. He'd promised to do the cooking if we built a nice grill for him.

"I wish I could offer you some tea," I said, "but they've cut the electricity to the kitchen and we don't have a bite of anything in the house."

"Well, that's what I was coming over for. I want you to come to my place for supper when you're finished here," Elsa said.

My surrogate grandmother had watched out for me since my parents died when I was fifteen and wasn't about to stop now. We agreed to be there by five.

ᏕᎦ ᏕᎦ ᏕᎦ ᏕᎦ ᏕᎦ

By ten o'clock the following morning we were on the road again, headed north in two vehicles. The sky was a deep blue, the roads were clear, and the drive went quickly. We were in Taos by twelve-thirty so we stopped for some lunch and a quick trip to the grocery store. I picked up salad ingredients, lean chicken breasts, and a few other staples. On the drive to Albuquerque we had both decided that we needed to start exercising and watching our diet. The idea loosely took the form of a New Year's resolution, which we realized put us in the same category with about a hundred million other Americans this time of year. I had a feeling that, along with at least ninety-nine million others, I would be doing good to stick with it a month.

The *Taos News* caught my eye in a stand outside the store and I bought a copy on impulse. I'm normally not a big newspaper reader, having learned that half the contents are usually designed to depress or infuriate me and the other half are there to lure me into stores to buy stuff I had no idea I needed until I picked up the paper. I jammed the paper into a grocery bag and wheeled everything out to the Jeep. Drake had gone ahead in his pickup truck to make a stop at the hangar and find out whether Eloy had any flights lined up for him.

The ski valley road was clear until I turned off onto the county road, which was shaded and snowpacked. I switched to four-wheel drive for the climb and pulled into the cabin's drive a few minutes later. Rusty bounded ahead, treating this place as much like home already as our own house. After carrying the grocery sacks in, turning up the thermostat, and checking the answering machine—where the only message was from Fred Montgomery, telling me that he'd done a fine bit of detective work by stealing Hope's water glass from the dinner table—I stacked a few logs in the fireplace and struck a match to them, then settled in to have a cup of hot tea and browse the newspaper. A headline on page three caught my attention.

ST. AUGUSTINE LOSES FATHER DOMINGO
Father Alphonse Domingo, 86, of the Taos parish church of St. Augustine, died Friday night in his room at the rectory. At this time, details are unknown as to the cause of death, although church officials say Father Domingo was in excellent health for a man his age. The county coroner may order an investigation to determine if the elderly priest died of other than natural causes. A funeral mass is planned for Monday afternoon at 2:00 P.M.

I felt a pang of sadness for the old priest, whom I'd found to be kindly and helpful. But the hint that he may not have died of natural causes bothered me. I reached for the telephone.

"Father Sanchez? You probably don't remember me," I said, introducing myself. "I visited Father Domingo last week."

"The young lady with the silver crosses," he answered. "Yes, of course. Father Domingo told me about it."

"I'm concerned about what became of the crosses. The newspaper hinted . . . well, Father Domingo's death . . . was it suspicious? Oh, gosh, I'm not putting this very well . . . I . . . my first thought was that someone might have killed him and stolen the crosses."

The line was silent for a fraction of a second too long.

"No, my dear. I don't think it was anything like that," Father Sanchez said. "I know Father Domingo had the crosses shipped to the Vatican right after your visit. I helped him pack them up and Father Ralph was here when Federal Express picked up the box."

"But his death. The coroner's office might start an inquiry?"

"I can't really tell you what they are planning," he answered. "I know his soul is in God's hands now."

Yeah, well, that might be fine. But if someone killed him I wasn't convinced that God would lock the guilty party in jail.

"Father Sanchez, may I ask one favor? Would it be all right if I looked through Father Domingo's papers? When I visited, he showed me some files that were connected with a case I'm working on right now. It would be most helpful if I could take another look at them."

He hesitated a moment, but agreed. Not wanting to give him a chance to change his mind, I told him I'd be there in an hour. I left Drake a note and Rusty and I climbed back into the Jeep.

Fifty-six minutes later we pulled up to the historic church and I hurried to the old priest's office. Father Sanchez met me in the hallway as I was trying the doorknob.

"Good afternoon, Ms. Parker," he greeted.

His manner seemed cordial, if reserved. I got the feeling he wasn't sure whether he could trust me. He pulled a key from the pocket of his black slacks and unlocked the office door.

"We never used to have locks on any door in the church," he said sadly. "But times have changed. It's unfortunate when we must distrust everyone."

"Please stay with me while I look at the files," I offered.

He pulled open the lower drawer of the desk, the same one where Father Domingo had gotten the file he'd shown me.

"I think most of Alphonse's personal papers are in this drawer," he said. "Here, please take his chair."

I felt a little strange, sitting in the chair so recently occupied by the older priest and looking at his open file drawer. But I had a feeling that there was somehow a connection between the dead priest, Ramon Romero, and the theft of the silver crosses. And this old man knew more about it than anyone else I'd run into so far. I pulled out the file he'd shown me the other day and began flipping through the neatly clipped articles.

Father Sanchez watched me for a couple of minutes then left the room, leaving the door standing open. I heard him enter another office across the hall and sit down in a creaking chair. Perfect. I'd know if he arose and came to check on me.

With the open file still spread out on the desk, I hurriedly riffled through the other files in the drawer. The headings didn't seem pertinent, but I paged quickly through the contents of each to see if I might find anything of help. The edge of one file caught as I tried to withdraw it and I pulled at the drawer handle to open it a bit farther. The old desk's drawers were heavy wood sliding against wood—no rollers or bearings to help them along—and it took some extra strength to open the drawer fully. At the back of the drawer was a narrow space between the edges of the files and the wooden back of the drawer. It contained a pint of Jim Beam and a small leather book. I glanced up at the doorway before lifting it out. It was a diary.

The entry I turned to read like a lurid novel. Apparently the old priest didn't trust his memory regarding his parishioners' confessions so he'd made notes. I wasn't sure why he'd need to remember so many details, but he'd obviously wanted to. I came to a note about Father Ralph, saying that the younger priest had confessed an attraction to one of the parishioners, who was only referred to by initials. I glanced again at the doorway.

Obviously Father Ralph didn't know this book existed or he would have removed it. And Father Sanchez wouldn't have left me alone at the desk if he knew about it. With a vague feeling of guilt I slipped the leather book into my purse and zipped it shut. As closely as the old priest had followed the story of the theft ring, I had no doubt that any inside information would be noted somewhere in here. I pushed the heavy wooden drawer back to the point where the back compartment didn't show.

None of the other files in the drawer appeared to be directly connected to my investigation, but I did want to read the articles about the thefts in more depth. I carried the folder to Father Sanchez's office and tapped on his doorsill.

"Do you have a photocopier here?" I asked. I didn't think he'd have any objection to my making copies of the articles. After all, they had been published in magazines I could access if I had a vast library at my disposal and about two hundred hours to spend looking them up.

He looked up at me questioningly and I showed him the folder.

"I'd like to read these when I have a little more time," I explained, "rather than staying here and bothering you several more hours."

He took the folder and flipped through the articles.

"I don't see anything here I'll need," he said. "Just take the folder with you and bring it back when you are finished."

I again felt that small pang of guilt over the diary in my purse, but promised the Jesus hanging on the wall that I'd also bring it back.

Rusty was waiting anxiously in the Jeep, fogging the windows with hot doggy breath, when I returned.

"Hey, buddy. We're ready to go now."

He wagged largely and leaped from the front seat to the back.

The sun painted the sky in shades of gold, orange, and coral on the western horizon. Magenta rimmed the few small shaggy clouds with a brightness that was nearly painful to look at, turning the adobe buildings in town pink in their glow. By the time Rusty and I arrived at the cabin the temperature had dropped to the teens and the valley had settled into deep blue-gray shadow.

Lights glowed at the cabin windows and the scent of cedar and pine woodsmoke drifted from the chimney. The heady scent of something meaty grabbed me as soon as I opened the door. Rusty, unhampered by having to remove snowy boots and jacket, zoomed straight to the kitchen.

"Hey, I was beginning to wonder about you guys," Drake greeted. "Start to worry when my sweetheart is out alone after dark."

Rusty thwapped Drake's leg with his tail, reminding him that I'd not been out alone.

I showed Drake the folder and the diary, but didn't admit that I'd helped myself to one of them without permission.

"I hope this will give me some clues about these thefts of artifacts and whether Ramon was involved." Of course, I still had to prove that Eloy wasn't connected with Ramon's death and that was yet another whole set of problems. But somehow it just felt right that Ramon'd had some enemies out there other than his own brother.

Drake dished up plates of beef Bourguignon, buttered noodles, and fresh asparagus spears, which we carried to TV trays in front of the fireplace.

"Eloy had good news for me when I got there," Drake said. "He got a call from a tour company that's bringing in a busload of forty people. They've presold them helicopter rides as part of their New Mexico tour."

"Hey, that's great!"

"They'll arrive day after tomorrow. It should be good for at least three or four hours of flight time."

I was pleased that his business here was going so well.

"After dinner, I'll sit down with some maps and work out a nice route I can do for them. I want to show them some really spectacular scenery, but I have to be sure I can fly the route in the amount of time they're paying for or I'll lose money on the deal," he said.

The food and wine soon took away the chill I'd acquired driving through the shadowy canyon with the stolen diary in my possession. Somehow, the sooner I read it and returned it, the better I'd feel. Drake became occupied with his maps, and I settled down on the sofa to read Father Domingo's diary.

The old man's shaky writing filled about three-fourths of the book. I opened it to the final entry. It told of the return of the crosses to the Vatican authorities. So the book was very current. Father Domingo had died only two days later.

Flipping backward through the pages, I noticed that there were not entries for every day. Probably only two or three per week. Sometimes the entries skipped a few weeks, once in a while it skipped an entire month or two. Although the dates were listed with only a month and date—no years—it appeared to me this book went back about three years. Had the old man been keeping diaries like this during all his years in the priesthood?

I started at the beginning and found that most of the entries pertained to church business—plans for holidays, memos to himself about visiting dignitaries, the arrival of Father Ralph, whom Domingo didn't like much when he first took his post at St. Augustine. Interspersed with the day-to-day doings at the church were little tantalizing bits of scandal. Nothing big, just mentions of things heard in the confessional, things overheard at diocesan conferences. Face it, the old padre was a gossip lover. I worked my way through the first twenty pages of his wavering longhand. No mention of Father Ramon.

I had to assume that other diaries existed, books that dated back to the time of Ramon Romero's stint at St. Augustine, books that laid out Father Domingo's personal views of the theft of valuable artifacts. Any man who took the trouble to collect magazine and news articles on a subject would surely hold deep feelings about it. Or maybe his gossipy old mind would have just rambled in speculation. Either way, he must have written it down.

Scanning now, looking for any mention of the artifacts or of Father Ramon, I came to only one entry containing his name.

Cornelia Baca came today, ridden with guilt. She has never told her husband of the real reason for their marriage, the fact that José is not his son, that she rushed into the marriage knowing she was pregnant with another man's baby. She wants to know if she should tell him. I asked who the father is, was he a man of the community? This is the point where she breaks down completely, falling to the floor and begging God's forgiveness. No, I finally learn. The father was the young priest, Father Ramon. Sadly, I am not shocked. The vow of celibacy is such a burden for a young priest. Many fall. Cornelia was only sixteen when this happened. What good would be served by telling her husband? Ramon is dead now, her son knows only one father, the father only one son. I counsel her to pray God's forgiveness but to reveal her secret to no one else.

So Ramon the saint had another dirty little secret besides the affair in Albuquerque. I wondered whether there was any way this could tie in to his death, and how many years had gone by since this affair. I scanned forward through the book to see if Cornelia Baca's name or that of her son came up again. There was only one other entry.

Young José Baca is a cause of concern. He confessed today that he is tempted to join a gang. It has not happened yet and I counseled him to stay close to his family, to honor his father and mother. If he only knew about his father. My burden grows heavy with the weight of the parish's secrets. I am growing too old.

I closed the diary and rubbed my eyes. It was after ten o'clock. Drake had put his maps aside and I could hear him in the bathroom brushing his teeth. I locked the doors, turned out the lights, and jostled Rusty from his stretched-out position on the rug in front of the fireplace.

"Hey, lazy butt, let's go to bed," I said softly.

I snuggled under the covers next to Drake but couldn't seem to fall asleep right away. I kept fighting off this nagging thought that there were more diaries somewhere among Father Domingo's possessions.

ELEVEN

It was pitch dark in the room when I rolled over for the fortieth time and looked at the clock. Five A.M. I *really* didn't want to get up that early, but I was weary from trying not to thrash around so much that I'd awaken Drake. I finally gave up the warm covers, pulled on a pair of sweats and tip-toed to the bedroom door. Rusty heard me and rose from his rug on the floor. We stepped onto the landing and I gently closed the door before switching on the stairway lights. The dog immediately raced down the stairs with a thunder that only a seventy-pound dog on wooden stairs can create. I had no hope whatsoever that Drake could have slept through it, but heard not a peep from the bedroom. I ducked into the bathroom, used it without flushing, then swished some mouthwash and ran a brush through my shoulder-length auburn hair, wishing the sleepless night had not left those dark circles beneath my eyes.

As quietly as possible I opened the front door and let Rusty out to do his business, while I put a pot of coffee on to brew. Like I needed to be any more awake than I already was. I glanced at my watch—5:06. I paced back to the front door, let Rusty in and paced back to the kitchen. It was going to be a long day unless I did something. And the thing that continually played in my mind was that I wanted to go back to that church and try to find Father Domingo's other diaries.

There are times when we tell ourselves that an idea is really stupid but we seem to have no power to put it behind us. And no matter how stupid the idea, I knew deep down inside that I was going to act on it. Drake would probably sleep until at least eight o'clock. And, in case the sound of my car leaving woke him, I would leave a note telling him what I was doing.

It was still a dumb idea.

I hastily wrote the note, grabbed my coat and gloves, and slipped my feet into my snow boots. In that certain way our little human brains have of justifying anything we really want to do, I told myself that Father Sanchez would undoubtedly be conducting early Mass by the time I got there and I could just tippy-toe back to the offices and have a tiny little look around. Just a little bitty look. It really wouldn't take but a minute.

Predawn is about the darkest time there is. Even the covering of pure white snow did little to light my way to the Jeep. I crunched my way over the crystalline surface in the subzero air with Rusty trotting along behind. He looked at me quizzically as I yanked twice at the door handle to get the thick frost to release it. Inside, the vehicle was not one iota warmer than the outside air. I inserted the key into the ignition and held my breath as the engine groaned twice before starting. It sounded like a roaring monster truck as it warmed up in the absolutely silent mountain air. There's no way Drake is sleeping through this, I told myself.

I reached for the travel mug of hot coffee I'd poured.

Steam wafted up through the small drinking hole and I sipped carefully at it. No additional lights appeared in the house during the few minutes I sat there allowing the car to warm up.

The drive into town was becoming very familiar and it went quickly with no other traffic on the road. Even the usually clogged intersection at the plaza was completely devoid of activity. As I'd hoped, there was a scattering of cars in the church's parking lot, indicating that a few devout souls attended early Mass. I parked at the edge of the cluster, near a small side door that looked as if it led to the priest's offices. 6:15. I hoped the two priests would be busy for a while.

Rusty watched anxiously as I locked the car doors and told him to stay there. He isn't accustomed to our making predawn trips and this place didn't have much potential as a fast-food joint, as he tested the air with his nose. I'm sure he thought I'd totally lost it, and I must admit I was beginning to wonder the same thing.

I glanced around, feeling nervous as a cat burglar, before gingerly trying the doorknob. I caught myself holding my breath, since the only alternate way I knew to get in here was to walk right through the middle of the church. Fortunately, this door opened. I pushed inward, willing it not to squeak, bump, or grind. I let my breath out only after I was inside with the door closed behind me.

I was standing in a short hallway, flanked by coat and hat racks on both sides, that intersected another hall ahead of me. The floors were brown saltillo tile, which I realized would show my every footprint with the graphic details of my boot treads outlined for the police, who would no doubt love to throw me in the slammer for breaking and entering on holy ground. I shook my head to erase the images I was scaring myself with. At this moment all I had to do was find my way to Father Domingo's office. One step at a time.

The halls were deadly quiet and colder than you-know-where. The long hall, which intersected the short entry where I stood, stretched for perhaps thirty feet in either direction, with a series of heavy carved wooden doors along it. All were firmly closed. Which way? I took a chance on going right, toward the chancel. I seemed to remember that Father Ralph had led me only one or two doors up this hall to the office on my last visit. I tried one door on my left. It was a bathroom. Guess even holy men have certain bodily needs.

The next door was the correct one and I slipped in and closed it behind me. Pulling a flashlight, which I'd had the presence of mind to bring, from my purse, I switched it on and shined it quickly around the room. I pretty well knew what the contents of the desk were so I aimed my attention to the other furnishings.

The room contained, in addition to the heavy old wood desk and its crackly leather armchair, only a side chair, a bookcase of pine carved with New Mexican-style squares and diagonals, and a four-drawer Hon file cabinet, circa 1950. I flashed my light over the bookcase, which appeared to be filled with Bibles in about thirty different bindings and a stack of back issues of *Roman Catholic Today*. The file cabinet looked like the better bet.

The top two drawers contained modern hanging file folders, all neatly tabbed and alphabetized. The subjects ranged from Accounts Payable to Web Site Information.

Strictly business. I had a hard time imagining old Father Domingo surfing the web, and assumed there must be an office staff that handled some of these more secular matters.

Drawer number three contained a neatly folded cassock. Beneath it were a spare pair of black shoes and a black beaded rosary. No diaries.

So as luck would have it, the last drawer must be the one. I always tease Sally when she tells me she found something in the last place she looked. Because why would you keep looking anywhere else after you'd found what you wanted? I opened the bottom drawer to find it—empty. Now what? I switched off my flashlight and sat in the dark for a minute thinking about it.

I decided that the worst thing I could do would be to wait around until the other priests finished with their parishioners and get myself caught. I slipped the stolen diary out of my purse and back into the drawer cubbyhole where I'd found it. I listened at the door a moment then carefully opened it with only a tiny click of the latch. Now, which way? Figuring that speed was of the essence, I stepped back into the long hall and began trying doorknobs. I already knew which was the bathroom, and Father Sanchez's office was directly across from Domingo's, so I headed away from them.

Open, flash light in, close. The other doors revealed two more offices, one with computer, copier, and other modern equipment; a coat closet full of priestly garb; and a storage room. Three doors remained—one for each priest, I assumed.

The first opened into a small bedroom with an unmade bed, shoes on the floor, an open book on the nightstand, and the lights left on. Father Ralph's domain, no doubt. It was somehow nice to know that even priests must get up in the morning and throw on their clothes to rush off to work. I would have pictured him arising in the wee hours to make his bed, tidy the room, then say a few prayers and reflect upon weighty matters before entering the church to minister to his flock. Just shows what I know.

I closed the priest's door quietly and approached the next one just as I heard voices at the other end of the hall. No time to make a decision; I scampered inside and closed the door behind me, standing with my back against the door, willing myself not to pant. I kept my ears tuned to the hall outside until the voices became muffled. It sounded like Father Ralph had taken someone into his office. I risked switching on the flashlight.

It was indeed another bedroom and I was, luckily, alone. I wouldn't let myself think of the possibilities had it been otherwise. The single bed was neatly made, but a slight dip in the center of the mattress made me wonder if this was the final imprint of the old priest's body. I didn't want to think about that. The other furnishings consisted of a nightstand with a lamp, a dresser, a crucifix over the bed, and a small statue of Jesus on the dresser. No personal possessions were visible and I feared for a moment that someone might have already cleaned out his room.

Apparently the old priest was just a better housekeeper than the younger one because I did find the dresser drawers were filled. As quietly as possible, I slid each one open and patted down the contents. My efforts were rewarded on the third try, when that drawer opened to reveal two stacks of diaries. It was, of course, the last place I looked.

There was no way I could take them all with me. Not

only would they be missed, probably, but they wouldn't fit into my purse. I'd have to settle for one or two and I better pick the right ones. I lifted the cover of the top book. Entries ended just prior to those in the diary I had taken home with me. The next one preceded this one chronologically, beginning five years ago. The one below it ended at that point and had started seven years ago. They all fit the time frame that included Ramon's death and the investigation of the art thefts, so I decided to risk taking all three. I stuffed two into my purse and the other inside my parka, rearranging the remaining ones in the drawer so that, with any luck, no one would realize they were missing.

"Today might be a good day to clean out Father Domingo's room." The female voice was right outside the door.

My heart stopped, along with my ability to breathe.

TWELVE

I switched off the flashlight as the doorknob turned. A wedge of yellow light from the hallway cut across the bare tile floor to the bed on the opposite side. My head swiveled around, looking for a hiding place. There was no closet, only a few pegs on the wall with identical black shirts and pants hanging from them. A pair of black shoes sat on the floor beneath them. Priests didn't have extensive wardrobes, I decided.

The only possible hiding place in the room was under the bed and I calculated my odds of diving for it before the woman at the door saw me. They weren't good.

A muted voice came down the hall. "First I need the quarterly contribution reports," Father Ralph was saying.

"Okay," she answered. "I can do the room this afternoon."

She closed the door and her footsteps clicked away on the tile floor. I remembered to breathe. My arms felt like jelly as I pushed the dresser drawer shut. I dropped my flashlight into my purse and rubbed both hands shakily down the length of my face. How was I going to get past the two of them and back to my car?

The small window over the bed was beginning to be outlined in gray. I looked at my watch but couldn't see it without getting my flashlight out again. It felt like I'd been here all day, but it was probably closer to an hour. If I hadn't awakened Drake when I drove out, he would be getting up soon anyway. I doubted that my note would reassure him, although at least he'd know where I was.

I tiptoed across the room to the door, pasting myself to the wall where I'd be behind it if someone opened it again. Voices drifted toward me now and then, apparently the secretary and Father Ralph conversed between their offices without benefit of an intercom. I never heard a third voice so Father Sanchez must have been occupied elsewhere. The room was growing lighter—the gray at the window turned to pearl white, then to yellow as the sun peeked over the mountains. I fidgeted, wondering whether mine was now the only car in the parking lot and whether someone would notice and question why a lone dog was waiting in it. What if they decided to tow the car? What if Rusty got out and was lost in a strange town? What if, what if.

I knew I had to get out of here soon.

It was almost eight o'clock and I'd left the cabin almost three hours ago. Surely Drake would be getting concerned. As if by ESP, from somewhere deep in my purse, my cell phone rang. Oh, God! I fumbled with the zipper and delved my hand down past my stolen booty. It rang again.

"Dora, did I hear a phone ringing?" Father Ralph's voice came through clearer than before.

I snatched up the phone and clicked the button. "I can't talk right now," I whispered frantically. "Call you right back." I hit the END button.

". . . somewhere in the building. I'll go check," Dora said.

I heard her heels clicking on the tile floor. Oh, shit. There was no reasonable explanation for my being in Father Domingo's room with his diaries in my possession. I had to make a move now. I eased over to the doorknob, turning it carefully and hoping it wouldn't squeak. Edging the door open a tiny crack, I risked a look. My heart pounded and a rushing sound filled my ears.

No one was visible.

I pulled the door open a few inches more. Dora was walking down the hall toward the chancel, her back to me. No sign of Father Ralph. Presumably he was back at his desk, letting the secretary investigate the unknown noise. The side door, my escape hatch, stood this side of Father Ralph's office. He wouldn't see me unless he came out. But I had a lot of distance to cover without Dora spotting me. I moved quickly.

Taking care not to let my rubber-soled boots squeak on the tile, I made for the short alcove by the side door. I had a good ten feet to go when I heard her heels clicking their way back. I sprinted and ducked into the short hallway leading to the outside door.

"Don't see anybody there," she said. Her voice sounded about ten inches from where I stood pressed against the wall and doing my best to resemble a coat on the rack.

"Okay." Father Ralph sounded preoccupied.

The door to Father Domingo's room. Had I closed it behind me? I couldn't remember. She would surely notice if it were standing open.

Apparently she didn't, because I heard her move away from my alcove, in the direction of her own office. I let out my pent-up breath as slowly as I could, reached for the side door and eased it open. Once I was outside with the door safely closed behind me I dashed for my Jeep. Rusty sat in the backseat, his eyes fixed on the spot he'd last seen me, staring through foggy windows. I was never so glad to see anyone.

I started the car and pulled out of the church's parking area before I found a spot to stop and take a deep breath. I was getting too old for the life of a cat burglar. I pulled out my cell phone again.

"Charlie! Where are you?" Drake demanded. "Your note said you had an errand in town, but what kind of errand is important at five A.M.?"

So I *had* awakened him when I left.

"I'm sorry, sweetheart. I'll explain when I get there. Are you up for some breakfast?"

"I would be, but I got a flight. That's what I was calling to tell you. I'll be gone until about noon."

"Lunch then?"

He sighed. "Okay. It's just . . . You gotta . . . Oh, never mind." He hung up without saying good-bye.

I dialed right back. "Drake, I love you," I said.

"Love you too."

It was a ritual we performed unfailingly. A few months ago I'd met a woman whose pilot husband didn't come back one day. A fatal crash. Drake and I had vowed then that we would never part angry at each other and that we'd never fall out of the habit of saying we loved each other. The possibility that any separation could be final ripped through me now and I cursed myself for taking so many chances.

I drove extra carefully on the way back, but the cabin was empty and dreary when I arrived and I roamed around lethargically for a while before I finally settled in. I fed Rusty

his usual scoop of nuggets—the other reason he was await-
ing our return so anxiously—then made myself a mug of
hot chocolate and toasted a bagel. Finally I pulled the diaries
from my purse and settled on the sofa with them.

It was slow going, reading the old man's wavy handwrit-
ing and trying to pick out only the names I was interested
in, without getting bogged down in reading everything. I
found myself being caught up in the furtive titillation the
priest clearly felt as he listened to other people's secrets. I
didn't want to get into that. I began scanning the pages for
the name Ramon. Finally, I found it in an entry dated in the
spring of the year Ramon was killed.

*The young priest, Ramon Romero, came to me today. He is
home visiting his mother. He is very troubled and came to me
for confession. I believe he feels more comfortable telling this old
priest of his secrets. He had an affair, years ago, with a parishioner in Albuquerque. It is sad, but not surprising. His problem now is that some unscrupulous people have discovered this
and have blackmailed him into doing things he did not want
to do. He admits that he took many valuable items when he
served at the Vatican. Even more when he was in Israel.*

So Father Domingo had suspected Ramon's involvement
in the theft of the silver crosses. No wonder he followed the
published stories so closely.

*Now my young friend is deeply in trouble. The evil men are
pressuring him to take more items but he is no longer in a position with access. So they want him to take his mother's property and get money for them. Ramon knows the knowledge of his
sin will kill his revered mother. And he fears that if he takes her
property, his brother will kill him.*

This was written only a few months before Ramon was shot to death on the steps of his church in Albuquerque, and he specifically named Eloy as someone who would be mad enough to kill him. This wasn't looking good.

Although I believed the men in the theft ring had something to do with it, the police were going after the most available suspect and this would be damning evidence indeed. So how much trouble was I going to be in if I concealed this diary? I was beginning to feel like quicksand was sucking at my feet.

I started to take a swig of my hot chocolate, but it was like cold sludge. I carried it to the kitchen to reheat it.

What was Ramon thinking? First having affairs, then stealing valuable artifacts from the church, then contemplating robbing his mother of her land, taking his siblings' inheritance. Ramon the saint. I almost had more respect for a mugger in a dark alley. At least he's making no bones about his intent. But a man of religion, praying and leading a devout life by the light of day while secretly falling to the depths of deception. Too bad the justice system was concerned only with the man who actually pulled the trigger. Too bad the man they arrested was someone who was good-hearted and caring.

I paced the living room with my mug of chocolate in hand, trying to shake off the quicksand feeling. Stop trying to make moral judgments here, Charlie, and just deal with the facts, I told myself. You, who've not been above a little larceny this morning.

The file folder of clippings Father Ralph had loaned me was on the dresser in the bedroom upstairs. I retrieved it and carried it to the kitchen table. Spreading them out, I began reading. I lost all track of time until the phone rang.

"Hi, hon, ready for that lunch now?" Drake asked.

Noon already. "Sure, whatcha got in mind?" I rubbed at my eyes to relieve the gritty feeling.

"Why don't you come by the hangar? I'll put the aircraft away, and we can go somewhere in town."

"Do you have anything else scheduled this afternoon?" I asked.

"Want to catch a movie?"

"Maybe something like that. Just something fun for the two of us." Actually I had in mind that it might be nice to go pick out our rings at the jeweler's. After this morning's tiff, I was feeling fragile, I guess.

I straightened the papers I'd been reading and stuck the folder, along with the stolen diaries, into a kitchen cabinet. I left a couple of lamps on and convinced Rusty that he'd be happy to stay home and watch over things here for the small payment of a bone-shaped treat.

Over a plate of steaming tortillas and chicken smothered in green chile at Michael's Kitchen, I filled Drake in on my escapade of the morning, leaving out the heart-pounding moments when I'd nearly been caught.

"Couldn't you have just asked Father Ralph to let you borrow the diaries?" he asked.

"I really doubt he knows they exist. Or if he does, he probably doesn't know that the older priest was writing down things people told him in the confessional." I speared a bite of chicken with my fork. "And if he knows *that*, he surely wouldn't let me out of the place with them."

He shook his head, a what-will-I-do-with-you look on his face.

"I'll take them back," I promised. "I'll figure out a way to sneak them back in so no one ever knows I had them."

He met my eyes silently.

"Okay, so I shouldn't be reading them. I really haven't read much other than the parts where I found Ramon's name. I have to know that much so I can help Eloy." I knew I sounded like a five-year-old who'd taken candy from the store.

"You'll do what's right," he said enigmatically. Meaning, you better do what's right.

We finished our lunch on another subject, but somehow it wasn't the best day to choose wedding rings. I didn't even bring it up. We found a movie that sounded good at the Storyteller Theater, then picked up a few grocery essentials before heading back up the mountain. By dinnertime we were snuggled together on the couch, a plate of cheese and fruit and two glasses of wine on the table before us, the day's previous tension gone. Drake turned to me, just about ready to jump my bones when the phone rang.

"Sorry to be calling in the evening," Ron said. My brother has always had excellent timing with his phone calls. I think it's because he has no romantic life of his own.

"What's up?"

"I got an answer for you on those prints Fred Montgomery sent. The water glass."

I'd forgotten all about the Montgomerys in the past couple of days. "So what's the word on Hope Montgomery?"

"Nothing conclusive. The prints you sent aren't on file with any law enforcement agency I can access. I got Kent Taylor to run them through FBI, NCIC, and the state of California. That's where you said the lady lives, right?"

"Among other places. But that's where her primary home

is and supposedly where she spends most of her time."

"Well, they don't know about her. Criminally, that is."

"Okay, thanks. I'll see what else I can dig up."

"Yeah, that would help. If she's a petty crook, she might have prints on file with some municipality. Just hasn't made it national yet. See what you can get on her background."

I told him to thank Kent Taylor, our favorite Albuquerque Homicide cop, for his trouble. I'm always surprised at the information Ron digs out of Kent; I suspect they have some kind of mutual favor-trading arrangement that I don't know about. By the time I hung up, Drake was trailing kisses across my stomach, pushing his head under my loose sweater. I switched on the answering machine and succumbed to his attention.

🐾 🐾 🐾 🐾 🐾

The bedroom was pitch dark when I woke up—suddenly and wide-awake. The red numerals on the clock said 2:43. Drake snored softly beside me and Rusty snored, not so softly, on the floor at my side. I rolled onto my back and listened carefully, wondering what had caused me to awaken. There was no sound at all. No car sound, no siren, no human voice interrupted the mountain's deep night.

My mind, however, was active and vibrating. Ron's phone call replayed and I wondered how I would go about finding more information on Hope Montgomery. I could hardly walk up to her door and demand to see identification, but I would have to get near her to do any snooping. Little did I know that by morning fate would deal me an ace.

THIRTEEN

The coffee was dripping into the carafe and I was dragging myself around the kitchen when the phone rang. After lying awake for more than two hours in the middle of the night, I'd had a hard time gearing up for action today. Drake was in the shower and I was in the mood to do nothing more energetic than to sit around in my sweats all day.

"Is this the helicopter service?" a female voice asked.

"Yes, it is." I'd forgotten that Drake's business calls were being forwarded here and hadn't answered with the company name.

"Oh! Is this Charlie?"

"Yes."

"Charlie, this is Hope Montgomery. Is that wonderful husband of yours available?"

In what sense of the word, I fumed. Why was it that this woman always set me on edge?

"Not at the moment," I told her, leaving out the part about his being in the shower. "May I take a message?"

"Well, dear, I've got a couple more houseguests who would *love* to take one of his tours," she gushed. "You know the boys just said it was *fab*ulous."

I willed myself not to growl. "He's pretty well booked up

today," I said. "An entire tour group. How about tomorrow?"

"Oh. We couldn't just sneak them on with the others?"

I told her I didn't think so, but would check with Drake and call her back. She left her number with me.

He emerged from upstairs a few minutes later, all warm and smelling of soap and aftershave. He planted a kiss on me that reminded me of the hot time we'd had the previous night. Pouring two cups of coffee, I told him about the call from Hope Montgomery.

"Not today," he said. "I've got my flight times calculated out to the minute and, *if* we don't have any weather glitches it'll take me most of the day to get this tour group done. Would you mind calling her back and scheduling something for tomorrow?"

"You'll have to *really* make it worth my while," I teased suggestively.

"On a brighter note," he said, "seeing her again might give you a way of finding out something for Fred and Susie." He poured cereal into two bowls and sliced a banana over them.

"I'm not sure how," I grumbled. "But I'll work on something." I handed him the milk from the refrigerator. "Is Eloy handling your flight-following today, or do I need to stay near the phone?"

"He'll do it."

We sat at the kitchen table, crunching on cereal while Rusty stared at me then at Drake. His begging policy includes nondiscrimination.

"I may run into town," I said, dreading the thought. "Or not. I have an idea on this identity thing and need a couple of supplies. Maybe I can find them here in the valley."

He set his empty bowl in the sink and went to the ski porch to get his jacket.

"Okay, just be careful. I got worried about you yesterday."

"You too."

Rusty and I watched from the window as his truck headed down the long driveway.

Now, I just had to figure out exactly how I was going to find out more about Hope Montgomery. One of the other thoughts that had rumbled around in my head during the night was the possibility that Fred and Susie might be the real imposters here. They looked sincere, but that Texas charm could all be contrived and there was always the chance they were wanting to catch a free ride on a wealthy woman's coattails.

I placed a quick call to Ron and asked if he could get hold of the court records for the case Fred and Susie had brought against Hope. Monty's will had supposedly left everything to her, but had he specifically excluded them? Had they been mentioned at all? Ron said he would work on that aspect of it and gave me a couple of research projects I could perform myself.

Still in my flannel pajamas, I wasn't at all in the mood to run into town again, so I decided to see how much I could accomplish on the internet. First was to use the phone book listings to verify that Fred and Susie Montgomery really existed in the Dallas area. That checked out, along with the information on the business card Fred had given me. Hope Montgomery had unlisted numbers in La Jolla and New York. Her Taos number was in the local phone directory. I had another idea, but would have to go to the library for that.

I'd no sooner disconnected the modem hookup than the phone rang.

"Gonna spend the whole day talking?" Ron asked.

"Sorry, I was on the internet and don't have two lines here," I told him.

"I've got the California motor vehicle people sending me a copy of Hope's driver's license. I'll fax it to you."

I almost blurted out that I didn't have a fax machine here, but remembered that my computer had that capability. I'd just have to figure it out.

"Even if you're dealing with an imposter, no doubt it will be this lady's picture on the license," Ron said. "Surely even the dumbest criminal would know better."

"No doubt. But maybe there'll be some other detail I can gain from it."

"Get a picture of her if you can," he suggested. "There's probably a lot we can do with that."

Two reasons to go into town. Guess I'd have to bite the bullet and go. We hung up and I went upstairs to get dressed. Thirty minutes later I was halfway down the mountain, headed for the Taos library, where I settled into the reference section.

Who's Who carried a lengthy profile on Monty Montgomery, including his work on the microchip processes he'd invented, his service on the boards of a couple of well-endowed charities, and his family connections. The only child listed was a Hope Montgomery. Her birth date was given, so that would be easy enough to cross check with her driver's license. The book also had a listing for Hope Montgomery, although no picture. Her biography listed her mother's name and a few personal details that Monty's listing didn't cover, along with the obligatory charity work that got her into the book in the first place.

I read the profiles three times then paid a dime for a copy

of the page. I don't always trust my memory on details.

Next, I drove to the newspaper office where I accessed the archives, hoping there would be news of the Montgomery family since they were local big shots. A mention of Monty when he'd bought the house was the extent of it. A photo showed him with a blond woman of Hope's size and build, and the caption said she was his daughter. I couldn't swear it was the same Hope I'd met, but I couldn't swear it wasn't either. The photo was too grainy. The article had run fifteen years ago and the photo might have been even older.

I made one final stop at Wal-Mart for a disposable camera, and a stop at McDonald's for a Big Mac and Coke. Life in the mountains didn't have to consist entirely of nutritious meals, for heaven's sake.

Wiping the last of the special sauce from the corners of my mouth, I used my cell phone to access the answering machine at the cabin. I was kind of hoping Drake might have checked in between flights to say hi. Only one call, from Eloy.

"Hey, Charlie. I'm just sitting around the hangar waiting for Drake's next flight to come in . . . and I wondered, uh . . . whether you've got any news about my situation. Uh . . . call me if you know anything. My cousin Steve, the Taos cop, mentioned that he's gonna stop and visit my mother tomorrow. I, uh . . . I'd sure like to get out of this mess before she finds out. Thanks. Bye."

I sat in the Jeep in McDonald's parking lot, thinking back to the diaries I'd read yesterday. It might not be a bad idea to see what the local police knew about the theft ring and about Ramon's death. The police station was just a few blocks away so I took a chance on finding Steve Romero in.

After a minimum explanation I was shown to his desk.

"Officer Romero? Could I have a minute of your time?" I asked, introducing myself and my purpose.

"Friend of Eloy's, huh?" he said, rubbing his hands over tired-looking eyes.

He was about Eloy's age, early forties, but softer and rounder than his athletic cousin. His diet of beans and tortillas had settled firmly in the middle of his tan uniform and the once-handsome face was round and unlined.

"Have you seen this?" he asked, tossing a copy of the Taos newspaper faceup on the desk.

I turned it to face me. The headline read: LOCAL PRIEST LOCATES VALUABLE CROSSES. An old file photo of Father Domingo smiled benevolently at me. I slipped into the chair beside Romero's desk and quickly read the article. It told how the old priest had recently returned the two silver crosses to the Vatican after they'd been missing for nearly ten years. Thankfully the priest had not mentioned my name or the possible connection with Eloy. It did say that Ramon's death five years earlier was still being investigated. I glanced at the byline. The story was off one of the major wire services. Father Domingo must have given an interview the day before he died.

"Know anything about this?" Steve Romero asked.

"Ramon's death? Only what Eloy's told me," I answered. "Which is why I'm here. Did Eloy tell you he's hired my firm to investigate?"

"No, he didn't." One black eyebrow went up in surprise.

"He's really most concerned that his mother not find out he's been arrested for Ramon's death. He's worried that it might kill her."

"Knowing how she felt about Ramon, I think that's not

too far off the mark," he said.

"Eloy said you were going to visit her—"

"I won't say anything," he assured me.

"What do you know about Ramon's murder?" I asked.

He grinned with very white, straight teeth. "You sure know how to phrase a question, don't you? C'mon, you know I can't tell you everything we know."

"Okay," I conceded. "I just want to be sure Eloy's getting a fair shake here, you know. Has his attorney been given the evidence against him?"

"Actually, this whole thing is Albuquerque jurisdiction, since that's where the crime took place. It's only because Mike Ortiz and I have vouched for Eloy's not being a flight risk that he's not in jail down there right now. Aside from that, I really don't know too many details about the case. Wish I did."

"I just can't imagine how this gun, which Eloy says is always in his closet, got taken away, used in a crime, and put back without his realizing it was ever missing."

"I know, I know," Steve said, rubbing his hands through his dark hair.

"Someone had to have access to Eloy's house. Who would that be?"

"Maybe the whole town of Taos." He chuckled. "You haven't been around here long, have you? Nobody locks their doors in this town."

A far cry from Albuquerque custom, where you not only lock them but lots of people also have iron bars on the windows and doors. It would take a long time for me to get used to this small-town casual attitude.

"Eloy told me he locks his," I argued. "Said he leaves a

key out for the cleaning lady once a month or so."

"Maybe he locks them now," he countered, "but I bet that hasn't always been the case."

His phone rang and he reached for it.

"Yeah. Uh-huh. Here? Hmmm. Okay. You got it."

I wouldn't have thought anything of the one-sided conversation except that Steve had turned the newspaper back around to face him as he listened. He was staring at it as he hung up.

"An update on the case?" I asked.

He glanced around the room to be sure no one else knew he was letting a secret out of the bag.

"Leon Palais, the head honcho behind this artifact theft ring. He's been spotted here in Taos."

The suspect mentioned in the article in Father Domingo's folder. My pulse quickened. "Really?"

"Some FBI guy in Albuquerque got suspicious and came up here. Said he had reason to believe the thieves might be on the move again. Some lady called him last week asking a bunch of questions."

Me. I hoped my face wasn't giving away my thoughts.

"The wire service broke the story about the two crosses; it hit Albuquerque a couple days ago. Knowing the crosses came from Taos, this Fibbie started nosing around. Figured Palais might show up. And sure enough. Unfortunately he eluded the FBI guy when he ducked into an alley."

"I—I'd *heard* that no one knows what Palais looks like any more because he'd changed his identity and his looks."

"Well, I don't know how they did it," he said impatiently. "Maybe some computer thing where they can add a beard, take it away, change hair color . . . whatever. Anyway, we're supposed to bring him in for questioning. FBI is faxing us his picture."

"Could I get a copy of it?" I asked.

He shot me a look that basically said butt out.

"Well, I could show it to Eloy and see if he recognizes the guy."

"*I* could show it to Eloy," he said.

"Yeah, but . . ." I shuffled a little in my seat. "I know where he is and in fact I'm heading that way now."

He got up from his chair and walked toward the back of the room, muttering something that included the word nosy. He came back a couple of minutes later with a sheet of flimsy fax paper.

"You still here?" he questioned, laying the fax down so it faced me.

It was Anton Pachevski.

"Ohmigod! I know this man," I said.

"What?"

"He's Anton Pachevski, the famous art critic. I met him at a gallery show here right before Christmas."

Romero suddenly wasn't so anxious to be rid of me. I gave him the details of the show at the Dumont Gallery and told him I'd also seen Pachevski at Hope Montgomery's after-Christmas party. He took a few notes.

"It makes sense," I said. "This guy is part of the art world, so he shows up here."

"People often change their looks, but it's hard for them to change their interests," he said. "You'd be surprised how many guys get caught doing just this—guy loves the racetrack in his old life, you'll find him at a racetrack in his new identity."

"Exactly." I looked at him like I'd already thought of this and had just delivered Leon Palais to him on a silver platter. "There you go." I shrugged.

"I think I'll nose around and see what big New Year's Eve parties are going on tonight," he said. "Maybe I can get men into some of these fancy society do's and scout around. This Palais/Pachevski sounds like the kind of guy who'd get invited to something like that."

I opened my mouth but didn't get a word out before he shushed me. "Now don't get any ideas about looking for him yourself. You know what the FBI said—he's slippery. And he could be dangerous. He went to pretty great lengths to disappear before."

❧ ❧ ❧ ❧ ❧

The canyon was already well in shadow when I started back to the cabin at three o'clock. I'd completely forgotten about it being New Year's Eve until Steve Romero had mentioned it, but I'd stopped at the grocery for some champagne and other goodies before leaving town. I would put together something special for our first New Year's together. Passing the hangar, I noticed that the aircraft wasn't in yet. Drake's tour group must have been larger than he expected.

Rusty greeted me like I'd been gone forever when I walked into the cabin. I let him outside to romp in the snow a bit, while I put the groceries away. Outside the window, I caught motion at one of the huge pine trees and saw that he'd chased a squirrel; it was now ten feet up the trunk, chattering at him like a bad-tempered schoolteacher. I called the dog back inside.

By the time Drake got home I'd prepared a salad and two baked potatoes, and steaks were seasoned and waiting to be put under the broiler.

"Big day, huh?" I asked.

"Almost like doing those endless tours in Hawaii," he groaned. "Reminds me of why I wasn't unhappy to leave that kind of work behind."

I took his jacket and rubbed his shoulders. "Would you like a nice hot shower before dinner?"

"No, I'm starved. The other thing passengers seem to think is that pilots never eat. We're just expected to keep flying through lunchtime, while they get taken to the lodge for a big buffet."

I waved the plate of steaks in front of him. "Here, pour a glass of wine for each of us and I'll have these ready in just a few minutes."

An hour later, he emerged from the shower looking well fed and much more relaxed. I'd cleaned up the kitchen, made coffee, and sliced a carrot cake.

"Want to go do New Year's Eve on the town?" I asked as we settled on the sofa with our dessert.

"Not unless you really have your heart set on it," he said.

"I'd rather celebrate here, just us two. Three," I amended, noticing that Rusty was giving my plate the big stare-down. I told Drake about the champagne, Brie, and paté I'd picked up for midnight.

"I gotta quit eating like this," he said, shoving a big hunk of cake into his mouth. "Married life isn't supposed to make me fat."

"We're dieting, starting tomorrow," I reminded him.

We put a video in the machine and turned on the television set for the first time since we'd been here. It was a classic romance film that I normally wouldn't watch on a bet, but somehow it fit in with our holiday honeymoon. By the end of it I was sniffling and Drake was ready for action. We decided to open our champagne since it was almost midnight. Toast first, then action.

FOURTEEN

New Year's morning saw me stretching lazily between the covers, wanting to stay snuggled in with Drake and ready to waste the whole day away. After all, it was only ten o'clock. Unfortunately, the telephone thought otherwise. It rang just as I was draping myself over his muscular chest.

"Hello," he said, stretching himself over me to reach for it.

I took advantage of the new position by shifting slightly under him and pressing my hips upward.

"Hi, Hope," he said.

My arms flopped to the bed. Ugh. Hope Montgomery had the worst timing. Served me right—I'd forgotten to call her back and schedule the flight for her guests.

"Tomorrow? Yes, our schedule's open." He pulled himself off me and reached for a notepad on his side of the bed. "Uh-huh. That'll be at *least* fifteen hours of flight time, plus expenses. Okay." He finished scribbling some notes.

"The flight for Miss Big Bucks," I said, without much attempt at keeping the snotty tone out of my voice.

"Hey, hon, I don't like her either. But this is gonna be good money. She wants me to fly her and some houseguests to *Las Vegas*, wait while they gamble for a day or so, and bring them back."

"Wow. And she knows how much this will cost?"

"I told her."

"Life must be something else when money's no object," I said.

"*Our* life is something else," he murmured into my ear, taking a little nibble while he was at it. The rest became a blur of warmth and sensation.

෨ඁ ෨ඁ ෨ඁ ෨ඁ ෨ඁ

"You sure you don't want to come on the trip?" Drake asked the next morning as we drove to the hangar. I'd offered to help check in the passengers.

"Nah. Besides, you just watch—they tell you there's only three people and they're staying only one night, but I'll bet they bring enough baggage for two weeks. You'll be lucky to get out of here under gross load."

"Hey, you're starting to get the hang of this business," he grinned. "I'm purposely going out light on fuel, for that very reason. I can top off at the Taos airport and again in Farmington if I need to."

Passengers never had a clue how important the weight load was in a small aircraft. Invariably they'd lie about their weight—some being offended that you'd even ask—or think they could carry all the luggage they wanted to. And it never failed that the heaviest man would insist upon riding in the front seat, which threw the center of gravity off so badly that it created a real danger. Pilots often had to make unpopular decisions for everyone's safety. Hope's group probably wouldn't be happy about the extra fuel stops, but those were the breaks.

"You just don't let that rich lady talk you into anything,"

I said, pressing against Drake for a good-bye hug.

"Don't you worry," he assured me. He knew that I knew she'd been making moves toward him. "Hey"—he brightened—"you're a commercial pilot. Want to take the charter yourself?"

"Oh, no, no." I laughed. "I'm not any crazier about lifting out of these mountains with a full gross load than you are." Winter flying in the mountains was still a bit beyond my comfort level.

The sound of a vehicle outside told us the group had arrived. As predicted, Hope's guests were a couple of extremely well-fed men, each tipping the scale at over two-fifty, and they'd each brought two heavy bags. I weighed all the pieces and handed over the figures to Drake to do a weight and balance calculation. By the time we'd loaded the bags, distributing the weight properly between the back and front seats and the cargo compartment in back, the sun was topping Wheeler Peak.

"Okay," I said, "let's get a picture of the group." I herded the three into a huddle and aimed my disposable camera. "One more shot." This time I honed in on Hope's face and clicked off two quick snaps before she could figure out what I was up to. I dropped the camera into the pocket of my parka and shuffled each passenger to his assigned seat.

"You take care of things," Drake told Rusty, ruffling the dog's ears before he picked up his own small bag. "And you" —he turned to me—"take care of yourself. We're gonna go pick out those rings when I get back."

A lump formed in my throat as he climbed into the aircraft, looking trim and professional in his khaki flight suit and leather jacket. For someone who thought she didn't need anyone in her life a year ago, I'd become awfully attached awfully fast. Now I couldn't imagine my life without him.

I waited while Drake climbed into his seat and fastened his harness. The aircraft's turbine engine whined to life, the rotors slowly sweeping the air. He pulled pitch a couple of minutes later and I turned my head aside as the rotor wash kicked up a flurry of loose snow. Rusty and I climbed into the Jeep as the blue and white helicopter gently lifted above the building and headed west out of the valley.

I shook off the low feeling that tried to settle over me when I arrived back at the empty cabin. There was lots of work to do. I'd keep busy and the two days would go by quickly. I looked around. The breakfast dishes were done, the living room tidy, and I'd already made the bed. Okay, so there wasn't *lots* of work to do. I'd just have to make up some.

Rusty went with me on this trip to town, where our first stop was to drop off the disposable camera at the one-hour photo place. On a whim, I called the Holiday Inn to see if Fred and Susie Montgomery were still there.

"Well, hey there, Charlie-girl," Fred's booming Texan voice greeted. "Any news for us?"

"Nothing definite," I admitted. "We've ruled out a couple of things, though." I told him that we'd run the fingerprints through the national crime records and found no matches.

"Well, that's something anyway," he said. He turned away from the phone to relay the information to Susie, repeating, "Ain't that something, Susie?" to her.

"Fred, I just had a thought. Hope's out of town right

now. Do you suppose there's any way we could get into her house?" I nearly bit my tongue as I said it. Hadn't I learned all I needed to know about sneaking around in other people's territory? Drake would surely come unglued if he found out I was doing this.

"I s'pose we could," he said. "I mean, she ain't given us a key or nothin' but I'll betcha someone's around."

"We'd have to be very careful about the household staff," I cautioned. "Couldn't let them know we were snooping around but I'd like about fifteen minutes alone in her bedroom."

"Okay. I got an idea," he said. "Can you come up there about eleven? Just park down the hill a short way. Toot your horn once then come up to the door. I'll be listening and I'll let you in."

True to his word, Fred Montgomery quietly slid the front door to Hope's mansion open for me at 11:05.

"Only person here's Bertha, the housekeeper," he whispered. "Susie's got her busy in the kitchen. Bedroom's down this hall. It has its own door to the outside—some little patio thing. You can go out that way and through a little gate. She'll never know you been here. I'll lock the door behind you."

"Bertha isn't suspicious?"

"Nah, we told her Hope'd invited us for lunch and musta forgot. Susie got right insistent with her that we want some food." He chuckled. "Personally, I don't think she speaks too gooda English. She kinda gives ya a blank look."

The poor Spanish Bertha probably couldn't decipher his Texan, which even I had to listen to carefully.

Whoever said this is like déjà vu all over again certainly

nailed it, I thought as I entered Hope's bedroom. I couldn't believe I was snooping into someone else's dresser drawers twice in two days. If I weren't careful, it would be pretty easy to slip into a life of crime.

The room had the same feeling as a hotel, beautifully decorated but not really lived in. The décor theme was southwestern, done in shades of turquoise, coral, mauve and tan, with a high cushy bed and carved bleached-pine furniture. Few personal items lay about. There's something about rich people. The more money they have, the less clutter. Probably the fact that they own several homes; the clutter can be distributed among them. I wasn't at all sure what I was looking for—something so dear to her that she would carry it everywhere, or perhaps something so incriminating she wouldn't let it out of her sight. In either case, she might also have taken it to Las Vegas with her. But I couldn't give up now.

I started with the dresser, opening a drawer at a time, patting down the lacy undies and feathery cashmere sweaters, looking for something out of place but trying to leave the contents exactly as I found them. Women are funny that way; we usually know at a glance if anything is out of place.

The dresser netted nothing so I went to the closet. A single neat row of expensive skirts, jackets, and slacks in richly textured fabrics hung with precision. Nothing unbuttoned, everything facing to the left, color coordinated outfits hanging together. I wondered if Hope was a neatness fanatic herself or if Bertha was paid to be fanatic for her. Twenty-three pairs of shoes and boots—I confess, I took the time to count them—were precisely aligned on the floor. The shelf above contained two folded blankets on the left end and a stack of bulky Nordic sweaters on the right. I ran a hand under the sweaters and came up with—voila!—a scrapbook.

This time I didn't dare take my find with me, so I sat on the only imperfect surface in the room, the floor, to page through it. The first page was dated at the top, 1961. A professional black and white photo was mounted with paper corners below the date. The name Monica Francis was printed in the border below the image. It showed a young woman, late teens or early twenties, dark hair and striking makeup, eyes smoldering at the camera, a pouty smile luring the cameraman. Stuck into the next page was a playbill from a minor New York theater. Monica Francis had the role of "Shopgirl."

The following page contained another professional photo, probably done at the same time as the first, this one with Monica's head flung back slightly, lots of teeth showing in the smile. Another photo showed her full-figure, in a slinky evening gown of the type Jackie Kennedy might have worn had she been somewhat less cultured. Monica had a figure that men would have called dynamite.

More playbills followed. Sometimes Monica moved up in the cast of characters, sometimes back down. She never seemed to make it to a leading role.

Two-thirds of the way through the book there was a letter from a producer at Universal Studios inviting the young actress to Hollywood for a supporting role in the remake of a film that had originally starred Grace Kelly. Obviously, Monica wasn't yet up for the Kelly role—it specifically said "supporting." The letter was dated 1982. Twenty years had gone by and Monica would now be in her forties. Probably too old for the young ingénue roles and too young to start playing somebody's mother. The professional photos had been updated, showing Monica now as a redhead, face still nearly perfect with only a hint of tiny lines at the eyes.

She'd obviously decided to move to Hollywood. Snapshots showed her in front of Grauman's Chinese Theatre and at Disneyland. In one picture, she stood in a bathing suit holding one end of a ribbon that some important-looking man was about to cut with oversize scissors. Her figure was still fabulous.

A few pages later a movie poster was folded into quarters to fit into the album. I unfolded it. A glowing picture of an older Jimmy Stewart with his arm paternally around a younger actress, whose face I knew but whose name I couldn't come up with, filled three-fourths of the space. Monica's name was in the middle of a list of six supporting actors in the film. The copyright date on the poster was 1983.

The following pages contained a few more movie promotional items, none of them mentioning Monica by name. Next came a few more playbills, again with her name falling low on the cast list.

Was this just more of Hope's movie memorabilia? I didn't think so—it was much more personal. Was Monica Francis a close friend? A relative? Or could—I flipped hurriedly back to the redheaded photo of Monica—could Hope actually have *been* Monica?

FIFTEEN

I stared hard at the photo, looking for the resemblance. The age would be about right. I'd estimated Hope to be in her fifties. But everything else seemed different—the hair, eyes, figure. How much cosmetic surgery would millions of dollars buy? How thorough a makeover could be done if the price was right? On the other hand, Hope *could* just be a big movie fan. I imagined the young girl, raised alone by her mother, not having much money. Movies might have been her escape, her passion. I thought of the movie memorabilia downstairs. Hadn't Steve Romero told me that people seldom change their interests?

A glance at my watch told me I'd way overstayed my welcome. I'd been in the room for nearly a half-hour, well beyond my allotted fifteen minutes. I looked again at the picture of the redheaded version of Monica. Did I dare? What the hell, I decided. I was already in so deep a little more trouble wasn't going to make much difference. I slipped the photo out of its little corners and shoved it inside my parka. Closing the album and making sure nothing looked out of place, I slipped it back under the sweaters on the closet shelf.

I listened at the bedroom door, heard nothing, and

opened it a crack. Still nothing. I closed it again and slipped to the French doors on the far side of the room. It was just as Fred had described; the door led to an adobe-walled enclosure with a private outdoor spa, covered now for the winter. The adobe wall had a small gate—with a padlock. Dammit, Fred, how was I supposed to deal with this?

I debated going back through the house but didn't trust my luck to sneak down another hallway. Two days in a row was pushing it. I looked again at the wall. It was about six feet high. Bertha's voice suddenly outside the bedroom door made the decision for me. In less time than it took me to formulate the idea, I'd bolted out the French doors, closed them behind me, and dashed for the wall. Some gymnastics class in the distant past came back to me and I ran for the wall as fast as I could, put my hands on top and vaulted. Unfortunately the vaults we'd done in phys ed weren't six feet high and I hit the wall with the bottom edge of my ribcage. It was good enough. My legs scrambled for purchase and my arms worked frantically to hoist me higher. It wasn't pretty but I was interested only in getting away, not in winning a gold medal. I landed on my butt in the snow and slid about ten feet down an incline before coming to a stop no more than six inches from the lethal spines of a yucca. My lungs grabbed for air.

"God, what am I doing?" I moaned.

Rusty waited anxiously in the Jeep at the bottom of the hill. My lower back was already getting stiff by the time I reached the car and I had a feeling a hundred muscles would be screaming at me by nightfall. I fished my keys out of my jacket pocket and checked to see how the photo inside had fared. I was surprised to find, given the beating my ribs had taken, that the photo was still in one piece. Ripped at one lower corner, but basically intact.

"Hey, kid. Doing okay?" I asked, rubbing the dog's ears and accepting a few smelly kisses. "Boy, am I glad to see you."

I twisted the key in the ignition and made a U-turn to avoid going up Hope's driveway. Ten minutes later we were at Burger King where we splurged on cheeseburgers all around. Rusty gulped his burger in two bites then tried to look starved so I'd share mine. I didn't fall for it.

The one-hour photo shop where I'd left the film was on the right side of the main drag as we left town. I belatedly remembered my film, and jerked the wheel roughly to pull off in time. The girl behind the counter couldn't find the pictures and I was beginning to wonder if this bad luck would be my fate for the day. I waited, not too patiently tapping my nails on the counter. When I reminded her that I'd dropped the film off less than two hours earlier, she thought of one more place to check.

"Wouldn't you know it." She giggled. "They were in the last place I checked."

I held my tongue, just pushed a ten dollar bill toward her.

Out in the car again, I flipped through the pictures. It seemed like a waste to pay for developing only three shots, but I hadn't wanted to wait until I had time to take the entire roll. All three pictures came out clear and sharp. I compared the new photo of Hope with the one I'd nabbed of Monica Francis. If they were the same person, I couldn't see it.

Face it, I told myself, Monica is probably Monica and Hope is probably Hope, and Fred and Susie are probably full of shit. I knew my sore muscles were making me grumpy and the fact that Drake would be away tonight wasn't adding to my peace of mind. I decided to go home, take some drugs, and put everything else out of my mind.

Three ibuprofen and a hot shower did wonders for my mental state, especially after I'd curled up on the cushy sofa with a mug of hot chocolate and the book I'd started reading a few evenings earlier. In keeping with the spirit of our new diet, I ate a microwave low-fat meal, then read my book until eight o'clock when I decided I could legally justify it being bedtime. I stripped out of my sweats and crawled between smooth sheets that still smelled of Drake's aftershave.

Raucous, wild, crazy barking awakened me with a terrifying suddenness that made my heart stop. It started up again with a pounding intensity and I looked at the bedside clock. Just after midnight. I spun around in bed, trying to get my bearings in the pure blackness. Drake kept a flashlight on the nightstand and I reached for it. Then remembering that I was clad only in a pair of panties, I reached for my robe at the foot of the bed before switching on the light.

I was alone in the room.

The barking continued, unrelenting, and I turned my head sideways to figure out where the dog was. Rusty is not normally a barker, not for the pleasure of it anyway except when he'd treed that squirrel yesterday, or when he's on guard duty. This barking signified an intruder.

I tightened my belt around my waist and crept around to Drake's side of the bed. Feeling under the mattress I came up with his nine-millimeter Beretta, checked the magazine to be sure it was fully loaded, and flicked off the safety. I edged toward the bedroom door, grasping both the flash-light and the pistol awkwardly. Finally, I figured out the two-handed grip I'd seen the police use in the movies so I adopted that. I stepped out to the landing and shined the light quickly around the living room.

Rusty stood at the door leading to the ski porch, back hair bristled, barking furiously. The bark rolled back to a growl when the light hit him. He glanced back quickly at me then pointed directly at the door. I shined the light at the window panel in it. The ski porch appeared to be noth-ing more than a black hole. Quickly I aimed the light toward each of the living and dining room windows. More black holes. My heart finally slowed to the point where I could no longer hear it. I tiptoed down the stairs, one at a time.

I kept my back to the wall, watching all the windows at once, keeping an eye on the door. Outside, an engine start-ed with a roar. I raced down the remaining steps and across the living room to a front window. A large, dark vehicle swept a wide turn in the driveway and headed down the drive without benefit of headlights.

"I hope you run off the road," I muttered, although on second thought I wanted them as far from here as possible. The black hulk rounded the bend in the driveway and its sound gradually faded.

Rusty remained rigid, nose pointed to the door, his growl quiet now. I reached out to him.

"It's okay now," I assured him. "They're gone."

I laid the flashlight and pistol on the floor and knelt to bury my face in the dog's ruff. He licked my forearm and wiggled away, trotting to the living room window to place his forepaws on the sill and stare out into the blackness. I sank to a cross-legged position and held my head in both hands, my legs suddenly too trembly to hold me. I'd felt so safe here, completely isolated in the mountains. I'd become like other rural people, not closing drapes when I was alone, not worrying about whether the door was locked. Now I felt vulnerable all over again. I got up and checked the front door. It was locked. Thank goodness I hadn't forgotten all my city paranoia.

Turning on a lamp, I switched off the flashlight and went around the room, checking all windows. Nothing seemed disturbed. I pulled the drapes closed at each dark orifice. According to the indoor/outdoor thermometer on the wall, the outside temp was hovering just below zero. Not the kind of conditions for casual drop-in visitors or even for kids playing pranks. Eloy had told me that lone cabins were sometimes targets for teens who wanted a place to take a girlfriend or those with the more sinister motive of a little larceny. The objects of their break-ins were usually the home's stash of liquor, maybe a TV set or VCR. Kids usually picked places that were obviously unoccupied and paid their visits during daylight hours. This didn't feel like teenage pranksters.

I opened the front door into the ski porch. I'd left the outer door unlocked and there were chunks of snow on the floor. The intruders? I couldn't be sure. The snow could have just as easily come off my boots hours earlier when I'd come home. In the unheated space it might not melt for days.

Rusty had shoved his way past me and stood with his nose pasted to the outer door, whining to get out. I debated. If there were footprints in the snow that could help us identify the intruder, I didn't want him messing them up. On the other hand, there were already prints from Drake, Eloy, and me from recent days. And was I really going to call the sheriff's office to report that I'd been frightened by a noise in the night? I let the dog out.

He trained his nose to the porch and steps, taking deep whiffs of the stranger's scent. If only he could talk. He could probably tell me exactly who it was. The trail took him across the covered porch to the living room window, then down the steps to the open area where we parked our cars. He honed in on a spot where fresh tire tracks made a wide arc in the drive. Next, he sniffed his way over to my Jeep, then to Drake's truck. Neither of those held his interest, thankfully. I hadn't even considered the possibility that someone might have tampered with our vehicles.

My furry red detective sniffed the ground back to the new tire tracks, gave a long thorough analysis of them, then lifted his leg and peed on the spot. So there.

Happy that he'd reestablished his territory, he trotted back to where I waited at the door. I'd been so wrapped up in watching his investigation I'd forgotten that I was standing on a frosty wooden porch barefoot, with only a loose terry-cloth robe as protection against the subzero temperature. Gingerly I stepped back into the warm cabin.

I knew I was too keyed up and too chilled to go back to sleep right away. I found a thick pair of socks and some of Drake's felt boot liners for my frigid tootsies, then went around and turned on several more lights. I made some hot chocolate and unearthed a bag of fresh peanut butter cookies I'd bought in a moment of weakness. This felt like as good a time as any to indulge myself a bit. I poured a little of the warm milk in Rusty's bowl and treated him to half of one of the chewy cookies. There. Much better.

Now that I'd done all the little comfort motions I could think of, I had to face the question of who might have been prowling around and why. Hope Montgomery drove a large, dark vehicle but I decided I could pretty much rule her out, since she was at this moment in Las Vegas gambling her little heart out with her friends. Couldn't think of any reason she'd want to frighten me or anything she could hope to get from me. But hadn't I just done the same thing? Entered her home and searched through her things and taken the photograph from her scrapbook? You're not entirely innocent here, Charlie, I reminded myself.

And what about the other case? Had someone at the church figured out that Father Domingo's diaries were missing? Had I left behind some scrap of evidence that pointed the finger at me? And, if so, how did they know we were staying in this isolated cabin miles from town?

For that matter, how did anyone? The only person who *knew* we were here was Eloy.

I didn't like where my thoughts were leading because Eloy was our client and, above all, we were supposed to trust that he was being straight with us. Besides, the dark vehicle whose tail-end I'd seen leaving here certainly wasn't Eloy's old battered white pickup truck. Did that get him off the hook? I wanted to think so but couldn't be entirely sure.

All this speculation hadn't netted me any answers, I decided, setting my mug down and brushing the cookie crumbs off the front of my robe. I crossed the kitchen floor a couple of times, while Rusty watched with head cocked, waiting to see if I'd weaken and reach again for the cookie sack.

The only conclusion I reached was that there was a lot of my investigatory information stored nowhere but in my head. That wasn't smart. If the intruders had gotten in or I were to disappear, all my work would be wasted if I didn't have some backup. I fired up the laptop computer.

It was nearly three in the morning when I finished typing up the details. I saved the document twice, on two different floppy disks. One, I put with the diaries and the photo of actress Monica Francis into a large brown envelope that I planned to keep under my pillow at night. The other, I wanted to keep off the premises but hadn't yet decided where—maybe Drake's hangar or in the glove box of my car. As an extra safeguard I also attached a copy of the document to an e-mail which I sent to Ron in Albuquerque, along with a cover note telling him to print it and make a case file. Without too many other ways to protect the information, I double checked both outer and inner front doors and the back door, then picked up the Beretta and flashlight and called Rusty to come upstairs.

Finally, I thought, I could sleep.

SIXTEEN

Nine o'clock found me groggy from lack of sleep and last night's mental exertion, and I probably wouldn't have awakened even then except for the insistent ringing of the telephone. I raised my head off the pillow and groaned.

On the fourth ring the answering machine downstairs picked up and I heard Eloy's recorded message, which we'd never bothered to change, droning instructions to leave a message. When Drake's voice came on, I rolled over and picked up the bedside phone.

"Guess you got an early start," he was saying, "so I'll just . . ."

"Hi," I said breathlessly as I grabbed the instrument.

"Hey, sunshine. Just getting up?"

"Kinda. I had a sleepless stretch in the middle of the night." No way was I going to worry him with the truth at this point. There was nothing he could do about it anyway.

"Well, I just had to call and tell you I love you," he said.

"I miss you like crazy. When are you coming back?"

"Not sure yet. I haven't talked to Hope or her group yet this morning, but they were still partying hardy last night at midnight. I walked through the casino on my way to call it a night and saw them all gathered around the craps table."

So Hope and her two burly friends had alibis.

"I imagine they'll want to gamble as long as they can today too," he added. "We'll have to be out of here by noon to be home before dark. I'll call you and let you know what they decide."

I pulled one curtain aside to check the weather. "It's snowing here right now," I told him. A half-inch of new powder covered the surfaces of the steps and the cars.

"I'll check the weather service," he said. "That may be another factor in our getting home today."

"Okay, hon, let me know." I hung up.

Too awake now to get back to sleep, I opened the drapes to brighten the cabin. Rusty had trotted down the stairs and was standing at the front door expectantly. I opened it for him and watched as he followed his previous trail, now covered by the new snowfall, to the spot where the tire tracks had been. He re-marked the spot and scanned the rest of the area before coming inside.

I padded around listlessly, filling his food bowl and freshening his water supply, but not having the energy to do much else. Deciding that a hot shower would help, I stood under the spray twice as long as I normally would, washed and conditioned my hair, and did a minifacial with some wonderful-smelling stuff Drake had given me for Christmas. Pampering myself is usually low on my priority list, so the special routine perked me up a bit.

I dressed in jeans and a fluffy sweater, a Christmas gift from Ron and his three sons. Made the bed and tidied the bedroom, stashing the brown envelope of evidence under the mattress. After blowing my hair dry and letting it fall plainly to my shoulders, I was in the mood for a decadent breakfast. Something like eggs Benedict. But that wasn't going to happen so I settled for two frozen waffles, toasted golden and topped with blueberry syrup and chopped pecans.

The phone rang as I was stuffing the last bite into my mouth.

"Charlie, it's Eloy."

"What's up?" I listened for any hint of guilt in his voice, remembering that the thought had flitted through my mind that he might have been our visitor last night.

"I was wondering if you'd heard from Drake," he said. "When's he coming back?"

"It might be this afternoon," I offered cautiously.

"I have a tentative ski charter lined up for him tomorrow. I'll need to contact them if he's not going to be available."

"I'll call you as soon as I know," I told him.

"Okay, leave a message on my machine at home," he said. "Since I don't have to be at the hangar this morning, I'm going skiing."

I hung up, chiding myself for ever suspecting Eloy. His voice had held no trace of guilt. And anyway, if he wanted in the cabin he had a key. He could just find out if we were here and come in any time the coast was clear. I switched on my computer and set up a password to prevent anyone but myself from accessing any of the files. Then I took the envelope of evidence out from under the mattress and put it by my purse. I'd carry it with me wherever I went. Not that I didn't trust Eloy, but I've learned that you never entirely trust anyone.

Deciding to see what else I could find out, I dialed the Holiday Inn and was put through to Fred Montgomery's room.

"Hey, there, Miss Charlie," he said. "Meant to get back to you yesterday but then we never did see you leave. You get any evidence?"

"I'm not sure," I hedged. "Have you ever heard of an actress named Monica Francis?"

He paused a few seconds. "I don't believe I have. She in the movies?"

"Some. She's also done some stage acting."

"Well, I don't rightly think I've ever been to a play on the stage," he said. "Want me to ask Susie? She's right here." He turned away and repeated the name to her. "Nope, she ain't never heard that name either."

"Okay, I didn't really think you would have. I get the feeling she was a minor player who never really made it big."

We ended the call with my asking the two of them to keep me posted with any new information they might get. I told them Hope would likely be home this evening or tomorrow morning.

I hadn't detected any hesitancy in Fred's voice, which made me suspect that he and Susie had nothing to do with my nighttime caller. At loose ends, but feeling that something would break soon, I fidgeted around the kitchen for a few more minutes. Then I had an idea of someone who might answer some questions for me. I dialed Information for Santa Fe.

"Milagro Productions," the male voice answered.

"David?"

"Speaking."

David Santillanes had booked a charter flight with Drake about a month earlier, acting as go-between with a producer in Los Angeles. The flight was for a music video

filmed in the open desert west of Albuquerque for a potentially hot new country music star. David's company had
been in charge of handling the myriad details from arrang-
ing a helicopter for the aerial shots to making sure lunch was
catered on time. I introduced myself and he remembered
me immediately.

"Sure!" he said. "How's the helicopter business going?"

"Just great," I told him. "David, I wonder if you might
be able to answer a question for me?"

"I'll try."

"I'm trying to locate an actress who did a couple of
minor film roles back in the eighties. I wonder if she's still
working or is out of the business."

"A wannabe star?" he joked.

"Maybe. She did some stage work too. But I don't think
she ever really made it big."

"Well, if she's still working she'll have an agent. Are you
on the net?"

I confirmed that I was and he gave me an internet
address where I could search for available talent.

"Pictures?" I asked.

"Oh, yeah. They'll have publicity photos and bios
online."

"What about older stuff? This particular lady may not
have worked in films for a long time. I'm pretty sure she has-
n't done anything in at least three or four years."

"You may have to go to print if it's been very long," he
said. "There are books with the same information, but if it's
been more than ten or fifteen years you may have a hard
time finding anyone who has an old book. I keep mine for
only a couple of years."

I thanked him for the information and reminded him that we'd love to do business again on his next film shoot. I logged on to the internet as soon as I'd hung up and went to the address he'd given. It took a bit of navigating to learn the system, but I'd soon figured out that I could search for an actor by name or by the name of their previous jobs. I keyed in Monica Francis. After a few seconds of hard-drive chattering, a photograph began to appear, line by line. It showed a woman in her forties. She had neither the red hair of the photo in the scrapbook nor the blond of Hope Montgomery and her nose and lips were different, but I could see a resemblance around the eyes and in the jawline.

The biographical information listed her last film in 1989 and a few stage plays after that. I printed the page and wrote down the name of the film, then went to a search engine and keyed it in. Since the star was a major name, I thought there might be more details about the movie itself. I came up with four sites, a couple of them being fan clubs for the big star and one that appeared to be geared toward fans of this particular film. Clicking that link I got four pages of fan-type trivia, but nothing I didn't already know about Monica. I logged off and retrieved the stolen photo from the brown envelope.

Holding the two pictures side by side, I could see that they were of the same woman. I got the pictures I had snapped of Hope Montgomery and held them next to the others. There were similarities, yes, but it would be hard to identify them as being the same person. A woman in her forties would not normally change this much with an extra fifteen years in age. If Monica had changed her looks, she'd had more help than just hair color and makeup.

I slipped one of the Hope photos in an envelope with the web address where I'd found the more recent Monica photo, then wrote a note to Ron telling him to look up the picture on the internet, print out a laser copy, and see if he could find an expert who could compare the two and give a definitive answer. I'd mail it the next time I went into town. Tomorrow, maybe. I was restless from waiting around the cabin for word from Drake, but not restless enough to make the long drive into town again.

Strapping on the snowshoes and bundling into my parka helped me focus on something else. I hid my little cache of evidence in a kitchen cabinet and took care to lock all the doors, tucking the key into my pocket, something Drake and I had never bothered with when we'd previously left the cabin. Rusty bounded along beside me as I headed into the woods behind the cabin. We plowed our way uphill for a short distance then paralleled the road below the driveway for a while. My heart was pumping by the time we reached an opening in the tall ponderosa pines at a tiny overlook.

Taking gulps of the thin mountain air, I stopped to look around. Below, the highway wound like a black serpent through the bottom of the valley. On my right I could see the blue roof of the metal building that was serving as Drake's hangar. It looked tiny from this altitude, hard to imagine an aircraft fitting inside. The windsock he'd erected was a minuscule orange triangle at the end of the building. Farther along the winding road, lodges and restaurants appeared sporadically. The village of Taos Ski Valley was out of sight beyond several more curves in the road, but I could picture the tiny alpine town with its Swiss-style hotels and condos nested into the base of the mountain. Skiers would be riding the lifts, getting ready to tackle the steepest slopes in the state.

"Pretty cool, huh," I said to Rusty.

He waved his tail slowly back and forth, eyes fixed on the panorama below us.

"Let's check out a different way back," I said. He followed me as I turned away from the overlook and followed the terrain downhill, back in the general direction of the cabin. We stayed to the left this time, since we had approached the overlook from the right. Fifty yards or so down the hill we came to a path that must have been cut purposely; it was much too open to be there by chance. I plodded my way to it and took the downhill lie. Rusty bounded onto the path, where the snow was again up to his chest since there weren't as many trees to shelter it. My sense of direction made me think we were headed generally toward the Romero cabin, but would probably come out below it, somewhere along the driveway.

Another hundred yards along the path, Rusty's attention diverted and he dashed across in front of me and headed to a small clearing. I started to call out to him but found my own attention captured.

A huge boulder sat at the edge of the clearing. Shaped like a bus and nearly as big, it was at least five feet high—I could barely see the top surface of it. I glanced uphill and could see the ragged edge of the overlook we'd just stood on. It probably fell from there, but this rock had been here a long time, at least a few hundred years, maybe a few millennia. Scrub oak flanked two sides of it, the sturdy branches firmly entwined in the cracks of the big rock. Its surface was pocked with places where smaller chunks had broken out of it and more than one set of young lovers had chipped their initials into its surface.

The boulder itself was interesting but what had caught Rusty's attention was a squawking blue jay. It was sitting on the chimney of a small fireplace built of round gray river rock that sat at the base of the huge boulder. Cocking its head toward me, the bird fixed its sharp black eyes on the dog and squawked again. I wanted to speak but held back, fascinated by the interaction between the bird and the dog. Rusty glanced at me and I gave my head a little shake. His eyes darted once more to the bird, then he lost interest and began sniffing the snow at the base of the little fireplace. The bird watched him for a minute then flew to the high branches of a pine tree.

On closer examination I noticed the fireplace was really a barbeque grill, built here probably by the Romero family as a place for family picnics. I gazed around, picturing the area in summer, with pine needles instead of snow on the ground, a folding table laden with packages of hot dogs and buns set up in front of the grill, children in shorts and T-shirts chasing each other and screaming.

A breeze stirred the tall trees and shook loose a clump of snow that landed on the tip of my snowshoe, reminding me that I was getting cold.

"Let's head back," I said to Rusty.

He dashed down the path, rounding a curve out of my sight, while I plodded slowly behind. He was waiting patiently when I reached the driveway, but raced toward the cabin as soon as I caught up with him.

"You're a fun hiking partner," I called out, "taking a nice break for yourself. Racing off right when I deserve a rest."

My snide comments didn't slow him down. He was sit-

ting on the cabin's front porch when I got there. I unbuck-
led the snowshoes and stowed them on the ski porch.
Inside, there was a message from Drake on the machine.

"Hi, hon. Sorry it doesn't look like I'll be home tonight.
Couldn't get the group moving fast enough. We'll leave here
about midafternoon, but will plan on staying overnight in
Farmington. I don't want to fly into the mountains after
dark with this heavy a load. I don't think there will be much
to lure them into staying long in Farmington, so we should
be airborne early in the morning. I'll call you."

Okay. I knew these kinds of things would happen. And I
wasn't going to let myself consider the possibility of another
unwanted visitor tonight. I'd simply leave a few lights on in
the cabin and sleep with the gun under my pillow, that's all.

I made a sandwich for lunch, then decided that I could-
n't just sit around all afternoon. I needed to be doing something. By two o'clock Rusty and I were headed toward Taos.
First stop was to drop the envelope to Ron into a mailbox.
Then I headed for the Dumont Gallery.

A small bell tinkled as the door closed upon the hush of
the gallery. The Sam Begay show was still hanging, although
there were quite a few red "Sold" tags visible. His rock for-
mations still looked like body parts to me. I was alone in the
place, so I browsed some of the other artists' work. The
place was deathly quiet except for the sound of my shoes on
the wooden floor as I stepped from one painting to the next.

"That's a lovely piece, isn't it?" Daphne Dumont's voice
startled me, coming from just over my right shoulder.

Some detective I am, I thought, letting her sneak up on
me like that. What I said was, "Yes, just beautiful." As
before, Daphne's white hair was pulled up in a complicated

twist at the back of her head and secured with a turquoise and silver thing that reminded me of a dagger sticking through a loaf of bread. Her broomstick skirt and velvet tunic were also turquoise, and a number of silver and turquoise rings cluttered her fingers.

The painting in question was a typical New Mexico landscape, with sagebrush and chamisa, a mountain in the background, and the edge of an adobe wall at the right edge, indicating that there was probably a house just outside the picture. I'd seen dozens similar to it over the years, but no doubt some tourist from back East would snap it up.

"We've met, haven't we?" she asked.

"I was here for the Sam Begay show," I told her. "And weren't you at Hope Montgomery's holiday party?"

"Yes! Darling Hope. Isn't she just such a dear?"

"You've known her for a long time, I suppose?" I tried to pose the question in the very most casual way.

"We've become quite close," she hedged. "She started coming in last summer and has bought several very nice pieces."

"But you didn't know her before that? Perhaps in California?"

She drew herself up. "I hardly see how that's any of your business."

I sighed and handed her one of my RJP Investigations business cards. "For purposes of an investigation we're conducting, I need to find someone who's known Hope Montgomery for more than two years."

Daphne brought a hand adorned with four chunky rings to her chest. "My goodness!" she exclaimed. "Whatever for?"

It was my turn to be enigmatic. "If you've known her a

long time, maybe you can tell me a little about her. If not, then I guess you can't be of any help to me."

A greedy spark glinted in her eye. Daphne was clearly not the type to accept being left out of the loop. On the other hand, she didn't want to gossip indiscretely. I watched the battle taking place behind her polished façade and I waited to see who would win.

"Hope and I have corresponded for years. It began when she requested our catalog by mail. She said she had visited the gallery and was very impressed with the artists we chose. I didn't remember her personally, but was happy to oblige her with the catalogs. Each year she picked out several favorite pieces and ordered them."

"Did she pick them up here or did you ship the paintings to her?"

"We shipped them. She would send a check and as soon as it cleared the bank we shipped the painting. Most of them went to California, a few to New York. I think we shipped one to Europe once."

"But you never met her face to face."

"Not until last summer. Actually I hadn't heard from her in over two years. There was that dreadful bit with her housekeeper in California, and she simply wasn't able to make the trip here."

"What dreadful bit was that?" I asked.

"The poor woman died. Monique . . . Frasier was her last name, I believe. She had been with Hope for a couple of years, I think, and Hope had really come to rely upon her."

Monique. Monica. I was detecting a strong fishy odor about the whole thing.

"I gathered she was more than just a housekeeper in the

strictest sense of the word," Daphne continued. "She had taken over a great deal of Hope's paperwork too. I seem to remember that it was Monique who sent the check for the last painting we shipped to California."

"And she died?" I prompted.

"Hope was extremely torn up about it. Of course, she'd just lost her father six weeks earlier and losing her right-hand person was simply too much. She wrote to say that she was going away for a while. Went to a lovely spa in the desert for several weeks, I think she told me. Then she'd become almost a recluse in her California home for a couple of years. She's just now finding the strength to get back out into the world again."

"Did Monique sign any of the checks?" I asked.

Her brow flexed into a pair of horizontal lines. "I really don't remember. Maybe Hope signed the check and Monique wrote the cover note." She shrugged slightly. "I just don't recall."

I thanked her and left the gallery, questions zipping around in my head like a pinball. In the car, I pulled my cell phone from my purse and dialed the RJP number.

"Ron, I mailed you a photo today, but before it gets there, I've got some more background information on this Hope Montgomery situation."

"Okay," he said.

"See if you can get a Social Security number for a Monique Frasier. Or Monica Francis. I have a feeling they're the same person. Monique was Hope Montgomery's house-keeper until a couple of years ago. Unless it was some kind of cash-under-the-table deal, Hope would have had to take withholding taxes out of her pay. See if you can get her dates of employment. And, supposedly, she died about two years ago. See if Social Security has any record of that. And find out who her beneficiaries were."

"Yes, ma'am. Anything else?"

"I've got some other theories about this. I'll do some more checking on my own."

I ended the call and turned to Rusty, who had been patiently waiting in the backseat. "One more stop," I assured him. "Then we're heading home."

Officer Steve Romero was sitting at his desk, a phone to his ear, when I walked in. The uniform he wore today must have been from an earlier season in his career. The button-holes were pulled tightly across his midsection. He glanced up at me and finished his call quickly.

"Ms. Parker. What can I do for you today?" he asked.

"I thought I'd stop by and see if your round of New Year's Eve parties the other night helped locate Anton Pachevski."

"Pachevski? Oh, Leon Palais." He shook his head. "Not yet. He's keeping low right now. We've had a couple of offi-cers who thought they spotted him, but we can't get a line on where he's staying and we haven't been able to get close enough to actually get our hands on him. You see him around?"

"No. I stopped in at the Dumont Gallery a while ago but Daphne Dumont didn't mention anything about him." I didn't admit that I'd forgotten to ask in my quest to learn more about Hope Montgomery.

"We've got all the galleries covered," he said. "I don't know if we'll get much cooperation. These art folks tend to stick together. On the other hand, I doubt any of them want to face jail time for harboring a felon so I doubt they're actually hiding him. I think they just don't know where he is right now."

I told him I'd let him know if I learned anything.

It was nearly six when I got back to the cabin, but I'd had a hunch on the drive home and decided to try to follow it up. It was still not quite five o'clock on the West Coast. I pulled out the page I'd printed off the internet, the one with Monica's picture and bio. Along with that information was the name, address, and phone number of her agent. This would be interesting. If Monica was really Monique, and Monique was dead, I'd like to know when she'd had her last acting job.

"Maury Schultz." The voice was abrupt, with a Jersey accent.

"This is Charlie Parker at RJP Productions in New Mexico," I lied. "We're casting the extras for a film here and came across one of your clients on the internet."

"Yeah?"

"Her name is Monica Francis. Her face is just what our producer is looking for in one of the supporting roles. I'm wondering if the picture on the web site is current?"

"Monica, Monica. Hold on." The phone clattered noisily to a desktop and papers began to rustle in my ear. "I'm checking my Rolodex here. This Monica, she ain't been around for a while. I gotta . . . hang on."

This time the blank silence of a line on hold greeted me. I was beginning to wonder if I'd been disconnected when Maury came back.

"Miss? Guess I can't help you with Monica Francis. Just called the number I got in my file. It's somebody else and they never heard of her."

"But her picture was on the web site," I countered.

"Hey, what can I say? These people get outta date books and post this stuff."

"But don't you still represent her?"

"Look, I got clients bringing me in a lot more than her. Years ago, I thought she might get somewhere. But she didn't. Not my fault. I got her a few parts but, hey, some make it and some don't."

"So she hasn't been in touch with you in a while?"

"By the notes I got here on the card, I'd say the last time I talked to her was four, five years ago."

I thought I had a pretty good idea why.

"Well, thank you for your time."

"Hey, I gotta lotta actresses here. I can get you somebody else."

"We'll let you know. Mr. Parker was really set on this one."

I hung up before he could pitch all his other clients to me. The phone rang nearly the instant I set it down.

"Hey, I got some pretty good information on your Monica Francis," Ron said. "She was working off and on in the movies from the 1960s until about ten years ago. Had a dry spell, I guess, because her next four or five employers were restaurants and hotels. Took waitressing work to get by on. Five years ago she went to work as a housekeeper for—guess who—Monty Montgomery. When he died, she stayed on, working for his only heir, Hope Montgomery."

"Aha! I knew there was something weird going on here."

"There was some mixup about that time with her Social Security number. Guess she tried using Monica's number but with the name Monique. It wasn't close enough to suit the government so she legally changed her name." Amazing the amount of information he could pull from normally obstinate bureaucrats.

"Okay, I think we've got something here. You should get a packet from me tomorrow morning. Act on it right away."

I placed a quick call to Fred Montgomery, with the message that they shouldn't leave town because I thought we'd have some answers soon.

It was pitch dark outside now and I found myself listening carefully for vehicle sounds and feeling vulnerable with the lights on inside. I pulled all the drapes closed and double checked the locks on all the doors.

"This is bull," I told Rusty. "We're here in the mountains. We shouldn't have to feel like someone's going to break in on us."

He wagged mightily and turned toward the kitchen. When I didn't follow, he pawed once at my shoe and turned to the kitchen again.

"Okay, okay, I get it." Obedient pet that I am, I filled his food dish.

ઝ ઝ ઝ ઝ ઝ

The following morning dawned clear and cold. The sky sparkled with ice flecks against Wedgwood blue. Yesterday's fresh snow lay undisturbed on the ground, and more whipped cream weighed down the tips of the pine branches. The sun glinted off thousands of faceted crystals.

Drake called at nine to say they were leaving Farmington, would be in around noon and if I'd pick him up at the hangar, he'd take me to lunch. I phoned Eloy and left the message to have him schedule the ski charter accordingly.

Ron called at ten to say the photo had arrived and he knew just the expert to give it to. My heart rate quickened.

"Tell him if we can have an answer by noon we may have a criminal in custody by the end of the day," I said excitedly. Before I hung up I told him what to do if the photo expert came up with the right answer.

"Okay, buddy," I said to Rusty. "Drake's coming home and we're about to solve one of our cases, anyway."

By eleven-thirty I'd neatened up the cabin, put fresh sheets on the bed, and done two loads of laundry. Fifteen minutes later I drove up in front of the hangar. Eloy's truck was already there.

"Hey, Charlie, how are things?"

"Great. Did you enjoy your ski day yesterday?"

He was maneuvering the small electric tug that they used to wheel the aircraft in and out of the hangar. "It would have been more fun if I didn't have this thing about Ramon hanging over my head."

I filled him in on some of the details I'd learned from Father Domingo's diaries. "I think I need to stop in at that church the next time I go to Albuquerque," I told him. "There's more to this than the matter of a priest having an affair with a married woman. And I'd like to see if our homicide detective contact will let me take a look at the file on Ramon's killing. There has to be other evidence we don't know about yet."

Eloy sighed, like the news of Ramon's affair was no surprise to him. He pushed the tug toward the large door where Drake would land. "I sure hope so, Charlie. I don't know what I'm gonna do if they take me down there for a trial. There's no way I'll be able to hide that from my mother."

I patted his arm. "Don't worry about it just yet. You're lucky your brother-in-law lawyer and your cousin on the police force are standing up for you. Not many people get that kind of advantage. We'll solve this soon."

The distinct whopp-whopp of the JetRanger's rotor blades came softly from a distance. I dashed outside like a kid watching the circus come to town. I looked toward the west but the sky was almost painfully bright and I didn't spot the aircraft immediately. Rusty cocked his ears, picking up the sound more clearly than I could. I looked again. There in the distance was a tiny dark speck. I blinked to be sure my eyes weren't tricking me. The speck became larger.

We stood beside the Jeep and watched the speck become a shape, the sun reflecting off the steady motion of the blades. I grabbed Rusty's collar as Drake brought the aircraft to a hover over the landing pad then set her gently down. He lowered the rotor rpm and the turbine whine gradually wound down. I let the dog go and he raced to Drake's side of the helicopter.

Another sound penetrated my consciousness. Sirens.

Two county sheriff's cars and one from the town of Taos wheeled into the driveway and roared to a stop just short of the landing pad. I saw the concern on Drake's face and put my hand up in a "stop" gesture. Eloy stood rigid beside me.

"Ray Tenorio," he muttered through clenched teeth.

"Don't worry. I don't think this has anything to do with you," I said.

I trotted over to Steve Romero's car.

"Is this about Hope Montgomery?" I asked.

He nodded.

"She's in the front passenger seat," I told him.

"Stay here," he said, guiding me to the other side of his car.

He made a couple of hand motions to Tenorio and the other officer. They stood behind their car doors, hands poised over pistols. I held my breath, praying that the pistols would stay holstered. Steve approached the aircraft and opened the passenger door.

"Monica Francis, also known as Monique Frasier, also known as Hope Montgomery," he recited. "You are under arrest for murder."

SEVENTEEN

He went on, reciting the Miranda rights by rote, while the two men in the backseats eyed the other officers nervously. Drake attended to the switches on his console. He'd learned by now to expect nearly anything when I was on the scene.

Hope blanched so white I thought she might faint. This certainly wasn't the way she expected her fun Las Vegas weekend to end. She glanced to her friends in the backseats, gauging their reaction. Neither would meet her eyes. She climbed docilely from the aircraft and hung her head while Steve clipped a pair of handcuffs on her. Ducking to avoid the still-spinning rotor, he led her away from the helicopter to one of the sheriff's department cars.

Before the officers could guide her into the backseat, she spun on them with venom in her eyes.

"You swine!" she spat. "How dare you!"

Gone was the cooperative manner, gone was the genteel face. The actress had slipped out of character.

Ray Tenorio and the deputy placed hands on her shoulders and forced her into the back seat of one of the squad cars. She was still ranting vehemently as the deputy backed his car and turned it around. I saw him saying something to her as he passed us and she appeared to return fire. He showed her who was in charge by turning on his lights and sirens as he pulled onto the highway. Let her suffer the humiliation of arriving at the county jail in a blaze of attention. Tenorio followed, grinning with large white teeth.

Hope's two guests had hustled their baggage out of the aircraft and into the car they'd arrived in two days ago, and were now only a few yards behind the second sheriff's car.

"Murder?" I said to Steve as they rounded the first curve in the road. Drake had finished shutting down the engine and had brought the main rotor to a complete stop. He walked up next to me to find out what was going on.

"Interesting lady, Monica Francis." Steve smiled. "And I have to offer compliments to you and your brother. He dug up a hell of a story and put some wheels in motion very quickly."

And? My raised eyebrows conveyed the unasked question.

"Seems that Monica Francis started out like so many other pretty young girls—wanted to be an actress so much she could taste it. Didn't do too badly. She got a number of minor roles, but that wasn't what she wanted. She was after real fame and, mostly, big money. Waiting tables and cleaning hotel rooms was bearable when she was twenty, but by the time she was pushing fifty, with no fabulous prospects in sight, she began to get desperate. She laid her plans well. Found a rich old man who needed a housekeeper, went to work for him. Hoped to clean out his bank accounts and skip but he complicated things by dying only a few months after she went to work for him. So she started to work on his heir, the real Hope Montgomery. But old Monty's daughter was no fool. She realized that things weren't right—valuable objects were missing, bank accounts were low. Deciding to expose Monica was, unfortunately, a fatal move for her.

"According to the LAPD, Monica couldn't have planned it much better. She and Hope Montgomery were close to the same age and not dissimilar in size and coloring. She drugged Hope with a bottle of sleeping pills, switched all their ID, and took Hope's body out to the ocean. Before dumping her off a pier, she battered her face so badly that no one would positively identify her. With Monica's wallet full of credit cards and identification, it was assumed that Monica had drowned and the surf had beaten her body against the pilings."

"But how did Monica fool Hope's friends?" Drake asked.

"Right away she disappeared. Left word with Hope's closest friends that she was checking into a clinic to deal with the depression she was feeling over her father's death. Actually she went to a doctor who performed a few surgical miracles, then to a spa where she acquired the right weight, hair color, and makeup techniques. She was an actress preparing for the role of her life."

I shook my head in disbelief. It was still a gutsy thing to do.

"Remember," Steve continued, "the real Hope hadn't been in California all that long. She'd appeared on the scene only a few months earlier, after Monty died. Monty himself was somewhat of a recluse, the inventor who stayed in his lab, so Hope didn't have too many people to deal with. And even Monty's lawyers and the other people involved with his estate had met her only a couple of times. Monica believed she could pull it off and she did."

Eloy had finished tying down the rotor blades and hooking up the tug to pull the helicopter inside. He joined us just as Steve was leaving. They shook hands and Steve murmured a few encouraging words to his cousin. He drove away while Eloy rolled the aircraft into the hangar and Drake filled out his logbooks.

I called Fred Montgomery at his hotel and briefed him on everything that had happened.

"Boy, oh, boy," he said. "I betcha she nearly panicked when we brought that lawsuit. Nobody had really questioned her until then, I'll bet. Here we thought she was afraid she'd have to give up some of that inheritance, and all along she was afraid we'd known the real Hope and could tell the truth about the imposter."

"You got it," I confirmed. "Well, now that we know what happened to the real Hope, it looks like you just might get that inheritance after all. Call your attorney back and see what he can do for you."

"I sure will, Miss Charlie," he said. I could practically hear his wide grin over the phone and I grinned with him. "And you send us the bill for your time on all this. We just cain't tell you enough how much we appreciate everything."

Drake and I decided to have a celebratory lunch in town, so we headed for Michael's Kitchen for another dose of chile.

"Speaking of attorneys," I said.

"Were we?"

"New train of thought. Telling Fred to contact his attorney reminded me that Eloy's brother-in-law, who is supposed to be representing him, has been awfully quiet recently. Maybe I should plan to pop in on him and find out what's going on."

Still feeling at the top of my game, I told Drake I also thought it would be a good idea to visit the church in Albuquerque where Ramon was killed. Seeing the spot might give me a better feel for what might have happened. Our food arrived just then and we concentrated on digging into stuffed sopapillas with chicken and green chile.

Mike Ortiz's office building looked quiet, again giving the impression that he didn't have much of a practice. Drake opted to wait in the truck and listen to his favorite country music station on the radio while I went inside. The reception area was silent except for the gentle hum of a computer; his receptionist was not at her desk. I stood in the middle of the room, looking around at the shabby furnishings, assuming the secretary would appear any moment now.

Mike's voice trickled through the open door to his private office, coming to me in bits as he apparently paced back and forth.

"Don't worry about . . . be okay . . . resolved soon . . . I know. Bye." The handset clicked down definitively and he muttered an expletive.

I tapped on his doorjamb.

"Mike?" He was visibly startled. "Sorry to interrupt. Your receptionist doesn't seem to be here."

He flopped down in his chair and raked his fingers through his hair. "Oh. She must not be back from the bank yet."

"I was in town anyway," I told him, "so I thought I'd see how things are going with Eloy's case."

"Nothing much new on it. You knew the judge in Albuquerque set the trial date for April."

"No—that soon?" It wasn't giving us much time to get evidence to clear him.

"Yeah. And my wife"— he glared at the telephone— "keeps bugging me about what I'm doing to save her dear little brother." He shuffled a couple of folders on the cluttered desk. "So what can I do for you?" His tone let me know that I was just one more interruption he didn't really want.

"I'll keep it brief," I said. I filled him in quickly on what I'd learned from the diaries, although I didn't say how I'd gotten the information.

"I don't exactly think this is hold-the-presses news," he said sarcastically. "There were other rumors about women over the years. The part about the artifacts is news to me, but I don't know if I could call it surprising."

"So Ramon the saint wasn't—except in his mother's eyes."

"And his sister's," he added glumly.

"Well, I'm still working on it," I assured him. "I'm not sure how or why Eloy's gun comes into it, but I think these other guys believed Ramon was dangerous to them and decided to get him out of the picture. Or there's always the possibility that it was motivated by simple jealousy. That scorned husband had plenty of motive. How he could have performed the switch with the gun is the big question."

"I don't know either," Ortiz agreed. "I'm working on the legal aspects of it. Trying to find a precedent we can use to either get the case thrown out or get the sentence reduced if it comes to that."

So the truth didn't really matter, once the case got to court, nearly as much as finding a legal loophole. Guess that wasn't exactly stop-the-presses news either. I left the office not feeling very hopeful for Eloy.

Drake was dozing when I walked out to the truck.

"Siesta time?" I teased.

He stretched and yawned. "Guess I didn't sleep too well in that hotel room last night. And people like Hope and her friends wear me down with their constantly changing desires. 'Go here, go there' all the time. You know, they actually wanted to dash off to L.A. 'on the way home' from Vegas?"

I patiently let him rant. "You're tired," I said.

"Yes. Let's go home."

I had the feeling he meant really go home, to Albuquerque, to our own house. But that would still be a while. He had a commitment here and the contractors still had a lot of work to do before our place would be habitable. We started up the ski valley road again.

Back at the cabin, I spent a few minutes gathering the billing information for Fred and Susie Montgomery's file, which I e-mailed back to our Albuquerque office so Tammy could compile a bill and mail it. Drake took his time under the hot shower and emerged looking somewhat refreshed. We decided that he should take a nap, I would plan something nice for tonight's dinner, and then we'd spend a couple of days simply being lazy—at least until the phone interrupted. I turned off the ringer while Drake slept.

By the time the interruption came, Wednesday morning, we were feeling satisfied in just about every way. Plenty of food, plenty of sleep, and well . . . we *were* on our honeymoon, after all. I'd taken Drake to see the huge boulder and picnic area Rusty and I had found, and we trekked up to the overlook one afternoon. So the phone call, when it came, wasn't entirely welcome but it didn't really interrupt anything either.

"That was Eloy," Drake said, hanging up. "He just happened to get to talking with some guy in the bar at the Sagebrush last night, and this guy is a film producer doing a documentary. Wanted to know if there were any helicopters for charter around here."

"And Eloy set it all up?"

"No, I still have to call the guy and make the arrangements." He spent about forty-five minutes on the phone, with aeronautical charts spread over the kitchen table and a notepad rapidly being filled with numbers and scribbles.

"Okay," he finally said, after hanging up. "They want a series of shots along the New Mexico-Colorado border, all the way from here to Trinidad." He showed me the route he'd drawn on the map. "Looks like it'll be good for at least two days of filming, because they want sunsets in both these places," he said, pointing.

"That's great. Should be worth some money, huh?"

He punched buttons on his calculator. "Not bad. And they have all their own equipment, including the Tyler Mount so I don't have to rent one." The special helicopter camera mount that most professional film people used was so expensive that we'd not budgeted for one yet.

"If you'll be gone for a couple of days, I may just use that time to go back to Albuquerque and check on our construction project again. Plus, I have a few more people I want to question about Eloy's situation."

He looked at me sideways. "Just don't be taking a lot of chances for Eloy's sake," he cautioned. "That's what he has a lawyer for. And I don't want any of these desperate characters coming after you."

"Unfortunately I don't have a lot of confidence in Mike Ortiz," I said. "He doesn't seem to be doing anything to clear Eloy. He's just snagging at loopholes in the law." I hadn't mentioned the midnight visitor the other night and didn't do it now either.

EIGHTEEN

The traffic began building north of Santa Fe and became heavier and heavier between the capital city and Albuquerque. By the time I reached the outskirts of my hometown, it was bumper-to-bumper at seventy-five miles an hour. I let loose with a curse as a blue sports car, tired of riding the tail of the pickup truck in the left lane, zipped in front of me with centimeters to spare. Albuquerque's drivers are notorious for making frequent and rapid lane changes, the only apparent goal being to gain one or two car lengths and arrive at their destinations three or four seconds ahead of their rivals in traffic. The longer I stayed in the mountains, the less I liked driving in the city.

Although it was after five o'clock a sense of duty determined that my first stop would be the RJP offices. Just a few blocks from the downtown area, the gray and white Victorian waited with steady reassurance. The high-rise office buildings that sat in a small cluster around the cross comprised of the north-south railroad tracks and the east-west Central Avenue corridor which delineated the city's four quadrants had emptied by now. Commuters were clogging the two interstate freeways, as I could attest, in their rush to swarm back to the suburbs.

Someone had once commented to me that Albuquerque has very little "city" atmosphere. In the traditional sense, where a city has tall buildings, mom and pop restaurants and shops, and easy availability of cabs, that's true. It's more like a dime-size city centered on a tabletop of sprawling tract homes, strip shopping centers, and six-lane streets where fast-food joints segregate themselves from the car dealerships who segregate themselves from the hotels. Sprawl is the modern name for it, but mainly it means that to accomplish five errands you have to drive ten or fifteen miles.

I parked behind the office and let Rusty run around the backyard while I unlocked the back door. Tammy's car was gone but Ron's convertible was still here. I called out to him as I entered.

His answering bellow led me upstairs where I found him carrying a cup of coffee toward his office. He set the cup on his desk and turned to give me a hug.

"How's the honeymoon going?" he grinned.

"Just about perfect," I told him. "It would be absolutely perfect if work didn't keep interfering. But the tradeoff is that we get to be there three months instead of a week, like most couples get."

"True. Here, I think I have some info for you on your murdered priest." He reached across a remarkably neat desk to pluck a folder from the corner of it.

"Hey, what's this?" I gaped. "Giving up your slovenly ways?"

"Tammy. The girl's determined to reform me."

"And you let her?" I'd been trying to impress the benefits of organization upon Ron for years.

"She came in here one day and made me start sorting

things. Then she filed away all the old cases, brought the billing up to date, and organized the current cases by priority and set up a spreadsheet on the computer for them. She's making me enter my time and expenses every day." He looked slightly rueful as he said this. "Only thing is, I didn't let her touch my Rolodex."

Wow. Maybe Tammy would work out after all. She'd certainly gotten more accomplished in this room than I'd ever seen.

Ron took a sip from his coffee and offered to get me a cup. "I've got a better idea," I said. "I *really* need one of Pedro's margaritas. Let's get some dinner there and you can fill me in. Later, when I get back, I'll read through the file."

Salty margaritas, along with chicken enchiladas smothered in cheese and green chile are more of a staple in my diet than bread, and Pedro and his wife Concha make them like no one else. We found a spot in the tiny parking area in front of their adobe restaurant where they live in the apartment upstairs, just a block off the touristy Old Town Plaza. Two vehicles I didn't recognize were parked there, along with the familiar battered pickup truck of Manny, another regular. Manny is a man of few words. He always sits at a corner table, the opposite corner of our usual spot, and downs tequila shooters like he has the insides of a teenager. He lifted his grizzled chin in greeting as we walked in.

"Hey! There's our Charlie!" Concha greeted me with more than her usual exuberance, pulling me into a hug against her pillowlike front. "Where have you been?"

Obviously I'm such a regular here that not showing up for a couple of weeks created cause for great concern.

"On my honeymoon, remember?"

She beamed at me slyly. "And where is that handsome

groom of yours?"

"I had to leave him." I placed my hand solemnly on her forearm.

"No!" Her deep brown face almost went white.

I relaxed my expression. "Not forever, silly. He had a charter and I needed to come back to town to see how our house is coming along."

"Don't you tease me like that," she scolded.

I got the feeling that if Concha hadn't already been married to wiry little Pedro, she might have tried to give me some serious competition for Drake. From the moment I'd brought him here, she had fawned over him completely. Of course, she also fawned over me and Ron, like we're just a few more in the brood she and Pedro raised.

"Margaritas!" Pedro's voice announced the arrival of our favorite libation. He set them down on our usual table with ceremony, then put his tray aside to give me a hug. "It's good to see you again, *chiquita*."

"Now, you get back in that kitchen and make their enchiladas," Concha instructed him. She bustled off to check on her other tables.

Ron and I clicked glasses before I slurped mine, taking a good lick of salt off the rim. We munched on tortilla chips and Pedro's special salsa until the enchiladas arrived.

"So what did APD have to say about the Ramon Romero murder?" I asked.

"They chalked it up to a drive-by gone wrong. Back when it happened they interviewed just about everyone in the neighborhood. It happened on an autumn evening, weather was nice, and services at the church had been over for thirty minutes or so. The church is Our Lady of

Lourdes, down in the north valley, on Fourth Street, I think, but you'd have to check the file on that."

Fourth and Second are both commercial streets with a fair amount of daytime traffic but much quieter in the evenings. Surely the area was well-lit and not isolated.

"The parishioners of Lourdes live mostly within a five-mile radius, but there aren't any residences directly around it. The closest homes are a block or two off Fourth, on the side streets. So there weren't any eyewitnesses, no one really close enough to identify the shots or what direction they came from.

"The shots, three of them, were fired from some distance away. That is, there was no evidence of a close-range shot. The first supposition was that someone may have knocked on the door of the church to lure Father Romero out, then shot him. Flaws in that theory are, one, why would they knock? The church is unlocked and they could have gone in and done the dirty deed much more privately. Two, they would have had to knock on the door then run down to the street to fire the shots. Seems like it would have attracted less attention and been less chance of missing their shot if they'd stayed close up."

Pedro arrived with our plates just then and we waited until he was again out of earshot.

"So, instead, the police settled on a drive-by?" I mumbled with my mouth half full.

"There's also been gang activity in the area," Ron continued. "It's a part of town where there have been rumbles for decades, but until recent years the weapons of choice were usually limited to brass knuckles and chains. Now it's spray paint and automatic weapons.

"Lourdes had been a target of some graffiti tagging and Father Romero had been vocal in his declarations against it. Probably wasn't the most popular guy in the neighborhood."

So now the priest numbered gang members, a scorned woman and her irate husband, along with a possible ring of art thieves among his enemies. Sounded to me like Eloy might be pretty far down on the list. The only thing that really nailed him was the fact that the ballistics tests had confirmed his gun as the murder weapon and Eloy himself told me it hadn't been out of his possession. I still didn't have a handle on who might have gotten hold of that gun, who had pawned it, and how on earth they'd managed to replace it in his house after the murder, but I'd just about bet money that it wasn't Albuquerque North Valley gang members.

"After that pawn ticket with the gun's serial number led them to Eloy Romero, they backtracked on the drive-by theory and are putting together their evidence against him," Ron told me.

"And what do they have so far?"

"Nothing beyond circumstantial stuff, according to what I can get out of them. The matching serial number, the fact that Eloy has no alibi for that night, the missing gap of several hours when he says he was on the road but could have managed to duck down to Albuquerque and confront his brother. His motive is the fact that their mother's health is so bad and she always favored Ramon—it could be the inheritance proved to be a strong enticement."

I flipped through the file, writing down the address of Lourdes and the address of the Albuquerque woman Ramon had dallied with. I couldn't picture Eloy, the easygoing ski instructor, who was happy to live on very little, taking such a drastic measure for a larger share of an inheritance. My money was still on the larger forces at work here, those who had stolen the valuable religious artifacts and were blackmailing Ramon.

We finished our enchiladas and each polished off another margarita before I headed back to the office to settle into our temporary quarters. Drake had left a message on the answering machine, letting me know where he was for the night—Trinidad, Colorado—and the phone number of his hotel. I called him and we each rehashed our day. Afterward, I burrowed down into the covers and Rusty flopped down on the rug beside me.

I awoke early the next morning, realizing that I was hearing traffic sounds from Central Avenue two blocks away, strangely unfamiliar after my time in the mountains. I quickly showered and dressed, deciding to make the early Mass at Our Lady of Lourdes. Rusty looked at me curiously when I made him stay behind. He wasn't accustomed to staying alone at the office, but Ron and Tammy would be here within an hour or so.

The drive down to the North Valley was fairly easy at this time of day; most of the traffic was headed up the hill instead. I located the church, another traditional adobe with rounded shoulders and a wooden cross above its bell tower. A scattering of people were leaving, walking down the concrete steps, dressed for jobs they'd now rush off to. I hung in the background until most of them had left and I saw the priest hovering near the door. I walked up and introduced myself. Except for his clerical collar, I would have easily taken him for a high school kid. His freshly scrubbed face with traces of a few pimples and his brown hair neatly part-ed on the side reminded me of someone whose mother had insisted that he have a good breakfast before she sent him out the door.

"Glad to meet you, Ms. Parker," he said in a voice that still needed to come down an octave or so.

I explained that I was looking into the death of their former priest and asked whether he'd been here at the time.

"No, I'm afraid I was away at seminary then," he said. "I got this assignment two years ago, after the church had been through a series of temporary clergy."

"I understand the murder happened right here on the front steps," I said. "That must have been terribly hard on the parishioners."

"Yes. Many of them had a hard time accepting it." He looked down at the steps. "Actually I think these are new steps," he said, indicating the concrete. "The old ones were brick, but so much blood soaked into them that it couldn't be cleaned off. Some of the parishioners were so distraught that they'd fall down weeping whenever they saw it. Others simply stopped coming. One of my predecessors had the steps replaced."

"I don't suppose anyone's come into the confessional and admitted doing it?" I asked.

He stepped back.

"I'm sorry, I shouldn't have asked." I wasn't sure whether he was more offended at my flippancy, the thought that a person from his own church might have done it, or that I'd ask him to break the sanctity of the confessional.

I left a few minutes later, feeling like I'd gotten all the information he knew.

NINETEEN

Stella Chavez lived in a trailer park less than a half-mile north on Fourth Street. I followed the winding one-lane road, past signs that warned of slow children playing, to number forty-three. Like most of its neighbors, number forty-three sat on a bare patch of dirt. A large cottonwood tree behind it spread bare branches to the azure sky. In summer it probably provided one of the few touches of green in the park.

The Chavez trailer was a single-wide, like its neighbors, white siding with a stripe of pink running horizontally around it, like a belt trying to hold up the skirting around the bottom. It was successful in only a few places. I mounted warped plywood steps and knocked on the metal door. It was opened by a middle-aged woman in a flowered muumuu. Her once-attractive face had become pudgy and her hair was lank and unwashed. Long lashes framed large eyes the color of strong coffee, but the eyes were tired looking. Even at a glance I got the sense she was a woman who'd given up caring. The smell of pinto beans and tortillas wafted through the open door.

"Stella Chavez?"

She nodded confirmation.

"I have a few questions about Father Ramon Romero," I said, handing her one of my business cards.

She took a step back, her hand on the edge of the door.

"Please. I'm trying to find out the truth about what happened to him, on behalf of his family."

"Leroy hasn't left for work yet," she hissed. "Come back in a half-hour." She shoved my card down into her pocket and closed the door in my face.

I turned slowly. Her voice came faintly from inside the trailer. "Just somebody selling something," she was saying.

I climbed back into my Jeep and backed out of the spot where I'd parked behind their faded blue Chevy Nova. Watching carefully for the slow children, I backed to the first curve in the road and found a spot in front of a trailer whose occupants must have already left for work. The Chavez's trailer was visible and I hoped I could keep an eye on it without Leroy Chavez noticing my conspicuously shiny Jeep.

Ten minutes later, he emerged, a stoop-shouldered man in blue jeans, a plaid shirt, and worn sheepskin jacket carrying a black metal lunchbox. He climbed into the Chevy Nova without a glance my way and slowly ground its engine to life after three tries. He gunned a puff of blue smoke from its tailpipe then backed out and lumbered away in the direction from which I'd come. I allowed two minutes for him to rush back for any forgotten item, then pulled into the spot where he'd been parked.

Stella met me on the porch, dressed now in a pair of pull-on knit slacks and flowered blouse, with a quilted jacket on and her purse over her arm. Her hair had been hastily pulled back into a ponytail. She was visibly startled when she saw me.

"I didn't have anything else to do for half an hour," I told her. "Thought you might be able to offer me a cup of coffee."

She didn't look at all pleased that her escape had been aborted, but she didn't try to run. "I don't know if we have any. I was just going down to the market."

"That's okay. I really don't need any and I'll be quick." I blocked the plywood steps. "Could we go inside?"

Grudgingly she opened the door with her key and preceded me into a small entry with a haloed picture of Jesus facing the front door. In the living room, the furnishings were old but clean and everything inside was neat and orderly. Dark wood paneling and brocade drapes throughout made the place dreary and I could begin to understand why a woman locked in here all day would turn to a little outside excitement.

"I'm not looking for the lurid details," I began. "And I have no opinion on whether a priest having a love life is right or wrong. I'm just trying to clear a man that I think has been wrongfully accused of murder—if he's truly innocent."

She relaxed a touch. "I just remembered that I do have some coffee," she offered shyly.

I followed her into the kitchen and watched her pour from a silver electric percolator. We both stirred sugar into our cups.

"Did Ramon ever talk to you about his family?" I asked. "His mother or his brother Eloy, especially?"

"You'll never repeat this to her?" Stella asked nervously.

I shook my head.

"Ramon was his mother's favorite. He made no secret

about that. He worried that her health was not good and he was not close by to help her. He said his brother Eloy was a bum, wouldn't lift a finger to help out."

I thought of Eloy, working an extra job to afford the nursing home care his mother was getting. But I didn't say anything.

"His sister is married to a lawyer. Ramon hoped they would take care of the mother, but they're both so busy. I guess the brother-in-law isn't really successful, I mean, not like you think of lawyers making all this money. They get by okay, but she has to work. She's a secretary at an insurance company, you know. They both work forty hours a week and there's no one taking care of their mother during the day—"

I had to interrupt. "Actually now she's in a nursing home. She's getting excellent care."

Stella looked somewhat mollified. "Well, it wasn't like that back then."

"Did Ramon ever say anything about any religious artifacts? You know, crosses, things like that?"

Something closed off inside her. "No . . . I don't remember anything like that."

"I talked with an old priest in Taos. He had some documents that showed Ramon had gotten involved with some men who were stealing and selling valuable items. Did he ever mention a man named Leon Palais?"

"Oh, no, no. Never would Ramon be involved in something like that."

Her loyalty was touching, if somewhat misguided. I was surprised that she wasn't bitter toward him about the trouble that must have ensued when the church and her husband found out about her off-limits affair. I wondered whether she had instigated the romance, tired of her dreary life without promise, or whether Ramon had lured her into it, making it seem more innocent than it was. Either way, I doubted I would get any unprejudiced information out of her. She clearly still had feelings for him and wasn't about to say anything against him. I felt sure she knew something about the stolen artifacts but didn't intend to share it with me.

I thanked her for the coffee, returning my cup to the kitchen sink. I drove out of the trailer park, wondering where to turn next.

The day was one of those January oddities we get here in New Mexico. Although the temperature hovered in the twenties, the sky was deep and clear and the sun warmed my car to the point that I actually had to roll down windows to relieve the stuffiness. A storm front was predicted to move in by tomorrow, however, and all that would change. I decided to look in on our remodeling project, do a couple of errands, then head back to the mountains by this afternoon.

The traffic on Fourth had abated somewhat with the morning commuters now safely at work, but the little old lady shoppers were out in force. I zagged my way south on Fourth to Griegos, then out Rio Grande to Central. Our neighborhood is just south of Old Town, in the old Albuquerque Country Club area. The homes were mostly built in the forties and fifties, with large rooms on decent-sized lots. A touch below ostentatious in their day, nearly modest compared to some of the newer places today. I grew up in this area, where most of the neighbors are now old enough to be my grandparents. It's quiet, undisturbed, and I love it. It had nearly broken my heart to see our home almost consumed by fire, but I had to admit the new additions would be nice when finished.

I pulled up in front and found Hank Logan at work directing the delivery of a load of drywall.

"It's coming right along, Charlie," he greeted. "Come in and let me know what you think."

We walked through the cold rooms, the heat being cut way back to a level that would barely prevent the pipes from freezing. I admired the progress.

"We've finished the drywall in the guest room and study. We've just got the master bedroom and bath and the hallways to go. I've got the texturing scheduled for Wednesday and the painters early next week. After that, the bathroom fixtures come in—they'll take about a day—then light fixtures, carpet. You'll be ready to move back in no time."

I was ready now, actually.

After ascertaining that he didn't need anything else from me, I wandered next door to Elsa's. She greeted me at the back door, wearing a pink velour robe I'd given her for Christmas at least ten years ago.

"Why, Charlie! Come on in." She held the door and ushered me to the kitchen table. "I didn't know you'd be in town."

She bustled about, pouring me a cup of coffee and setting a plate of toast triangles in front of me.

"Here, have some breakfast," she insisted.

I didn't mention that I'd already had enough coffee to make me buzz. I took a half slice of toast and spread her homemade raspberry jam on it.

"How is that fine young man of yours?" she asked. "And Ron and his boys. I hardly see them anymore without you next door."

"Everyone's fine," I told her. "Drake's got a charter for the next couple of days, so I decided to come by and see how the remodeling is going."

"That nice builder told me it would be ready for you to move back in about a month or so."

"That's about right, I guess. The timing should work out with our job in Taos too. We've contracted to stay there until March first. But I'll sure be glad to get moved back into our own house. And I know Drake is enjoying the work up north, but doesn't want to miss out on anything around here either."

"Ron mentioned that you're working on an investigation up there?"

"I had two of them going, actually," I said. "I think we wrapped up one of them. The other one is more complicated."

I filled her in briefly on the situation with Eloy and his brother's death. "This priest certainly had a number of problems, though," I said. "His involvement with an art theft ring, the tension in the neighborhood over the graffiti problem, his family bickering over his mother's property, and then the scandal of that affair."

At the mention of Ramon's affair, Elsa perked up. "*That's* the priest you're talking about?" she asked. "Why, I followed that. I think I still have the newspapers. There was a lot more to that story than met the eye."

TWENTY

For a woman of eighty-seven, Elsa's memory is amazing. I followed her into the living room where she cleared a few items off the top of an old steamer trunk and lifted its lid. Inside were stacks of yellowing newspapers and magazines.

"What *is* all this stuff?" I asked incredulously.

"Oh, whenever I see a story that catches my attention I save all the issues and put them in here," she beamed. "I've got the Kennedy assassinations, the moon landing—although I think they staged that whole thing somewhere in Hollywood—and the time that one mayor got booted for his shenanigans with money."

"And the story of Father Ramon's illicit affair with a married woman," I added.

"Oh, that one was messy," she confided, digging into one of the stacks.

I shouldn't have been surprised. Elsa had followed a couple of favorite soap operas for years, although she wouldn't admit to exactly how much they titillated her. A few months ago I'd had occasion to bring some old files over and work on them here. I'd watched firsthand how she finished her gardening work every day by a certain time so she wouldn't miss "her shows."

Within a couple of minutes, she'd pulled out the papers she was looking for.

"There," she said triumphantly. "Look 'em over. You can bring them back when you're done."

I put on my jacket and tucked the papers under my arm. "Is there anything you need from the store?" I asked. "Any little chores around the house?"

"No, no, I'm fine," she assured me. "I always do my shopping on Wednesdays. Even if they don't give out trading stamps anymore."

Worried that the lack of trading stamps would start her on a new subject, I hurriedly said good-bye and told her to be sure to call Ron if she needed anything. I tossed the old newspapers into the backseat of the Jeep and drove the few blocks up Central to the RJP Investigations offices. Not planning to stay long, I parked out front.

Tammy was feeding Rusty half a donut when I walked in. She looked up at me guiltily.

"He really shouldn't have this kind of stuff, huh?" she asked.

"Well, let's not make it a habit," I said. She was doing such a good job getting Ron organized that I didn't want to nitpick the details.

We went over a few office matters, then I went up to Ron's office and peeked in. The phone, as usual, was at his ear, but he gave me a grin.

Across the hall, in my office-turned-bedroom, I gathered my overnight bag and the snow boots that seemed ludicrous here but would be a necessity back at the cabin. I carried everything out and stashed it in the back cargo area of the Jeep, Rusty following my every step. Donuts or not, I guess he wanted to be sure he wasn't left behind. Once the luggage went into the car, he knew I was leaving.

Ron was off the phone when I went back upstairs, and we spent thirty minutes in which I filled him in on the resolution of the Hope Montgomery story and thanked him for the quick legwork on that. I also told him about my interview with Stella Chavez this morning and Elsa's hints that Stella's affair with the priest had gotten quite messy. I left a few minutes later, with just a couple of stops to make in town before starting the drive back.

Broken cirrus clouds were beginning to show in the west, indicating the incoming weather front. It probably wouldn't arrive until this evening or tomorrow morning, but I wanted the three of us to be safely back at the cabin before it did.

Interstate 25 traffic wasn't bad this time of day and we were soon topping La Bajada Hill and looking down into Santa Fe. I pulled off at Cerrillos Road and lunched at McDonald's. I carried Elsa's newspapers in with me and scanned through the articles as I dipped fries into a puddle of ketchup I'd made on my tray.

The details of Ramon's affair had been thoroughly hashed out in the press. Stella Chavez had been a dutiful parishioner in his church for years. She had confessed to him regularly, praying with him, begging God to help her be a better wife. As she became comfortable with the priest, she admitted that Leroy verbally abused her, calling her lazy and worthless, convincing her that she had no friends. She told Father Ramon that she really tried to do better, but nothing was ever good enough. She continued to pray that she would become better.

The attraction had begun gradually, according to both

parties, but grew into a love that neither Ramon nor Stella could deny. The first time her husband hit her, Stella went to Father Ramon and ended up in his bed. A power beyond either of them kept them together, even though there was no possibility of a future together. They remained secret lovers for several years until the inevitable happened. Stella became pregnant with Ramon's child.

There was no option that was not a sin: divorce, marriage to a priest, abortion, suicide. She thought of them all.

Perversely Leroy would not let her leave him. As if to pour salt into her humiliated and wounded soul, he made her stay with him through the pregnancy. He took her to church every week, flaunting her condition in front of the community—and poor, miserable Ramon. Then, when at the age of forty-two, Stella gave birth to a baby with Down's syndrome, he publicly and loudly renounced the child, forced her to put it up for adoption, and moved out of their home. Two weeks later, Ramon Romero was shot dead on the front steps of the church.

Stella went into a depression so deep that she didn't leave her bed for months. Leroy was questioned in the priest's death, because the whole story had come out by this time, but he had a solid alibi. He moved back in with her and changed their membership to another parish, content now that both sinners had been punished.

I thought of the Stella I'd met this morning. She was clearly still terrified of Leroy, trying as she had to escape my visit, and making sure he didn't know I was there. Now, in her late forties, she looked closer to sixty—a worn-out woman whom life had dealt too much.

As I bit into my burger, I wondered why she hadn't simply walked out years ago. If she'd taken the drastic step of having an affair with her priest, why hadn't she had the courage to walk away from her marriage? I had the feeling that a strict religious upbringing, coupled with strong Spanish family ties, would make this seem impossible. And having watched another friend's situation that had gone bad, I knew what an illogical hold an abusive man could have over a woman. After alienating her from friends and family, she was likely to take his word for it that she was worthless and would never make it without him. Stella fit the mold. I felt sorry for her.

It was nearly two o'clock when I drove into Taos and the clouds had continued to build. It was completely overcast here. The intersection approaching the plaza bottlenecked into its usual stop-and-go formation, and I missed the yellow light by seconds.

Just ahead was the Dumont Gallery and my eyes caught a familiar face. Anton Pachevski crossed the sidewalk and ducked into the passenger side of an illegally parked black Suburban with its hazard lights flashing. I couldn't see the driver. The flashers went off and the dark vehicle jumped into the flow of traffic. I chomped impatiently for my light to turn green.

The creeping traffic allowed me to move only about four car lengths before I had to stop again, but the Suburban was large enough that I could still see it ahead. With no idea what I'd actually do with Anton if I caught him, and not wanting to risk a confrontation with potentially dangerous types, I was at least determined to find out where they were going. I didn't think Anton had recognized me, although he'd been only an intersection's width away. Even if he did, they couldn't move any faster in the clogged traffic than I could. I kept my eyes on their vehicle's black luggage rack.

At Civic Plaza Drive, they turned left and I got caught by the light again. I tried to watch their movements but there were two vehicles in front of me and I couldn't see far down the street. When the light changed I made a chancey left turn and raced west. No sign of the black Suburban. I scanned the driveways and tiny parking areas of the town government buildings that lined the street. Nothing. When I came to the T at Camino de la Placita, I had no idea whether to turn left or right. Just rounding the bend to my right, I glimpsed a dark vehicle so I opted for that direction. Two streets down, at a four-way stop, I caught up with it, but it was a dark blue pickup truck. I had lost Pachevski.

However, I did know he was in town and I could describe the vehicle reasonably well, so I stopped in at Steve Romero's office and told him what I knew.

"I'll put it all in the file," he said, "but I don't know how much help it'll be. This time of year, half of Texas comes to town, all driving Suburbans."

"I'm pretty sure this had New Mexico plates," I offered.

"Pretty sure?"

"Okay, I can't be certain. I guess without some numbers, it doesn't help anyway, does it?"

"Don't sound so discouraged," he said. "At least we know he's still around town. I'll put a few men on the lookout for him."

A cold wind had picked up by the time I left the building, and the clouds spat a few threatening granules. I headed north toward El Prado and the turnoff to the ski valley. At the hangar, both Drake's and Eloy's trucks sat outside and

I saw my husband loading his overnight bag into his. I tooted my horn and he waved. It was a relief to know that he'd returned before the storm set in.

The scattered granular snow had changed to full-fledged large flakes by the time I pulled into my parking slot at the cabin. Rusty bounded out of the car, happy to feel like he was home again. He raced around the yard, nose to the ground, and visited each of his favorite trees. At the steps to the cabin, he came to an abrupt halt, his nose glued to the wooden stairs.

I didn't pay much attention, reaching into the back for my bag and the stack of newspapers Elsa had given me. The dog didn't follow me into the house and when I came back out, he was still engrossed in investigating the stairs and porch.

"C'mon, you. Let's get out of this weather," I called.

After the second call, he came in. I busied myself setting out his food bowl and carrying my bag upstairs. I tossed the newspapers on the sofa, thinking I'd read them more thoroughly after dinner.

The changes were subtle, but they were there. In a kitchen cabinet, some pans were not as I thought I'd left them. Two throw pillows on the sofa were lying flat on the seat, not propped against the arms as they usually were. Just then I heard a vehicle outside and rushed to the front window. It was Drake.

He greeted me at the door with a kiss. "Well, that was an interesting job," he said. "And the aircraft is already due for a fifty-hour inspection. I left it with Frank, the mechanic at the Taos airport. He said he'd do it overnight and have it ready tomorrow."

"Yesterday morning, you left here before I did. Right, hon?" I asked. "Did you come back at all after that?"

"No . . ." He seemed puzzled.

I walked into the kitchen to put his dirty Thermos in the sink, glanced at the back door to the utility porch. The lock on the doorknob was locked but the deadbolt wasn't. I distinctly remembered locking it.

"Someone's been in here while we were gone," I informed him.

"Well, Eloy still has a key," he pointed out. "He might've come in to check on something."

"Could be, but I doubt it." I told him about the sofa pillows being out of place and the kitchen pans. "Why would he move any of that stuff?"

"Beats me. Call him."

I dialed Eloy's home number but he wasn't there yet. I left a message on his machine.

Upstairs, the disturbances were more subtle. The mattress on our bed, which I'd just remade with clean sheets before we left, was slightly askew. The bedspread was wrinkled. Sometimes my neatness borders on manic, I know, and I had not walked out of this house with these little touches out of place like this. In the vanity under the bathroom sink, a couple of bottles were tipped over, and some towels lay in a rumpled heap.

"Drake, Eloy didn't do this," I told him. "Someone's been going through everything in the house."

I continued to scout around while Drake started dinner. Parts of the house were undisturbed, like the second bedroom and the cabinets and bookshelves in the living room. I turned on my computer and it booted up. After giving my password I ran a log of recent entries and found only my own. If the intruder had searched here, he hadn't gotten very far.

"Nothing that common housebreakers usually take is missing—TV, microwave, my computer. They're all still here. So I have to believe the guy was after something very specific."

"And it doesn't sound like the way Eloy would look for something," Drake said. "Under our pillows, for heaven's sake."

The phone rang just then. "Eloy! I'm glad you called," I said. "Did you come up here to the cabin while we were gone?"

"Well, yeah, yesterday afternoon."

"Were you looking for something?"

"No, I didn't even go inside. Just wanted to check that the Scout had enough gas in it. Heard snow in the forecast and wanted to be sure you could plow the driveway if you needed to. Why?"

I told him what I'd found.

"Well, that *is* weird. But they didn't forceably break in?"

"Not that I can tell. All windows and doors are intact. I wonder if they quit before they were finished, though, because there are quite a few places that aren't disturbed." Or they found what they were looking for. Most likely in the last place they looked. "Eloy, you might want to come up here sometime and see if anything's missing."

He said he'd come out in the next few days but couldn't think of anything of value that wasn't out in plain sight. I hung up, still feeling unsettled, but relieved that I'd notified our landlord of the problem.

"Where's Rusty?" I asked, turning to Drake. It was dark out now and an uneasiness settled over me.

"I don't know," he answered. He called out to the dog but there was no response.

"Rusty!" I opened the front door and shouted. The rust-colored hulk didn't appear. "Where could he have gone?"

Drake looked concerned. "Check the house, just to be sure he didn't get shut in the bathroom or something. I'll look outside." He pulled on his parka and picked up his pistol and flashlight.

I raced upstairs, calling as I went. No dog in any of the rooms. I checked the utility porch and behind the major pieces of furniture. As I'd felt sure, he wasn't in the house.

"Charlie!" Drake shouted from outside.

I pulled on a coat and boots and dashed out.

"He's injured," Drake said. "We need to get him to the vet."

Rusty, my best friend and sidekick for nearly ten years, lay on the snowy ground, a nasty bloody gash on the back of his head. My fist went to my mouth and I bit my knuckle to keep from crying out.

"Oh, God, how did this happen?"

"Well, he didn't just bump into a tree," Drake stated. "Somebody's hit him."

I peered into the darkness nervously.

"Okay, go inside and find a vet with emergency services after hours. Call and find out where we have to go. Then close up the house. I don't want you staying here alone," Drake said. "And turn off the stove—I think I left it on."

I rushed in and did as he instructed. I grabbed a couple of blankets and the directions I'd written to the vet's office.

I closed all the drapes and left lights on, hoping that, even as we rushed around, the intruder wasn't watching from somewhere in the woods, although he easily could be.

Drake had placed the unconscious Rusty on the backseat of the Jeep. He trembled sporadically.

"You don't mind driving, do you?" I asked. "I want to keep an eye on him." My voice quavered as I said it.

I climbed into the backseat and placed Rusty's head on my lap, then wrapped the blankets around him.

"Sure." Drake took my keys and carefully backed up.

The snow came at us in gusts so thick it was impossible to see through them, like someone above was shaking the contents of a down pillow in front of our windshield. I stroked Rusty's fur and checked the wound to be sure it had not started bleeding again.

Only when something rammed us from behind did I realize that we had more than the weather and the injured dog to worry about.

TWENTY ONE

"What the hell!?" Drake shouted.

"What was that?" I looked at him for answers but he seemed just as puzzled as I was.

Bam! It happened again and Drake struggled to hold the Jeep on the narrow, snowy mountain road. He looked into the rearview mirror.

"Somebody's out there, ramming us," he said, "but I can't see a damn thing for the snow except some headlights. Do you have your seatbelt on?"

"Yes."

"Get one around the dog if you can."

I fumbled with the belt in the middle seat but twining a belt around seventy pounds of unconscious dog wasn't an easy feat. I finally looped the long end under his body and managed to find the buckle in the dark, purely by feel. It snapped into place and I cinched it as tight as I dared without restricting his already erratic breathing.

Bam! The rear end of the Jeep slid precariously.

"Watch out! The dropoff!" I screamed.

"I know," he answered tersely.

He was perfectly aware that the road dropped off thirty or more feet. There was no point in my reminding him. *I* knew that.

"Hang on!" Drake shouted.

He sped up as we entered a sharp curve in the road, then steered to correct the skid, then sped up again on a short straight stretch. Only his intimate knowledge of every bend in the road, from driving it every day for a month, kept us from sliding the wrong way. He kept up this dangerous speed-skid-correct tactic through several more hair-raising turns.

"I don't see their headlights anymore," he said.

"Keep going. They'll catch up," I prodded.

Rusty stirred for a second and vomited over the edge of the seat onto my shoe. Ugh. But at least he was still alive.

Drake kept glancing back in the mirror. Finally we reached a large open curve in the road and he risked turning his head to look back.

"I think they're off the road," he gloated.

"What?" I twisted my neck to look back. Sure enough, between gusts of snow I could see a pair of headlights shining up the hill at an awkward angle. They weren't moving. "Do you think they might be hurt?" I asked.

"Do you think I care?"

He was right. Whoever this was, they'd tried to kill us. While part of me hoped they weren't injured, another part of me hoped they were gone for good.

Drake made the turn onto the ski valley road, which already had a couple of inches of snow on it. We had to take it slowly because the visibility was so bad and there were no other tracks to follow. An hour later we pulled up at the veterinary clinic. I was feeling a little queasy from the curvy road and the stench of vomit. The smelly liquid had now soaked into my sock.

Dr. Virginia Nelson came out to the car which Drake had parked as near the front door as he could.

"Boy, this is a bad night for you folks to be on the road," she said.

"We wouldn't be if we'd had any choice," I told her.

I unfastened Rusty's seatbelt and my own and slipped out.

"Still hasn't come around, huh," Dr. Nelson said, gently running her hands over the dog and lifting his eyelids.

"Just once, for a few seconds." I showed her the evidence.

"Let's get him inside."

She dashed back inside and brought a wheeled gurney down the ramp and stopped it at the side of the car. She and Drake pushed and pulled as gently as possible to get the inert dog onto the gurney while I stood by helplessly with a golf-ball-size lump rising in my throat. I'd never seen my normally vivacious buddy so quiet. Even in his sleep he snored or chased rabbits. I blinked back wells of moisture that were forming in my eyes.

The two of them wheeled the gurney up the ramp and directly to a surgical room at the back of the clinic. Lights blazed in here and the doctor had already prepared a tray of instruments. She dabbed at the wound with gauze and cleaned away the caked blood in the surrounding fur.

"This is going to be easier for you folks if you don't watch," she said. "I'm going to clean the wound thoroughly and shave the area. With a head injury, I don't want to anesthetize him, so I'll use a local so I can get this thing stitched up. I'll put him on an IV of dexamethasone to reduce any brain swelling and concussion.

"The worst part will be when he starts to wake up. A lot

of dogs will cry constantly and he'll probably have to be on some pretty heavy-duty painkillers. At a minimum I'll need to have him here twenty-four hours, and it may be more like four or five days before he's able to go home."

Four or five days. I felt a murderous rage building inside me.

"With that weather out there, you might want to get a room in town tonight," Dr. Nelson said. "Call me in a couple of hours and I can let you know how he's doing."

It took all my will to turn my back and leave the room with Rusty lying on that table. Drake put his arm around my shoulders and squeezed a little life back into me. He guided me out to the Jeep and buckled me into the passenger seat. After he'd started the engine we both sat there, numb.

"Shall we follow the doctor's advice and stay in town?" he asked.

"I want to go back up the mountain and find that vehicle and choke the living shit out of whoever's in it," I growled. I glanced down into my lap and noticed that my fists were tightly clenched.

"Seriously?"

"Seriously."

He patted the pockets of his parka. "I've got the Beretta. Let's go."

The snowfall had lessened somewhat, but it was still slow going out of town and up the ski valley road. Drake kept the Jeep in four-wheel drive and took every curve carefully. By the time we'd reached the turnoff to the cabin, there were at least six new inches on the ground and I felt myself falling into a stupor of fatigue and numbness. A lot of the fight had gone out of me.

We came to the dark vehicle off the side of the road. It had taken the curve too fast and skidded sideways into the high snowy berm the snowplow had been piling up all winter. The headlights were off now; snow covered all the windows. The back left quarter panel had smacked solidly into a forty-foot pine tree, wrapping the metal around its thick trunk. There would undoubtedly be axle damage. They were lucky—the tree was the only thing that had saved them from plummeting thirty feet down the rocky mountainside.

Drake aimed the Jeep's headlights straight at the disabled car. It was a black Suburban.

TWENTY TWO

"Approach quietly," Drake said, keeping his voice low. "Yank open the passenger door, then duck for cover." He pulled the Beretta out of his jacket, checked the magazine, clipped it back in place, snapped off the safety and chambered the first round.

We carefully opened our doors and climbed out, never taking our eyes off the Suburban. Almost in unison, we pushed our doors closed but didn't let them make a sound. I crossed in front of the Jeep and reached for the Suburban's passenger door. Drake stood with legs apart, both hands on the Beretta. I grabbed the door handle and pulled, then ducked below the windows. My heart was pounding like a bass drum.

What were we doing? I closed my eyes.

"Nothing," Drake said.

I raised my head tentatively. "What?"

"There's no one in it."

I rose and peered inside. My breath whooshed out.

So where had they gone? I scanned the ground around the vehicle but there were no tracks. In the hours since the wreck enough snow had fallen to obliterate anything. I walked around to the mangled back end and brushed snow off the license plate. It was a New Mexico plate, Taos County designation. I memorized the number. I felt sure it was the same vehicle I'd followed earlier in Taos.

"What do you think?" I asked, turning to Drake.

"They must've gone for help. Choices would be, back up to our cabin—that's the easiest one." He scanned the surrounding mountains. "I doubt they'd get cell phone reception right here, but the odds would probably be better down on the main road, so they could've hiked on down. They could have also hoped to hitch a ride, either into Taos or up to the ski lodges."

"Pretty much a toss-up either way, huh?"

"I'd say so."

"I'd sure like to get the police up here to impound their vehicle before they can get a tow truck to rescue it," I said. "I'm a bit worried about going straight to the cabin, though."

"Well, there's no place to turn around until we get almost there anyway," he pointed out. "Let's head that way and see what happens."

Back in the Jeep I wrote down the plate number of the Suburban and we buckled up.

"Is there any way we can approach the house with the engine off?" I asked Drake. "You can hear a car coming for ages up there."

"We may have to stop along the road and hike the rest of the way in."

I was really beginning to wish I'd changed shoes this afternoon after my trip from Albuquerque. My standard running shoes with dog vomit spattered over the tops weren't much good for snow hiking. Oh, well.

"Drake, stop!" We'd just passed the narrow trail that led to the picnic site. "I think we could back in there and hide the Jeep. It's out of sight of the cabin but not too long a walk."

"I'll bet this is where the Suburban was hiding when we drove out. I wondered how anyone got behind us on this road without our seeing them," he said as he expertly backed the Jeep into the narrow slot.

"You better stay here," he said. "You don't have a gun."

"And wait for somebody to come trekking through the woods and find me sitting here defenseless in the car? I think not."

"Charlie . . ."

"I'll find a weapon. C'mon." I hopped out of the Jeep and began looking around. "How about the tire iron?"

"Okay, just stay behind me," he instructed. "You won't even get a chance to use that thing if they've got guns."

Being basically a chicken, this time I obeyed.

The falling snow had nearly stopped and we were able to follow the road by its white smoothness, without having to turn on the flashlight. The cabin looked just like we'd left it, which was little comfort, since I'd pulled all the drapes closed and anyone in the world could be inside without our knowing it. I looked for any sign of visitors. The snowy footprints on the porch could easily have been ours and nothing else looked out of place.

"Here," I whispered to Drake, pointing to a side window whose curtain didn't quite meet in the middle.

We detoured to the left, circling behind the parked snowplow and Drake's pickup, then cut quickly and silently across the open space to the window. By standing on a wooden crate, I could just look over the sill. Through the narrow crack in the drapes, I had a view of the dining area, most of the living room, and part of the kitchen. I took my time, looking carefully into every corner. I could see the bottom of the stairs but nothing of the bedrooms. Nothing appeared to be disturbed.

Using Drake's shoulder for balance, I jumped off the crate.

"It *looks* untouched," I whispered. "But I can't see upstairs or the kitchen or the utility porch."

He signaled me to follow him to the back and to crouch beside the steps leading to the back door. "Don't move until I come back for you," he said. "If you hear gunshots, get back to the Jeep as fast as you can, but don't run out in the open." He pulled out his key and quietly turned it in the lock.

It seemed like a couple of eons passed while I stooped in the snow, my butt becoming icy from the snow soaking into my jeans, and my limbs turning numb from inactivity. Finally, Drake reappeared.

"All clear," he announced.

I groaned as I unkinked myself from my frozen position and pulled myself up the steps. I handed Drake the tire iron and swatted loose snow from my clothing. Inside the utility porch, I removed my snow-filled stinking shoes and left them there.

"Hot," I moaned. "I need something hot."

He put a kettle of water on to boil and helped peel my parka from my arms. "You sit," he instructed. "I'll get you a hot shower started and then make you some cocoa."

He went upstairs and I could hear the water running.

"Okay, come on up," he called.

In the bedroom he helped me out of my frozen, wet things and steered me toward the shower stall. I stood there motionless for a good five minutes, just letting the steamy water course down my body. I heard Drake leave the room, presumably to turn down the flame under the kettle, then return. In another minute he was beside me, naked in the shower.

"I moved the Jeep back up near the cabin," he said, "and took a look at the damage."

I groaned. I'd forgotten about the probability that there would be repairs needed after the ramming we'd taken earlier.

"It's not too bad," he assured me. "The bumper absorbed most of the impact."

He grabbed the soap bar and began to rub my back with it, soothing and kneading the muscles. After he'd turned me around to make sure everything was rinsed, I did the same for him. We both emerged, warmed, but tired in body and spirit. We bundled into flannel pajamas and robes and went back downstairs for our chocolate.

"Has it been two hours yet?" I asked. "I'm dying to check on Rusty." The sight of his empty bedding on the bedroom floor had brought more tears to my eyes.

"I'm sure it has," Drake said. "Better call the doc before it gets too much later."

"He's doing as well as expected," Dr. Nelson assured me. "I found some wooden splinters in the skin and I cleaned them all out. He's had an antibiotic shot and is on IV fluids now. He woke up but is in a lot of pain, so I've also given him painkillers to get him through the night."

"As well as expected?" I quivered. "Is he going to be all right?"

"Well, head wounds are always dangerous," she replied. "But yes, I think he'll be okay. He's not in nearly as bad shape as some I've seen who've been hit by cars."

"No, I feel pretty sure he was hit by a human." The words grated. I felt the rage building again. "Whoever did this is going to be sorry."

"Well, feel free to call back in the morning and check on him," the doctor assured me. "And don't worry."

I hung up and gave Drake the details. He looked relieved.

I drained my mug of hot chocolate while he placed the call to the police. He couldn't get Steve Romero on the line this late, but told the dispatcher that we believed the vehicle was already being sought in another case, in addition to having rammed us and trying to push us off the road.

"Do you think they'll get here before Pachevski?" I asked.

"I don't know, hon. The guy I just talked to didn't sound in any big rush to act on it. Said he'd tell Romero about it in the morning."

"I have an idea," I said, taking the phone from him and pulling the phone book from the table.

I dialed the towing company with the largest ad in the yellow pages. There were only three listed.

"Yes, did you get a call for a black Suburban stuck off the ski valley road?" I asked innocently.

"No, ma'am," the tired-sounding dispatcher answered.

"Okay, thank you." I posed the same question to the next company.

"Yeah, but we're so backed up tonight, it's gonna be at

least another two hours before we can get up there," the man whined. "There's dozens of cars stuck in this storm and you're just gonna have to wait your turn."

"Actually, it's okay," I answered perkily. "My husband was able to get it unstuck and we're fine now. Just wanted to let you know you don't have to come."

"Well, thanks, ma'am. We appreciate you letting us know."

I turned to Drake. "That buys us some time, anyway."

"I don't feel too guilty about it," he said. "They're probably safe and sound up in one of the lodges, thinking their vehicle is being taken to a shop somewhere."

Suddenly I was bone-tired. It was nearly midnight. The drive from Albuquerque, the shock of Rusty's injury, and the encounters with the black Suburban had all taken their toll. We switched out the lights and I nestled into Drake's shoulder under the snug blankets.

TWENTY THREE

Dawn lightened the windows to pale gray when I awoke, suddenly, with that eyes-wide-open feeling and my thoughts running clear. Pachevski still wanted something in this cabin, I realized. Unknowingly, I must have interrupted the search when I arrived back from Albuquerque. They had hidden somewhere, but when Drake showed up, they panicked. They hit Rusty over the head so he wouldn't alert us and were probably planning on doing the same to us so they could finish taking the house apart. When we found the injured dog and rushed off down the mountain, they figured they could get rid of us permanently and make it look like an accident. Then they'd have all the time they wanted to search the rest of the place. The Suburban had probably been parked in the picnic area turnoff all along. Needles of anxiety pricked at me.

There was something big at stake here and Anton Pachevski wasn't going away until he got what he wanted.

With any hope of sleep gone, I slipped quietly from the covers and pulled on my flannels again. Drake rolled over and hugged my pillow but didn't wake up. I made my way carefully downstairs and started brewing a pot of coffee.

Okay, I thought, assuming they didn't find what they

wanted, where have they not searched yet? And what area of the house had we not already gone into? We'd pretty well spread out and used most everything. Surely we would have come across anything unusual.

I poured a mug of coffee and stirred sugar into it, slowly whirling the spoon, concentrating on the question. Taking a sip of the hot brew I stared around the rooms—kitchen, dining, living. My eyes fell on the bookcase where I'd found the funny yellowed scraps of paper in the photo album. I knew what they were after.

The album was still in place, the photo in the narrow folder in place when I checked it. Yes, the scraps were still there. I pulled out the slim plastic sleeve containing them.

Even if these truly were pieces of the Dead Sea Scrolls, though, would they really be that valuable? Valuable enough to kill for? I remembered hearing that there were thousands of scroll pieces. That scholars had put many of them back together to reveal new books previously not included in the Bible. I turned the plastic sleeve over in my hand. There weren't more than twenty characters printed on them, in total. I couldn't believe they would have that much Biblical importance, other than perhaps to an eccentric collector who might simply want to own a piece of history. No, there had to be something else.

The two silver crosses I'd given to Father Domingo. Now those had enough religious importance that he nearly went into tears at the sight of them. A large-scale investigation had been launched and rewards offered for them. And I remembered from the clippings in the old priest's file that many other artifacts had been stolen. That had to be it. Was it really possible that treasures from the Vatican and other

Catholic churches around the world might be hidden in this unassuming mountain cabin in New Mexico?

So where would they be? I slipped the scroll pieces back into the photo folder and put it back on the shelf. Then my hand stopped. I examined the way the bookshelves were constructed, built in on either side of the fireplace. I pulled the photo albums and books from the bottom shelf and set them on the stone hearth. Tapping on the rough-sawn tongue-and-groove paneling behind them, it sounded solid. I replaced the books and repeated my steps with the next shelf up. Centered in the expanse of the three-foot-wide shelf was a hollow place about a foot wide behind the paneling. I ran my fingers over the wood. There was a small door but it was well hidden. The upper and lower edges were flush with the shelves above and below, and the left and right seams were concealed in the grooves of the paneling. It was an excellent carpentry job. I touched around the edges of the opening, hoping to activate a spring mechanism but nothing happened.

At last I spotted it, a tiny hole meant for grabbing and pulling outward. The hole was nowhere near large enough for my finger to fit in it and to attempt it with a fingernail would surely mean death to the nail. I looked around for a tool.

A flat-bladed screwdriver from a tool kit on the utility porch made a perfect fit. Very carefully, I fitted it into the hole, which slanted at an angle enough to allow the screwdriver to get leverage. A gentle pull was all it took and the four smoothly finished edges let go and came toward me. Not high tech but very effective.

I took the wooden door in both hands and laid it aside.

Behind it was a cubbyhole roughly two feet deep, a foot wide, and eight or nine inches tall. The space itself was lined in felt and inside sat a hinged box of highly polished wood. I pulled it out.

Carrying the box to the sofa I sat with it on my lap and lifted the lid. Inside were two more silver crosses, simpler than the ones I'd found before but with exquisite workmanship that made me take a deep breath. The box was obviously made for them. It had special indentations where each cross fit exactly. The entire interior was lined with tarnish-resistant jeweler's cloth, and the silver gleamed without blemish. Wow.

There had to be more. I set the box on the sofa and pulled books from another shelf. It too had a hidden compartment and I quickly removed the door and pulled a wooden box from it as well. It opened to reveal a set of exquisitely shaped silver hearts with flamelike projections coming from the dip in the top of the heart. Sacred hearts, I thought they were called. Of the set of four, one had a detailed silver dagger through it, another was rimmed in tiny jewels, one was nearly solidly encrusted in jewels, and the other was burnished with gold.

"What are you *doing?*" Drake asked, emerging sleepily from the bedroom.

Like a deer in the headlights, I stared, frozen.

"Hon?"

"Look at this," I said, amazed.

"I know. I see you sitting there in your pajamas, with books all over the hearth, tools and wood all around you, and something that looks like Captain Hook's treasure spread out around you."

"I think this is what Anton has been looking for. He probably found out that I'd turned in two crosses to Father Domingo and he knows I must have found them here in the cabin."

He ducked into the bedroom to retrieve his robe then joined me.

"What if Father Domingo . . ." I couldn't finish the sentence, picturing the tactics they might have used to get information from the old man.

"Hon, I really doubt they'd go that far," Drake said, half reading my mind. "The old man was so innocent he probably just mentioned the crosses in passing and they figured out the rest. Besides, the police said he died of natural causes, didn't they?"

"Yeah," I admitted. "Okay, let's not think the worst about that. But I'm certain this is what they were searching the cabin for. And I'm pretty sure my coming home yesterday interrupted them. They were probably being careful, not absolutely ravaging the place, because they thought they had plenty of time and they didn't want to make us suspicious."

He strolled into the kitchen for a cup of coffee and stood at the side of the sofa grinning at me. "So what are you gonna do now?"

"Here, help me," I said, handing him another screwdriver.

I pulled the books from another shelf and showed him another hidden door. Demonstrating my expertise with the screwdriver, I opened it and extracted a soft velvet bag. Inside were more sacred hearts and a gold statue about six inches tall of Mary holding the baby Jesus.

"Feels solid," Drake commented, weighing the statue in his hand.

We found four more caches as he continued opening more cubbyholes, while I followed along, replacing the wooden doors and sticking books back on the shelves, piling the treasure on the sofa. Drake was just pulling the loot from the last hole when there was a loud pounding on the door.

"Shit!" We both said it together.

I stared at the door guiltily. Through the glass panel leading to the ski porch, I could tell that whoever it was had not come into that airlock, but was standing outside. But it could be only a matter of seconds before he'd decide to walk into the ski porch and tap on the inside door. Had I locked the outside door last night?

Without a word to each other and moving in amazing unison, I grabbed the newest treasure and added it to the pile on the couch. Drake replaced the hidden panel and jammed a couple of books onto the shelf.

The visitor pounded again, louder this time. "Police!" he shouted.

"Double shit!" I cursed.

I grabbed a fuzzy afghan from the hearth, planted myself in a corner of the couch and flung the afghan over myself and the goodies. "Tell him I'm sick," I whispered as Drake approached the door.

"I'm Officer Steve Romero."

I heard the voices clearly as Drake greeted him at the door.

"You called last night to report a wanted vehicle on your road?" he asked.

Drake ushered him inside.

"Hi, Stebe," I sniffed. "Don't cub dear be. I think I caud

a bad cold last dight." I dabbed at my nose with a tissue and mimicked a pretty decent sneeze.

"I just stopped by to tell you that we've got a wrecker down the road with that Suburban right now," he said. "Did you say you're pretty sure it's the one you saw Pachevski getting into last night?"

"I'm preddy sure." I grinned weakly. It really was a miserable cold.

"Well, I'll let you concentrate on getting well," he said. "You folks take care. We'll dust that vehicle for prints and run the registration. I think we'll have this Pachevski, Palais, or whatever his name is pretty soon."

"Thaks, Stebe."

Drake went as far as the front door with him, then came back in.

"Is he gone?" I asked, slipping out from under the afghan.

"Driving away now." He continued to look through the crack in the drapes until the police car was out of sight.

I got shakily to my feet and hugged him. "Now what?" I asked.

"Maybe we should have just showed him the stuff and let him deal with it," Drake suggested.

"Well, we didn't. So let's take our time and figure out how to handle this."

The phone rang.

"Charlie? It's Eloy." His voice sounded peculiar. "Tell Drake I'm really sorry but I won't be able to come to the hangar today. My mother passed away last night."

TWENTY FOUR

"Oh, Eloy, I'm so sorry," I said. "Hold on a minute."

I told Drake the news and handed over the phone. He spoke some soothing words and assured Eloy that his coming to work would not be crucial.

Not when we were standing here in Eloy's cabin with a bundle of loot, potentially worth millions, I thought.

"What are we going to do with all this?" Drake asked after he'd hung up.

"Well, I think we can rule out the idea of placing them around the room and pretending we're redecorating," I said.

"I think we can rule out sleeping at night until we're rid of it," he said.

"Let me think about it. You guard it while I get dressed."

I pulled clean jeans and a warm sweatshirt from my dresser drawers, then combed through my hair and bound it into a ponytail with a cloth-covered band. I knew we should probably just turn everything over to the police and let them handle it, but I could just envision all these lovely pieces in an evidence room somewhere for a couple of years until a trial could get under way. I couldn't help but feel that someone with the church should handle them, at least get them somewhere safe. Surely, for purposes of convicting Anton and his bunch, photos and appraisals would be proof enough. I expressed as much to Drake as we carefully bundled everything back into the wrappings in which we'd found them.

"So who you gonna trust?" he asked.

"Well, I know that Father Sanchez at St. Augustine helped Father Domingo return the first two crosses. He'd know what to do, I think."

"It's gonna be pretty nerve-wracking, heading into town with all this stuff in the car," Drake said. "Should you call him first and let him know?"

"In case we're hijacked along the way? Maybe so."

I looked up the number for St. Augustine and dialed.

"Father Sanchez?"

"He's out this morning. This is Father Ralph."

"I don't know if you remember me. I came to see Father Domingo about some church artifacts a few weeks ago."

"Oh, yes, Ms. Parker," he answered. "The two crosses that we sent to the Vatican. Of course, I remember."

"We, uh, we've found a few more things. I'd like to bring them to you, if that's all right. I think the Vatican should get these too, and maybe you can help me pack them up."

"Certainly, come anytime."

"Right after lunch?"

"I'll see you then."

I hung up and turned to Drake. "He sounded happy to hear about it," I said.

"I guess so. This'll make him an instant hero, probably get an upgrade to bishop or something."

I packed the artifacts into two ordinary-looking duffles

while Drake got dressed. We carried the duffles out to the Jeep and made the trip into town uneventfully, although I couldn't help watching out for any sign that we were being followed. With the sun out, last night's snow was melting rapidly here in town, leaving the streets wet with muddy water. When we passed the turnoff to the veterinarian's office, I stared wistfully.

"We can stop by and check on Rusty when we finish at the church," Drake suggested.

"Let's do. I'd feel better if I could at least see him awake." The memory of leaving his inert body with the vet, despite her reassurances, bothered me.

"I'd like to make one stop, if you don't mind, before we go to the church," Drake said. "Eloy said he would be at the funeral home around noon. He sounded like he could use some support. Do you mind?"

I wouldn't be entirely at ease until we had dropped off our treasure, but figured one stop wouldn't hurt. We pulled into the parking area of the Mitchell Funeral Home, an adobe-colored flat-roofed structure, and parked beside Eloy's truck. I made sure the duffles were on the floor in the backseat, out of sight of prying eyes, then locked the doors and double checked them. Surely right here on the main road through town no one would be brazen enough to smash their way into a vehicle.

The carved wooden front door swung silently inward, admitting us into a soothing room with thick beige carpeting, rose-colored drapes, and massive floral bouquets on Queen Anne tables. A discreet sign with changeable letters directed the way to various viewing rooms.

"May I be of service?" a smoothly polished voice

inquired. The man wore a light gray suit and plain blue tie. Everything about him was designed to comfort anyone who encountered him.

"Romero?" Drake asked.

"The family is in here," he intoned, directing us to the first room off a short hall. It was a graciously furnished office containing a cherry desk with four chairs arranged in front of it. No one was sitting.

"Eloy," Drake said.

"Oh, Drake, Charlie, I'm glad you stopped by." Eloy looked fit, as usual, but strain showed around his eyes and mouth. "We're just discussing the funeral plans."

He turned to indicate the two other people in the room. "You've met Mike Ortiz?" he asked.

I indicated that I had and shook Mike's hand. I introduced Drake.

"And this is my sister, Maria."

She was a miniature female version of Eloy, with his facial features, glossy dark hair, and small bone structure. At a little under five feet, she looked like a porcelain doll that you'd want to dress up and put on a shelf for safekeeping.

"Are you doing all right, Eloy?" I asked.

His eyes cut briefly to Mike. "Yeah, fine. We're just working out the details now. Her death wasn't unexpected, you know."

I glanced at Mike and saw the same lines of tension etched there that showed on Eloy's face.

"The funeral Mass will probably be on Saturday," Eloy said. "Please, come if you'd like."

"It will be if we can agree on anything," Mike broke in.

Drake and I both looked at him, startled.

"Well, Eloy seems to feel like money's no object here, and Maria and I just feel like we should be watching the pennies a bit." He put his arm possessively around Maria's shoulders to demonstrate their solidarity. She winced a tiny bit.

Drake and I shuffled a little, knowing this really wasn't any of our business.

"No," said Eloy, noticing our discomfort, "tell me what you think. Mama was always there for us as kids. I think we can spend a little to show our respect."

"And what? Take out a loan?" Mike retorted. "You won't have any of the old lady's money until some property gets sold."

Maria's mouth tightened at the term old lady, but she didn't say anything. Mike's arm was still tightly around her shoulders.

"Don't speak about my mother that way," Eloy growled, balling his fists. "If he had his way, he'd just toss her in the garbage." His voice cracked.

Drake subtly stepped between them. "Sounds like tempers need to cool a little here so you can work out a compromise."

Eloy dropped his hands and relaxed them. Mike was still glaring at his brother-in-law.

The funeral director had vanished and I wondered whether he shouldn't be here to referee. Surely he dealt with highly charged situations like this all the time. He could probably suggest something that would be agreeable to both sides. I glanced around, hoping to spot him.

"Look guys," I said, searching for a soothing tone of voice to use, "I'm sure they offer something that's a nice middle ground between all and nothing. Why don't you just sit down and talk to the nice people here about it. They'll help you come up with something."

I backed out into the hallway, caught the eye of the funeral director, motioning him to get his gray-suited little butt in here. He took a deep breath and entered the room with a deeply concerned look pasted to his face. I got the feeling that he desperately wanted to go outside and have a cigarette. I flashed him a look that said *straighten this out.*

He cleared his throat and directed the family members to sit. Drake and I edged out and fled to our car.

"Whew! Glad to be out of there." He chuckled.

"Aren't family occasions wonderful?" I started the car and headed south toward St. Augustine.

We each grabbed a duffle bag from the backseat and headed toward Father Ralph's office. The priest stood to greet us.

"So what do you have?" he asked.

I told him how we'd found the artifacts in the cabin, and how we suspected that members of the art theft ring had broken in and searched the place, then tried to run us off the road, in order to get the items themselves. I told how Father Domingo had kept clippings about the thefts and how Leon Palais, also known as Anton Pachevski, was here in town and was wanted by the police. I told him my theory of how the theft ring had blackmailed Ramon Romero into participating, using his prize assignment to the Vatican to gain access to the items he was forced to steal for them. How Pachevski had been forced to disappear in the Caribbean for several years, but that the FBI knew he was back and were again actively searching for him.

It was my first confession to a Catholic priest. I took a deep breath when I was done.

"Don't worry, my children," he smiled. "I know exactly what to do with this."

We picked up the two duffles and headed toward the hall. "Come," he said. He stood aside so Drake and I could precede him. "The last door on the left."

We walked down the tiled hallway and I reached for the handle of the last door. The room was dark.

"Set your bag down and you'll find the light switch on your right," Father Ralph said.

When I switched on the light, I found myself face to face with Anton Pachevski, who had a gun aimed right at me.

TWENTY FIVE

Instinctively I backed toward Drake, but Father Ralph nudged him in the ribs with a pistol and we both stumbled into the room.

"I should have thought of this in the beginning," Pachevski said with his hint of a French accent. "Having you find the treasure for us was so much simpler than looking for it myself. And it was so kind of you to deliver it, as well."

His white hair was still perfectly slicked back, his European clothing perfectly tailored, his cultured voice unnerving. I reached for the handle of the duffle.

"Push it over here please," he instructed.

I hesitated.

"Don't think I won't use this." His voice rose a touch as he corrected his aim so the pistol was pointing straight at my chest.

I thought of Father Ramon's blood soaking into the church steps.

"Yours too," he said to Drake. "Just set the bag down and push it toward me."

Drake kicked the bag gently and it slid across the tile, stopping just short of Pachevski's feet.

"Now, let's take a little ride," he suggested, as if this were a Sunday jaunt to the park. "Ralph, some blindfolds, please."

The priest nudged us both to the middle of the room so there was no chance of making a dash for the hall, then proceeded to tie a silk scarf around Drake's eyes and another to bind his hands together. He did the same to me, then I felt a jab in my ribs.

"Out to the car, kids," Ralph ordered. His normally soothing voice had turned ugly.

"So you were in on these thefts from the beginning?" I asked, turning to face the sound of his voice.

"Now!" he shouted.

"And did you cause Father Domingo's death too?" I taunted. "Just because the old man insisted on sending the first two crosses back?"

He shoved me roughly in the back and I stumbled.

"Do what they say, Charlie," Drake said quietly. He didn't sound submissive—more like he was formulating a plan.

Anton walked in front of us, Father Ralph bringing up the rear. We turned to our right, into the small side entry I'd used on my earlier visit. Cold air brushed my face when Anton opened the door.

"Step down," Anton coached. "Now, just follow my voice."

How could someone not notice that two bound and blindfolded people were being forced at gunpoint? It was the middle of the day, for heaven's sake. I wanted to scream or shout or cause a scene but had no way of knowing whether there was anyone within earshot. In the distance I could hear cars on the road, but that was nearly a block away, with buildings and trees between to muffle any noise I might be able to create.

I heard a car door open.

"Get inside," Anton instructed. "Duck your head."

I sat and he pushed my legs inside. On the opposite side of the car, behind the driver's seat, I could hear Drake doing the same thing. I leaned into his body for reassurance.

Cold air breezed the back of my neck. Behind me Anton was stashing the two duffles into a cargo area. We were in a sport utility vehicle of some kind. He slammed the hatch back down. From their voices I could tell that Father Ralph was taking the driver's seat, with Anton riding shotgun, undoubtedly keeping his pistol trained on us.

"You know where to go," Anton instructed Ralph.

The vehicle cranked to life and we bumped our way out of the rutted dirt parking lot. We made a right-hand turn and the road became smooth. I assumed we were on the paved highway, which turned into Paseo del Pueblo. From the traffic sounds around us and the number of stops and starts we made, we were going right through the middle of town. That meant we were heading north.

Didn't anyone notice that the car had two blindfolded people in the backseat? I hoped like hell that a cop would spot us. After several blocks, however, it became obvious that Anton and Ralph weren't worried. I began to assume the vehicle's windows were tinted so darkly that no one could see in. I concentrated on trying to picture exactly where we were. On TV the captured heroine can always later tell the police when they crossed over the railroad tracks and she'd hear the rushing water of every stream. In reality it didn't work that way. We made a series of twists and turns and I was thoroughly lost. I guessed that fifteen or twenty minutes had gone by, but in my current state of hyperalertness, it could have just as easily been five minutes or an hour.

Eventually the road straightened and the car picked up speed. We were on an open stretch of highway somewhere. Just as I was trying to calculate how many miles we might have gone, the car slowed and abruptly made a turn onto a dirt road. The first pothole lifted me off my seat, making me wish our captors had at least had the courtesy to buckle us in.

It seemed like we traveled miles on the dirt road, but then time flies when your brains are being jostled into Jell-O.

The car pulled to a stop and our doors were jerked open.

"Okay, the ride's over," Ralph said.

Gee, daddy, just when we were having so much fun.

A hand grabbed me by the elbow and pulled me out of the car, without bothering to remind me to duck my head this time. My forehead smacked the upper doorsill, sending a pattern of stars out my eyeballs. Car doors slammed all around and the gun barrel in my back directed me to walk straight ahead. The path was dirt and not very smooth. I stumbled a couple of times and Anton kept nudging at one arm or the other to correct my direction.

The air felt cooler and the sun hit my face on the left side at a low angle. It was past midafternoon. We mounted two shallow brick steps and I heard a key in a lock, followed by Ralph's voice instructing us to step forward.

"Drake?" I called out.

"Right behind you, babe. Don't worry."

"Shut up, you two," Ralph growled.

The door closed behind us with a firm click.

"Put them in separate rooms," Anton instructed.

"This way." Ralph led us down a couple of small steps then into a hallway.

He opened a door and shoved me into a room. My toe caught on something and I went down on my knees to a brick-hard floor. Pain shot up through my thighs and into my spine. An involuntary cry slipped out and I dropped to my side on the cold floor.

"Charlie?" Drake's voice.

"She's okay," Ralph hissed. "Keep going."

The door to my room closed with a distinct click. I heard retreating steps and another door opened and closed. Anton's footsteps didn't move away.

"Okay, now what?" Ralph asked a minute later, just outside my door.

"Not here, you idiot," Anton answered, this time without the French accent. They walked away.

I rolled toward the door and stuck my ear to the narrow space at the bottom of it. Squiggling my head a bit to shove my blindfold away from the ear, I could hear their voices becoming fainter as they walked away.

". . . the airport . . . gas up first." It was Anton's voice, the quieter of the two, and I was catching only a fraction of what he said.

". . . but . . . Ramon?" Ralph's voice became obliterated as someone turned on water in a sink.

I strained against the door.

". . . worry about it. Just do your job and I'll do mine." Anton's voice was right outside my door.

I rolled away from it just as the knob began to turn.

"Well, Ms. Parker," Anton greeted in an especially oily tone. "I'm very sorry that we can't stay and have a nice evening together. But we have an appointment we'll be late for if we don't get going."

We? Did he mean all of us?

"I'll be saying good-bye now," he said.

He unzipped my jacket and pulled it off my shoulder. I felt a sharp needle prick in my arm then everything went black.

TWENTY SIX

My head felt like someone had set an anvil on it, a crush-
ing, squeezing pain in my temples. I rolled to one side and
groaned. Fuzz blurred my vision and I blinked hard, rubbed
my eyes. My blindfold was gone and my hands were
unbound. I was lying on a bed, could feel the springiness of
a mattress under me. The room was pitch black except for a
dim light from the door to the hallway. I rolled onto my
elbow and gradually sat up. My head pounded.

What had happened? Anton Pachevski and Father Ralph
had brought us here from St. Augustine, I remembered.
Anton had come into the room, then the needle in my arm.
I held my throbbing head in my hands. How long had I
been out? Where was Drake?

I stood shakily and made my way to the door, my feet
feeling like lead weights. I didn't have any shoes on. I looked
around and found them beside the bed and slipped them
on. I was surprised to see that the room was fully furnished.
I'd expected that we had been taken to an abandoned building somewhere. In the hall only a tiny night-light burned.
Then the smell hit me.

Gas.

I dropped to the floor but the smell was stronger there. I

stood again and made my way up the hall, trying each of the doors until I found the room Drake was in. He, too, was lying on a bed in a nicely furnished bedroom. There was no trace of the silk scarves that had restrained us.

"Wake up, hon! There's a gas leak in the house."

He stirred groggily and rolled away from me. They must have given him a larger dose of the drug than they'd given me.

"Drake! Now!" I shouted. "We've got to get out of here now!"

I took his hand and pulled, trying to roll him over. God, what to do? I went to the bedroom's window and slid it fully open. A larger bedroom across the hall, presumably the master, had a sliding glass door leading to a small fenced yard. I opened it and cold air rushed in. Back in Drake's room, I closed the door to the hallway, hoping to keep the deadly fumes at bay until the room aired.

He groaned and rubbed at his eyes.

"Drake! Wake up!" I rubbed his arms and patted his cheeks. "They've set it up to kill us with a gas leak. We have to get out of here."

"Dark," he mumbled. "What time?"

"I don't know. I don't dare turn on a light to see my watch. C'mon, there's a room across the hall with a door. Let's get out."

He sat, in the same head-in-hands position I'd taken a few minutes ago, while I fumbled in the dark for his shoes.

"Can you stand up?" I asked.

He gave his head a quick shake and winced in pain. "Just a second."

I was hoping we had at least that much time.

"Okay, just across the hall," I coaxed. "Then we'll be outside in the fresh air."

He stood, shakily at first, but steadier as the air from the open window hit his face.

"I'm doing better," he said. "Let's get going."

We crossed the hall as quickly as we could, went through the master bedroom, and out to the yard. Both of us dropped to the winter-dead grass and took huge gulps of air.

"We better not stay around here," Drake said. "That whole place could blow."

"It's freezing out here," I chattered, suddenly realizing that we didn't have our coats on.

"Gotta be below zero," he agreed. "We won't make it very far without them. I'll go back inside."

"No. I think you got a heavier dose of that drug, whatever it was," I said. "Here, you get your boots on and I'll run back inside." I dropped the boots on the ground near him.

My nerves were taut as wires as I again entered the lethal house. I left the hall door open as I entered the room where Drake had been. There on the chair was his jacket. I grabbed it and ran to the other room. My coat was also on a chair in my room. For all their preparation, thank goodness they hadn't taken our coats away. They obviously hadn't planned on our ever needing them again. I dashed back outside and threw Drake's coat around his shoulders, then slipped my arms into mine. The parka's hood and the gloves I kept in the pockets helped tremendously.

"Ready?" I asked.

The adobe wall had a portal with a wooden gate. We slipped through and looked around.

"Let's get away from the house in case it goes sky high," Drake suggested, tugging at my arm.

He pulled a tiny flashlight from somewhere deep in his

parka. By its light we clambered over clumps of sagebrush to the front of the house, where we came to the empty driveway and were able to trot on its smoother surface. We slowed to a walk after about fifty yards, neither of us clearly in shape for any long-distance running. In the near distance, four or five miles away, the town of Taos sparkled with thousands of tiny gold lights. Beyond it, the eastern horizon was faintly visible over Wheeler Peak. Directly ahead of us, maybe a half-mile away, Highway 64 stretched southeast toward town and northwest to Tres Piedras. And coming up the road we were standing on was a dark vehicle.

We looked at each other.

"Uh-oh," said Drake.

We each dove for our side of the road. I crouched behind the dirt berm, telling myself that it wasn't them, it could be anyone, there were probably a lot more houses up this road. My heart was pounding anyway. I tucked my face under the dark green sleeve of my parka as the vehicle approached, hoping I looked like a bush.

It roared on past. I raised my head tentatively. Through the dust it kicked up, the car looked like a small sport utility with ski racks on top and four people inside. I let out a pent-up breath.

"Guess we ought to stick to the sides of the road," I said, brushing bits of tumbleweed and dust off myself. "Drake?"

"Over here," he groaned. "Doesn't look like I'm going to be walking anywhere," he said. He shined the light on his leg.

"Ohmigod, Drake, what happened?" Jutting from the meaty part of his calf was a large jagged piece of glass.

"Guess I fell on this," he said, picking up the top half of a shattered beer bottle.

"Is it bleeding much?"

"We better take a look," he said.

He carefully pulled the glass shard from his leg and his pant leg was immediately soaked in blood.

"Here—quick—take my knife and cut off the bottom edge of my jeans," he instructed.

Under the jeans he wore thermal long underwear and woolen socks. I sliced the knit cuff from the long underwear and stretched it around his leg above the wound to form a makeshift tourniquet.

"Hand me the material you cut off," he said. "I need to apply pressure directly to the wound."

I held the flashlight while he used both hands to cover the cut. After a couple of minutes he tentatively lifted the bandage and checked it.

"I think it's pretty well stopped," he said, removing the tourniquet. "But I don't think I better try walking on it. As soon as I stand up, it'll probably start gushing again."

I looked at him. His face was too white. Something inside me clenched up.

"I'll be just fine," he assured me, seeing the look on my face. "Let's just take this a step at a time."

I took a deep breath. "Okay. You're right. Is your cell phone still in your pocket?"

"I don't know." He patted his pockets. "Here."

He handed me the phone and I switched it on. There wasn't much life left in the battery.

"Okay, what? 911?"

"How you gonna tell them where to come?"

Good thought. We only knew we were on a side road off Highway 64, somewhere out in the sticks. I looked around, trying to figure out a plan. I could walk up the road, following the vehicle that had just passed us, hoping to come to a friendly house and they could tell me our location so I could get emergency help. Unknown was just how far away this house might be. Things here were pretty spread out; it could be miles.

Or I could walk down to the highway, which was within sight, call 911 and tell them to drive out, watching for a nearly crazed female in a dark green parka who would be waving frantically because her husband was injured, she'd just been abducted and drugged, and her dog was still in the hospital in unknown condition, and . . . Stop it! I brought myself back to center. Took another deep breath.

"Okay," I said. "I'll walk down to the highway and call 911 from there. Chances are, there's a road sign or mile marker, or some way of identifying this road. I'll be able to tell them where you are. Now, meanwhile, should I go back up to the house and bring some blankets down to keep you warm?"

"No, don't bother, I'll be okay," he said, flapping his arms and rubbing his legs to keep circulation going.

"Drake, it's zero or below out here. It'll only take a few extra minutes."

I ran back up to the house we'd just vacated. The gas smell was stronger than ever in the master bedroom. I held my breath and pulled all the bedding from the king-size bed—a comforter, blankets, and sheets. Bundling them into an unwieldy lump I shoved back out the door and through the wooden gate.

Drake was shivering hard when I got back to him and I was glad I'd insisted on getting the blankets. I spread them on the ground and made him climb onto the soft layer of cloth. Then I rolled the whole thing around him as many times as I could. His head was the only part sticking out. When I stepped back I had to chuckle.

"You look like a giant cocoon," I told him.

"It's better," he said. "Take the flashlight with you." His bone-weary tone worried me. He was still way too pale.

"I'll get someone here as fast as I can," I promised.

Walking away and leaving him behind was the hardest part. I didn't let myself look back, except once. Just made myself go as fast as my own pounding head would allow. I used the flashlight sparingly. Once my eyes adjusted to the darkness, I could see the pale tan dirt road and I kept to the middle of it. Once, I allowed myself a look at my watch. It was only six P.M. It felt like at least midnight. It had only been five hours since Anton and Ralph had abducted us from the church. I wondered . . .

I pulled out the cell phone again and took a chance. Dialed Ron at the RJP offices.

"Thank God you're still there," I breathed.

"Charlie? What's going on?"

"I don't have enough battery power to go into it. Call James Burns at the FBI there in Albuquerque. Tell him Leon Palais, aka Anton Pachevski, is probably trying to catch a flight out of there tonight. He'll be with a man known around here as Father Ralph. I don't know his last name or if that's his real name, but he's in this just as deeply as Palais. They're carrying a fortune in religious artifacts.

"I don't have any idea which airline or what time. I just heard them mention getting to the airport. After you've called Burns, then call Kent Taylor and tell him the same thing. I think these two also killed Ramon Romero. They left the Taos area about three hours ago, so tell them to do it *now*."

I'd hardly said good-bye when the low-battery signal beeped at me. I switched off the phone, hoping it still had enough juice left to make the 911 call. The highway was only another hundred yards now. That leaden feeling was coming back into my feet again and a fantasy of being able to lie down for a few minutes briefly flashed through my mind but I couldn't let myself do it.

At the point where my narrow dirt road met the paved highway, I started looking for landmarks. There were a couple of industrial businesses, dark and quiet now, and I could see the county airport's rotating beacon clearly. The entrance road must be no more than a quarter of a mile away.

I flipped open the phone and punched in 911. Busy.

Again.

Busy again.

What was going on? When were 911 lines busy? I tried to think ahead, to form an alternate plan. Just then I realized that an oncoming car was a police cruiser. I switched on my flashlight and aimed it at him, shining it toward his windshield and away in a series of flashes that I hoped resembled the code for SOS.

Whether they did or not, it worked. The car slowed and pulled over.

"Problem, lady?" the officer asked through the window he'd lowered just a crack.

"Yes! My husband's injured just up the road here and I've been trying to call 911 but can't get through. We need medical attention."

"Good luck. There's been a big pileup on that horseshoe curve south of town. Every emergency responder in the county is out there. Happened about thirty minutes ago, so it's gonna be hours before they're freed up. Then we got another one out here at Tres Piedras just now. Somebody T-boned another vehicle at the intersection. I'm on my way to that one now. You're gonna be better off just to take him to the hospital in your own car."

He wished me luck, cranked up the window, and sped off to the west.

My own car. Yeah. I'd last seen it when we parked it at St. Augustine, on the south end of town, I was now at the farthest-ass north end of town, a distance of probably twenty miles. How was I going to get there? And who knew if it was even still there? The two fugitives could have decided my vehicle would be safer to drive to Albuquerque. Drake's set of keys were probably still in his coat pocket but mine, along with my purse and my brown envelope of evidence, were under the front seat of the car. If they got into the Jeep they had free access to everything.

I started to dial 911 again but knew it was useless. The officer had told me what would happen. I wanted to kick the dirt, throw something, or sit down and cry.

The airport.

My pulse picked up as an idea began to form. Our helicopter was sitting at the Taos Airport, a little over a quarter-mile away, right now. Drake had told me earlier that he'd left it there for its fifty-hour inspection. A fifty-hour is pretty simple, oil change and inspecting a few items. *If* someone was still there, and *if* they didn't have the aircraft dismantled . . . New energy surged through me. I stuffed the flashlight and cell phone into pockets and I began to run.

TWENTY SEVEN

By the time I reached the turnoff road to the airport property, I knew I should be pacing myself—I was in no shape to be running full speed, especially at this altitude— but something pushed me on. There, at the end of the long access road, I could see lights in the FBO facility and in the hangar. I raced to the building and flung open the front door.

A startled dispatcher stared at me.

"Is Frank still here?" I gasped. "Oh, never mind."

I bypassed the empty passenger waiting area and pushed my way through the door leading to the maintenance hangar.

"Miss, you can't just . . ." the dispatcher stuttered, following me.

"Frank!" I shouted.

A sandy blond head appeared around the back of the fuselage of our blue and white JetRanger.

"Charlie? What's the matter?" The dispatcher backed away after the mechanic greeted me by name.

Although I'd met Frank Gardner only briefly when we first came to Taos, he remembered me and knew I was also licensed to fly.

"Are you finished with that fifty-hour yet?" I asked, working to make my voice sound normal and get my breathing back under control.

"Just about. I'm putting all the covers back on now." It was always amazing to me how many places on the fuselage of an aircraft could be opened up to get to the thousands of parts inside.

"I've got an emergency. Will she be ready to fly right away?"

"Sure. I was gonna call Drake to see if he could do a run-up and check everything anyway. But you can do it."

I walked the length of the hangar and back, forcing myself to calm down and concentrate on the steps I had to perform. Unlike Drake, I didn't have thousands of hours under my belt, so this didn't all come as second nature to me. I started the preflight procedure, making myself do each step without thinking of Drake lying out in the cold desert alone.

"Okay, shall we roll her out?" Frank said.

He hooked up an electric tug and gently backed the aircraft onto the tarmac. I climbed into the right seat as he backed the tug away and gave me a thumbs-up that I was clear. I turned the battery switch on, checked the fuel boost pumps, and pushed in the caution light circuit breaker, going methodically through my startup checklist. The turbine engine soon whined to life, the rotors slowly spinning up to speed.

In the course of my training I'd done only a couple of night flights so I looked around, planning what I'd do. It shouldn't be that difficult. From our flights in and out of the Taos airport I knew basically where the powerlines ran. The nearest ones had blinking red lights on the poles and I'd use my landing light to illuminate the ground and locate Drake. I brought the rotors up to speed and lifted off. Circling the airfield once while I gained altitude, I got my bearings and headed toward the road where I'd left him.

Crossing over a fenced maintenance yard full of trucks, I searched the highway for the turnoff to the dirt road I'd come down. I came upon it sooner than expected and had to circle back. With my bright light trained on the road, it was only a few seconds before I saw the blanket cocoon I was looking for.

Apparently Drake had heard me coming. He was sitting up, blankets still around his legs, waving his arms at me. He tucked his head into the blankets to avoid the upwash of dust as I turned the aircraft to face into the wind, flared, and brought her in for a perfect landing on the road. By the time I'd locked down the controls, he was up, bundling the blankets into a wad, and limping his way to the passenger's side. He shoved the blankets into the backseat and hoisted himself into the front.

"I'm trying to get some heat in here for you," I shouted over the turbine whine. "Are you freezing?"

He slipped his headset on and buckled his harness. "I'm doing okay, but the leg's still bleeding a bit."

"I'll head for the hospital, but I don't know how soon we'll get you in. There's been a bad accident on the highway. That's why I couldn't get a 911 response."

I radioed ahead to the hospital's dispatcher and informed him that I was bringing in a wounded patient by helicopter. He asked how soon we could be there; the highway victims were just starting to arrive. "ETA three minutes," I responded.

I pulled pitch and we made a direct line for the center of town. Navigating over the town was easy, with streets and plenty of landmarks to guide me and I set down on the hospital's helipad three minutes and ten seconds later. An ER team wheeled a gurney out and made Drake lie down on it.

"You got any other helicopters coming in tonight?" I yelled over the rotor noise.

"Maybe. With that pileup."

"Okay if I set this over there on the grass then?" I asked.

"Sure, I guess so." This was obviously not someone with enough authority to worry about protocol.

I moved the aircraft, set it on a nice level spot, and shut everything down. By the time I got inside, a technician had sliced Drake's jeans another twelve inches up the seam and was cleaning the wound with gauze. I guessed they were hustling to get the simple stuff out of the way before the really bad cases came through the door. Twenty minutes later, Drake had a neatly bandaged leg, a supply of antibiotics, and a whopping bill. I put the charges on a credit card, rather than try to hassle with insurance papers, and we were out of there as three ambulances roared up to the emergency entrance.

"Now what?" he asked.

"We need to see if my car is still at the church or if that's another whole set of problems to fix."

Poor Drake, he'd been through so much and I could tell he didn't need this.

"Come on. I know what we'll do," I said. He limped alongside me to the spot I'd left the aircraft.

I headed for the pilot seat and he didn't say a word, but went to the passenger's side. He watched silently, looking at me with either amusement or pride—I couldn't be sure. He made no comment as I lifted off and headed west, where I hoped we'd be able to tell if my car was still there. As we approached the church I switched on the landing light.

"There it is!" I cheered. Thank goodness we didn't have to track down a missing vehicle.

"Set her down," Drake said.

"What? Here by the church?"

"Sure. It's a big parking lot and there aren't any other cars."

"Won't this get me in trouble?"

"Possibly. Just do it quick and get back out before anyone has a chance to write down our tail number." He patted my arm. "I'm okay to drive the car. Let me out here and beat it back to the airport. I'll come out there and pick you up."

I looked at him again, checking to see if he was really okay. His color was much better. "All right," I said. "Get ready to bail."

As soon as the skids touched the ground, he jumped out. He cleared the rotor blades, pulled a key ring from his pocket and flashed it toward me, then gave me a thumbs-up. I took her back up and quickly gained enough altitude to avoid noise complaints from the townsfolk.

Five minutes later I honed in on the beacon at the airport and set the ship gently in front of the hangar. Frank towed it back inside after I tied down the blades and I spent a few minutes filling out my logbooks. Drake arrived about ten minutes later in the Jeep.

"Everything look okay with the car?" I asked.

"Just fine," he said.

"Want me to take over the driving?"

"If you don't mind. My leg's throbbing already."

The cabin sure looked good when we drove up. It wasn't even nine o'clock yet but I was bone tired and Drake looked just as bad. Inside, at least it was warm. I switched on some lights. I looked around the room and tears began to well up unbidden.

"It's too lonely without Rusty," I said. My voice came in a quiver.

Drake took me into his arms and I fell against him, sobbing for all the ordeals we'd been through in the last two days.

TWENTY EIGHT

The phone rang, startling me out of a catnap. Drake and I had slumped to the sofa together, arms locked around each other. I stared around the room, dazed for a minute until it came to me what I was hearing. Before I could force enough energy down to my legs to stand up, the answering machine had come on. Ron's voice came through: "Just wanted to let you know that the Feds caught up with your guys at the airport. They've recovered the church's treasure and there's even talk of presenting you with some kind of award for your valiant service to them. I'll call you in the morning with the details. Bye."

I jostled Drake and together we limped up the stairs, pulled off our clothes and fell into bed. By six A.M., although it was still dark outside, I was awake and restless. A hot shower took care of some miscellaneous muscle aches and the last vestiges of the headache that had lingered since I came out of the drug Anton had shot into me. I toweled off and dressed in soft sweats and went after my wet hair with a blow dryer until it lay cleanly around my shoulders.

Downstairs I brewed a pot of coffee and tidied the last evidence of yesterday's treasure search from the living room. I glanced wistfully at the telephone. It was still too early to call Dr. Nelson to see about Rusty's condition. But I could call Ron at home.

"What's this about some award from the church?" I teased, after his groggy hello.

"Umm, hold on a second."

In the background I could hear a toilet flush and water running in the sink. He returned in a couple of minutes. "Better," he said. "Well, we had a bit of excitement here last night, thanks to your tip. Have you seen the news?"

"No." We'd tried to receive the Albuquerque television stations when we first got here, but decided we were surrounded by too many mountains to get a signal.

"Last night at ten it was the late-breaking story. Feds and APD had the plane, on the taxiway, surrounded by armed agents."

"Oh, my gosh."

"Yep. They moved fast after you called. Got passenger manifests and found two men traveling together who had bought their tickets at the last minute: Paco Leon and Ralph Baldonado."

"So Anton used a mixed version of his real name."

"Guess he hadn't realized that you'd made that connection. This guy has more fake identities than Madonna's got hair colors."

"Plus, he probably thought Drake and I were dead by then." I quickly filled Ron in on how we'd been drugged and left in the gas-filled house.

"Oh, jeez, Charlie. I better give the Feds that information so they can add two more attempted murders to the list of charges. Anyway, these two were on a flight to Dallas with a connection to Bogota. It was another thing that made the ticket agent suspicious—an overseas flight and they each had only one carry-on bag."

"How'd they get the treasure past airport security?"

"Bluffed their way through. Told 'em it was cheap trinkets they were taking to the children of some Columbian village. They almost got away. The plane had pushed back from the gate and was second in line for takeoff by the time the authorities roared out there in cars and vans, strobes flashing and all that. Luckily for all the other passengers, the two of them gave up without a fight. Although the news stories so far have been full of somber reflection on the grave danger to everyone's safety."

"Doesn't surprise me." I'd recently read a poll that showed the second-least-trusted segment of our society were media people—right after lawyers.

"Oops, gotta go. My other line's ringing," Ron said. "I'll keep you posted."

It was still a bit early but I took a chance and dialed the vet's office. Got a recording stating their business hours and I started to leave a message when Dr. Nelson herself picked up the line.

"I heard your voice, Charlie, and I knew you'd be worried about Rusty," she said. "He's doing fine. Better than most head injury cases, actually. I'd like to watch him the rest of the day, but I think I can probably release him late this afternoon or tomorrow. Call me again around four and I'll let you know."

A couple of thumping noises from upstairs told me that Drake had awakened. I rummaged through the refrigerator for some breakfast and came up with eggs and ham. With some pancake mix from the pantry shelf, I set out to create a substantial breakfast. We'd had nothing since our coffee yesterday morning. It was no wonder we'd been totally wiped out last night.

The phone rang as I was stirring the pancake mix.

"You won't believe this," Ron said, without preamble. "They're not charging Anton and Ralph with Ramon's death."

"What!?"

"Kent Taylor tells me they both provided alibis."

"And they checked out?"

"Apparently so. Ralph was definitely at an ecumenical council in New York when it happened. Dozens of witnesses. And Anton, Leon, whoever he was at the time, was in St. Maarten."

"Can he prove that? He did a pretty good job of being unseen after he got there."

"He says so. He's provided a list of witnesses and they're still checking them out."

"What about the possibility that one of them ordered someone else to do the actual shooting? Some little punk out there could have done it for drug money."

"They're checking that out too," he said.

I hung up the phone, angry. This slimeball Anton. He disappears to a tiny island where he manages to avoid notice for years. Now, when it's convenient, he can come up with alibi witnesses. I knew I'd place no credence whatsoever in those witnesses, but the Feds would probably have to believe them.

My skillet was hot so I cracked the eggs and began scrambling them furiously. A nagging thought began to form. What if it was true—that neither Anton nor Ralph killed Ramon?

"Those eggs piss you off?" Drake teased, coming up behind me. "You're stirring them hard enough to wear a hole in the pan."

I set the skillet on another burner and turned to him.

"The police are checking out alibis for Ralph and Anton. They don't think they're guilty of Ramon's murder."

"What?" he said.

TWENTY NINE

Eloy's answering machine picked up. Unsure exactly what to say, I only left a message for him to call me back.

"Today is his mother's funeral, isn't it?" Drake said. He'd finished cooking the pancakes and was setting two full plates on the table. "Come eat, and then we'll figure out what to do."

I hadn't realized how absolutely ravenous I was until I started eating. Both of us put away eggs, ham, and pancakes in no time flat and followed that with coffee and a couple of somewhat dry Danish rolls we'd left in the breadbox.

"How's your leg this morning?" I asked Drake.

"Sore. Those stitches scratching against my pant leg are going to drive me crazy. But there's no inflammation. It's going to heal all right."

We continued to sit at the kitchen table, neither of us finding the energy to move. But I knew I couldn't sit there, with a killer potentially getting ready to make a move against Eloy.

"As much as a funeral would not be on my list of things I'd like to do today," I told Drake, "I think we should go."

He called the funeral home and got the times, while I stacked the dishes and pans in the sink.

"The funeral Mass starts at ten," he said. "I don't think we'll make that unless you want to tiptoe in after it's started."

I looked at my watch. He was right. By the time we dressed and drove into town, we'd probably catch only the last of it.

"Graveside services follow. That will be at a cemetery on the west side of town."

"Let's go there," I said. "I wouldn't mind watching everyone else arrive."

The small cemetery sat in a low spot, a few acres of dirt surrounded by a three-foot-high wrought-iron fence. Some bare-branched trees ringed the fence. Overhead, the sky was the color of lead, lending the whole scene a desolate quality. The only color came from small bunches of faded plastic flowers on some of the graves. Pale, tattered ribbons fluttered in the slight breeze. I shuddered.

We waited in the Jeep until a white hearse appeared, followed by a limousine and line of cars with their headlights on. The hearse stopped inside the fence's only gate. The other cars found places to park anywhere they could. Eloy emerged from the family limo, along with his sister and her husband. He looked haggard, his eyes red-rimmed. He spotted Drake and me and we walked over to him.

"Are you doing all right?" I asked, shaking his proffered hand.

He nodded but no words came out. He pressed his lips together. He and Drake shook hands and gave each other a manly hug with much back-patting.

"I've got lots to fill you in on," I told him, "but it can wait until another day." I wanted to warn him to be careful, but this was not the time.

"Everyone's going to Maria's right after this. There'll be lots of food. I should go for a while and you guys can come along, then we can go back to my place if you'd like."

Drake nodded agreement.

People were standing around the casket, which now sat on a platform above an open hole in the ground.

"I know you need to get over there," I said. "But one quick question. Did your mother have a will?"

"Sure. Mike drew it up for her a few years ago. Why?"

"Not important right now. Go ahead and join your family."

Drake and I waited on the fringes of the group. I spotted Officer Steve, Eloy's cousin, standing with head bowed, behind Mike, Maria, and Eloy. There were probably twenty people in the same age group—cousins, I assumed. There was one older couple and I thought I remembered Eloy once telling me that his mother still had a sister living. The woman appeared frail, her skin pale against the black lace mantilla she wore with a black dress and black wool coat. The man kept a hand on her elbow and she leaned on him frequently.

Father Sanchez's words, partly in Latin and partly in Spanish, drifted past me since I understood neither language. I scanned the crowd for clues while Drake shifted uneasily, taking the weight off his injured leg.

When the group began to break up, I turned to him. "Are you sure you feel like going to Maria's?" I asked.

"Sure. Let's go for a while," he said. "What am I going to do at home, anyway? Sit around and eat more."

"I'm curious to take a look at Eloy's house later. The layout, I mean. I want to know where this closet is from which his gun magically disappeared and reappeared. If my hunch is right, something's going to come to a head in the next day or two."

We walked back to our car and waited. When Eloy and family had climbed back into their limousine we followed it into town. The Ortiz's house was a decent-size adobe, a two-story territorial with a bright blue front door. It sat on a narrow lane with no room to park on the street. Cars had already filled the circular drive so we drove down the street. About a half-block away we found a vacant lot and noticed that several other drivers had the same idea. We parked beside another couple I'd seen at the cemetery and walked together back to the house.

Inside, it was graciously furnished with mission-style carved furniture mixed with contemporary pillowed sofas and chairs. Indian rugs covered the tile floors and the art was a pleasant mixture of well-known New Mexico artists like R. C. Gorman and Amado Peña, along with some beautiful landscapes by artists I didn't immediately recognize.

We relinquished our coats to a young girl who said she was putting them in the back bedroom, then found Eloy in the dining room. A lavish array of food was spread out— everything from pots of pinto beans to casseroles and salads.

"Here," he said. "Have something to eat."

We protested that we'd just eaten a huge breakfast, but I had to admit everything smelled wonderful.

"Your sister has great taste in furnishings," I said.

His mouth did a little twitch. "A little ahead of Mike's earning power, I think," he said. "But it's none of my business if they want to live off credit cards."

We had moved into a corner of the breakfast room, away from the others, Eloy with a fully loaded plate and Drake and I, amazingly, each taking a small bowl of green chile stew.

"I'm not going to stick around for too much of this family stuff," Eloy said. "You guys still want to come to my place?"

"If Drake's leg holds out we will," I told him between mouthfuls of the delicious stew.

I filled him in briefly on our adventure the previous day.

"So our cabin was full of stolen treasure?" he said incredulously. He shook his head in amazement. "I wonder how long it had been there? And who built those hidden compartments behind the bookshelves? My father built the cabin, probably forty years ago, but I sure don't remember ever hearing about any secret hiding places."

"What hiding places?" Mike Ortiz had come through the kitchen and stood beside Eloy.

"At the cabin," Eloy told him. "Remember when we were kids and went up there in the summer for picnics all the time? Did Dad ever tell you he'd built hidden compartments behind the bookshelves?"

"No. I never knew that. What about them?"

"Charlie and Drake found a bunch of stolen artifacts from the church in there. The police caught two men who were involved in a major theft ring."

"Unfortunately Ramon was involved in it too . . ." I began. Suddenly I knew exactly what had happened. I craned my neck to find Steve Romero but didn't see him.

"Excuse me," I said. I left the men chatting and hoped I looked like I was heading for the powder room.

I didn't find Steve in the living room or dining room. I didn't remember seeing him since the cemetery and decided he probably hadn't come. I couldn't very well make a phone call from here, but if we left we might just pop in at the police station before going to Eloy's. I followed a hall past a bathroom and a study and came to the bedroom with coats piled over the bed. I was rummaging through them, looking for ours when I heard the door click shut behind me.

THIRTY

"When did you figure it out, Charlie?"

I spun to find Mike Ortiz pointing a gun at me. I clutched my coat to my chest, my heart beating furiously.

"The clues have been there all along, Mike. You surely don't believe that I'm the only one who suspected you." I sure hoped someone else did, anyway.

He chuckled. "There's nothing to connect me. I've been very careful. For years."

"You don't think you left a single fingerprint when you built those hidden compartments?"

"My prints are all over that cabin, I'm sure. It's a family place. I've been there many times."

"It was pretty smart of you to insert yourself as a middleman, ready to take a cut of all the stolen artifacts, Mike."

His face became scornful. "Ramon was such a dupe. I guess he thought his saintly image would remain intact if he didn't deal directly with Palais and his bunch," he smirked. "He came to me for legal advice on the whole thing. He just didn't figure out that, with him out of the way, I'd end up with all his mother's property *and* all the artifacts."

"So why didn't you retrieve the stuff and sell it long before now? After you shot Ramon, no one else knew where it was."

"Well, I have to admit I was a bit intimidated by Leon. He stayed in regular touch over the years and let me know he was keeping tabs on my moves through a series of people he put in place here in town."

"Like the fine, upstanding Father Ralph."

"Him, and others. I was hoping Leon would disappear, or at least stop watching long enough for me to make a move. I owe you a debt of thanks on that. You got him out of the way for me. Unfortunately most of the treasure went along with him."

"There's more?"

"Enough to take care of me for a while," he said smugly. "And now I've got to take care of you because I'm not going to have the authorities chasing me down. A month from now I'll be on a beach in Mexico, blending into the population. It doesn't take much to live in Mexico."

"I can figure out how you got Eloy's gun from the closet and used it to kill Ramon, but how does the pawn ticket come into it?" I asked.

"That part nearly tripped things up," he admitted. "Ramon and Eloy'd had a big fight a few days before Ramon died. I thought it was a sure thing that the cops would suspect Eloy. I'd already returned the damn gun to his closet and I was just waiting for them to come get him. But it didn't happen."

"And?" I said, diverting his attention away from a noise in the hall.

"So I took the gun again and pawned it in Albuquerque, using Eloy's name. A couple of days later I retrieved it but kept the ticket, which I left at the church in Albuquerque. The cops were really working the murder case right then—

I just knew they'd find the ticket and make the connection. Eloy would get blamed for the murder, but no way could they tie it to me."

"But somehow the ticket got lost in the other priest's things and was found only recently," I finished.

"And of course I'd wiped the gun clean and put it back long before then," he gloated.

"A perfect frame," I said. "With both Eloy and Ramon out of the way, Maria would inherit everything. You'd get rid of her and end up with the whole inheritance, plus a fortune in artifacts." I gripped the cloth of my coat. "What about Maria now?"

"Let her *hardworking* brother support her. I've recently liquidated a lot of the real estate Consuelo owned, put the money in a separate bank account. Which, by this time tomorrow, will be empty. Maria knew I wasn't making it as a lawyer, but she insisted on nice furniture, fine art, hanging out with the upper crust of this town. Her credit cards are all maxed out. Let her figure out what to do next. When they read that will, they're both going to discover that their inheritance won't cover the bills for more than a few months." His perfect white teeth gleamed in a grin that showed no hint of humor. His eyes showed not a trace of compassion.

"So like I said," he continued, "now it's time to get rid of you."

He grabbed an overcoat from the pile on the bed and slipped his arms into it, keeping the gun trained on me all the time.

"Put your coat on, Charlie. We're going to pretend we both just decided to step outside at the same moment." He opened the bedroom door and stood aside. "Just remember that I'll have the gun in my pocket."

Experience does teach us things and one thing I knew was that I had no intention of being led away to my death twice in as many days. I lunged toward Mike and threw my coat over his head. Grabbing the doorknob I dashed into the hall and pulled the door shut behind me. Unfortunately he was quick and his gun hand made it to the edge of the door before it closed. The door caught him at the wrist and I spun to see the gun in his hand. With his index finger still in the trigger guard, the gun wafted about, pointing at the floor, then the opposite wall. I still had a grip on the knob so I gave it a hard yank, hoping to dislodge the gun.

Instead, his fingers contracted and the pistol went off.

THIRTY ONE

For a second the percussion rang against the walls and the tile floor. Then I went deaf. I kicked his hand and knocked the gun to the floor where it slid the remaining length of the hall and came to rest under a small table. My hearing gradually returned.

Mike pulled his hand back inside and slammed the door. The lock clicked.

"What the hell!?" Voices from other parts of the house clamored in surprise.

"Charlie, what's happened?" Eloy appeared at my side, with Drake limping right behind him.

"It's Mike. He's the killer."

Skeptical faces appeared, crowding into the narrow space. A crash from behind the closed door startled them all.

"Quick, he'll get away," I shouted. "He's going out the window."

Eloy threw himself against the locked door, splintering the frame, then dashed into the bedroom. Although Mike hadn't made lots of money as an attorney, he'd eaten well over the years and was a tad on the slow side trying to heft himself out the open window. Eloy the outdoorsman had no trouble grabbing him before he'd made any progress.

Drake rushed past me and by the time I looked into the room Mike was facedown on the floor with Eloy straddling his back and pinning his hands. Drake had his foot on Mike's neck for good measure.

"Is Steve in the house?" I called out to the crowd in the hall. "If not, call him. If you can't get him, get the police over here."

I left Drake and Eloy in charge of the prisoner and went to find Maria. Eloy's petite sister was standing in the kitchen, her face white with shock.

"Maria?"

Her eyes welled over and she turned to stare out the window.

"Did you know?" I asked gently.

She shook her head negatively, then gradually rolled the motion over into a nod. "I suspected."

"Want to talk about it?"

"No. I don't know." She reached for a box of tissues on the countertop. "He always talked about how we'd really be set for life one day. Every time I'd see something in the store I liked, he say, 'Buy it. We're going to have plenty of money soon.' It worried me." She hung her head. "I guess it didn't worry me enough. I kept buying things.

"I really thought he meant he would start making more money in his law practice. Maybe he had a big case going or something. I don't know. He never gave me details. After Ramon died, he told Mama she should redo her will. He got kind of pushy with her. When it was done, I sneaked a peek. He kept it in his study here at home.

"I don't know . . . I don't understand a lot of that legal language, but it looked like it included money for him, whether he stayed married to me or not. Like he'd get part of Mama's property even if he wasn't in the family anymore. He'd never said anything about us splitting up, but I started to wonder. I started to pay attention to little things, little comments."

She balled up one tissue and aimed it at the trash can. It missed but she ignored it. She reached for a fresh one.

"I started to think that he was planning to leave me."

"He told me he'd secretly sold a lot of your mother's property and he planned to be carefree on a beach somewhere within a month." I got the feeling my statement didn't come as a surprise.

A commotion from the front of the house told me that the police had arrived.

"Did you think Mike might have killed Ramon?" I tried to be gentle with the question but it wasn't the kind of thing you can phrase delicately.

"I suspected it at the time, but then I started to think I was crazy," she sobbed. "Right before Ramon died, he and Mike had several bad arguments. He'd come over here and they would lock themselves in Mike's study. I could hear voices through the door, angry voices. Once I caught the word 'stealing' when they were shouting at each other. Ramon would leave and Mike would stay in a foul mood for hours."

"Was Mike here the night Ramon was shot?" I asked.

"That's just the thing. No, he wasn't. He said he'd had a late dinner meeting with a client in Santa Fe and he'd just stay over. At first I thought there might be another woman. I was so obsessed with that idea that I didn't put two and two together. When Ramon died so violently it shook us all.

Eloy and Ramon had never been close—they were just too different. Mama and I had only each other to grieve with and I spent a lot of time at her house.

"It was only after Mike made her rewrite her will and a few other things came to my attention that I remembered he wasn't home the night Ramon was killed. The thoughts that came into my mind were just too terrible to think about."

A couple of other women came into the kitchen and I slipped out to find out what was happening down the hall. I arrived in the foyer to see Mike being hauled out in cuffs. He gave me a hateful stare. I'd wrecked years worth of his planning.

"Charlie, we'll need to come out to the cabin and see what other evidence we might find," Steve said, coming up beside me.

"Sure. I can fill you in on everything he told me. As a lawyer, I'm sure he'll know better than to give you guys a confession, but maybe some of the stuff he said to me will help you get the hard evidence you need."

He nodded and set a time to come out in the afternoon. "Glad to see your cold is better," he winked.

"Talk to Maria," I suggested. "Something tells me she might be willing to waive the right not to testify against her husband."

THIRTY TWO

Drake and I have settled nicely back into honeymoon mode. With his leg injury he can't do much flying, although it hasn't prevented him from doing anything *really* important. I've taken a couple of his short charters and am becoming a halfway decent pilot. We finally made it to Taos where we visited the jeweler and chose beautiful matching bands of gold and turquoise.

Eloy offered us the use of the cabin for as long as we want, rent-free. He said he couldn't thank me enough for saving his life and catching Ramon's real killer, and a bunch of other embarrassing stuff. Drake and I talked about it and decided that prolonging the honeymoon an extra month, until our house was finished, wouldn't be half bad.

Rusty is well on the road to recovery, joining us at the cabin again four days after our hurried trip to the vet. He's occasionally shaky on his feet, but I caught him barking at another treed squirrel, so I'd have to say he's quickly returning to his old self.

After Steve and his crew had finished searching the cabin, there were enough stolen artifacts, along with the now-verified pieces of the Dead Sea Scrolls, to put Mike away on that count alone. With the addition of the murder charge, the illegal sale of his mother-in-law's property without her knowledge, and the fraudulent changing of her will, Mike Ortiz will be spending a lot of time in Santa Fe, courtesy of the New Mexico Corrections Department.

Fred and Susie Montgomery sent Ron a check for the cost of the investigation of Monica Francis, plus a little extra they said was to be a wedding gift to Drake and me. They included a picture of themselves in lounge chairs by the pool of a southern California mansion, palm trees and tons of flowering bougainvilla in the background, toasting the camera with full champagne glasses. The inscription "Come visit anytime" was hand written on the back of the photo.

Ron and I had a nice long conversation. It seems Anton and Ralph are each facing their own sets of problems. Anton's include grand theft and flight to avoid prosecution. Ralph has a number of aiding and abetting charges. His jail time might not be burdensome, but I have the feeling the church's higher connections will deal with him.

Ron told me I'd received a letter from Rome, which he forwarded to Eloy's mailbox and I picked up yesterday. It was a letter on Vatican stationery, commending me for my dedication to the Catholic church and service to the Lord in returning priceless church property. And to think, I'd never even set foot in a Catholic church until a month ago. Included with the official typed letter was a thick, cream-colored notecard, embossed in gold, with a personal thanks from you-know-who, himself.